Patrick Stevens almost choked on his coffee when he read the meeting agenda

He couldn't possibly be that unlucky, could he?

"What's wrong?" The perennially smiling kindergarten teacher slapped him on the back, as if that would help.

"Did you see who's running for PTO president?"

She shrugged. "Some woman named Patterson."

"As in, mother of Jason Patterson." That should have said it all.

"And that's a problem because?"

She was obviously still too wet behind the ears to understand the implications.

"Jason Patterson, the kid who threw cherry bombs in the boys' toilets. Led his own gambling and extortion ring."

"I'm sure he wasn't *that* bad." She flipped her hair and gave him that sparkling, you're-just-old-and-burned-out smile.

At thirty-eight, he considered himself far from old. But she might have a point about the burned-out part. Summer break seemed very far away some days, especially when he thought about Jason Patterson. His ultimate failure.

Dear Reader,

Four Little Problems is my oldest son's book in so many ways. Not because he and I have weathered challenges, which we have. And not because I love him every bit as deeply as Emily loves Jason, which I do.

No, *Four Little Problems* resulted from one of those everyday conversations I suspect I don't appreciate nearly enough. My oldest son and I were discussing single mothers and dating. He mentioned how difficult some children make the dating process when they don't like their mother's potential boyfriend.

When I gave it some thought, I was impressed with the courage it must take for a single parent to attempt a relationship in the midst of juvenile guerrilla warfare. I wondered how a relationship could survive, maybe even thrive, under such stressful circumstances. Then I started the inevitable "What if..." and my imagination was off and running.

Emily and Patrick's story was born of that "What if..." Their relationship was so challenging from the get-go, even I wondered if they could pull it off.

On a side note, fate came full circle when my editor asked for title suggestions. My son proposed the title you see on the cover—*Four Little Problems*. I'm so proud of him and his contributions.

I hope you enjoy the story I've come to think of as *Luke's Book*.

Yours in reading,

Carrie Weaver

P.S. I enjoy hearing from readers by e-mail at CarrieAuthor@aol.com or snail mail at P.O. Box 6045, Chandler, AZ 85246-6045.

FOUR LITTLE PROBLEMS
Carrie Weaver

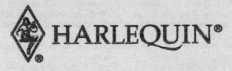

TORONTO • NEW YORK • LONDON
AMSTERDAM • PARIS • SYDNEY • HAMBURG
STOCKHOLM • ATHENS • TOKYO • MILAN • MADRID
PRAGUE • WARSAW • BUDAPEST • AUCKLAND

ISBN 0-373-78091-5

FOUR LITTLE PROBLEMS

Copyright © 2006 by Carrie Weaver

Books by Carrie Weaver

HARLEQUIN SUPERROMANCE

Special thanks to Mary Jane Brooke,
Superintendent of the Le Roy Central School District,
for being so helpful in responding to my questions.
She did her utmost to ensure that I had
accurate information. Any discrepancies are
mine, made in an effort to merge reality
with the fictional world I created.

PROLOGUE

"WHAT DO YOU MEAN my son needs a reality check?" Emily planted her fists on the substitute teacher's desk and leaned forward.

Mr. Stevens's eyes narrowed, but he held her gaze.

Something she had to admire despite his know-it-all attitude.

Topping five-eleven, Emily knew some men found her intimidating during the best of times. But today, suffering from PMS and hearing another childless moron offering advice on how to raise her kids, she felt darn near homicidal.

Or suicidal. Single parenthood sucked at times.

Mr. Stevens gestured toward a chair. "Please sit down, Mrs. Patterson."

"*Ms.* Patterson." She glared at him just long enough to let him know she wasn't ceding defeat. Then she wedged her rear end in the kiddie chair.

"Ms. Patterson, perhaps I started our meeting on the wrong foot. I'd anticipated Mrs. Wells's return from maternity leave by now. As a substitute, I'm at a bit of a disadvantage conducting her parent/teacher conferences."

Emily decided not to point out that her day hadn't been peachy, either. So, she went for a noncommittal "Mm-hm."

It wasn't her fault Mrs. Wells had extended her maternity leave. And it wasn't her fault this guy was experimenting with the idea of becoming a teacher. Rumor had it, Mr. Stevens was some well-known scientist, on leave from a high-paying job.

He flipped through a file folder on his desk. "Jason is an exceedingly bright child. His test scores are well above average."

"He's a smart kid."

"But he needs a firm hand if he's to achieve his potential. Perhaps his father should meet with us, too, and we can all formulate a plan for rewards and consequences?"

"Honey, if you can find Walt, you feel free to bring him in and have that conversation. Child services hasn't been able to locate him in seven years. But if you do, be sure to offer him a beer. That's the kind of reward he'll understand. And as far as consequences, he's not big on those. That's why he works under the table to avoid taxes and child support. *I'm* the one who administers rewards and consequences for four children." Emily ran out of breath, her chest heaving with emotion.

Mr. Stevens glanced around the room, at the ceiling and everywhere but at Emily. "I'm sure it's very difficult."

You have no idea. "Yes, it is."

"Maybe we could work more closely to ensure Jason makes the most of his opportunities."

Warning bells went off in Emily's head. Hadn't a boss once made a similar offer in mentoring her boys? And expected a game of slap and tickle with Emily in return? "Would you please clarify what you mean by working more closely together?"

"An accountability notebook would be a good thing. I'll write down Jason's homework assignments and you can check them daily to make sure he stays on task. I'll also include a section regarding his behavior in class. Consequences at home should help there."

Emily released a breath. "Okay. We can do that. He's a good kid, Mr. Stevens. For some reason, he's just gotten out of hand this year."

"He's gotten out of hand because he's been allowed to. If you're interested, I have a few brochures for the district-sponsored parenting classes." He opened his top desk drawer.

Emily's heart sank. If she didn't think he was right, she'd call him on his condescending attitude. As it was, she was too embarrassed to tell him that she'd already taken the courses and tried her darnedest to apply what she'd learned, but none of it seemed to work with Jason these days. Neither did any of the tactics she'd used when he was small. He'd turned into an alien creature almost overnight.

The teacher rummaged in his top desk drawer. "And I can give you a list of reading resources. Some parents find behavior modification quite helpful. Skinner, of course, was the—"

A muffled snap came from his drawer.

He jumped to his feet, cursing under his breath.

Emily tried to place the snapping sound— she'd heard it recently in another context.

Mr. Stevens brought his hand to chest level. "What the hell?"

Emily gulped at what she saw. A small mouse-trap gripped the teacher's middle finger, turning the tip an ugly purple.

Now she remembered the sound. Jason's ill-advised purchase at the dollar store. And how she'd instructed him to get rid of the mousetrap before he broke a finger.

Jumping up, she grabbed a pair of scissors, intent on prying the spring open.

"No!" Stevens jerked away.

"Stand still." Emily advanced, intent on saving him.

The door opened and the principal entered. "Mr. Stev— What's going on?" she asked. Her gaze skimmed over Emily, the raised scissors, the swearing teacher, the mousetrap.

The principal crossed her arms over her chest. "Ms. Patterson, I think it's best if you leave."

"Let me explain."

"*Go.*" Her voice brooked no argument.

CHAPTER ONE

Two years later...

PATRICK STEVENS GLANCED at the meeting agenda and almost aspirated his coffee right there in the teachers' lounge.

God, no.

He couldn't possibly be that unlucky, could he?

"What's wrong?" The new, perennially smiling kindergarten teacher slapped him on the back, as if that would help.

"Did you see who's running for PTO president?"

She shrugged. "Some woman named Patterson."

"As in, mother of Jason Patterson." That should have said it all.

"And that's a problem because?"

She was obviously still too wet behind the ears to understand the implications.

"Jason Patterson, the kid who threw cherry bombs in the boys' toilets."

No recognition.

"Led his own gambling and extortion ring."

"I'm sure he wasn't *that* bad." She flipped her hair and gave him that sparkling, you're-just-old-and-burnt-out smile.

At thirty-eight, he considered himself far from old. But she might have a point about the burnt-out part. Today, a little over two months into the second semester, summer break still seemed very far away. And other days, he couldn't imagine being anywhere else but in the classroom. It was a dichotomy that would have intrigued him if he had time to contemplate abstract thoughts. But, as it was, he barely had time to knock back a cup of coffee before his kids returned from music class.

Jason Patterson. His ultimate failure.

"The little delinquent told the playground aides the dice were for improving his math skills," he muttered under his breath as the newbie practically skipped out of the lounge. Obviously, she hadn't heard the mousetrap story and he wasn't about to enlighten her.

The girls' physical education teacher came in before the door clicked shut. Her eyes were on the prize—the coffeepot.

Patrick reread the agenda, hoping he'd been mistaken. No such luck. He suppressed a groan.

"What's your problem, Stevens?"

"Did you see who's running for PTO president?"

"The Patterson woman. You can kiss that field trip of yours goodbye. I doubt the woman can head up a fund-raising campaign. But with poor Mrs. Bigelow deader than a doornail, I guess we have to take what we can get."

"Yeah. A heart attack at thirty-three. Who'd have thought?"

"Mrs. Bigelow was such a nice woman, too. And her kids know how to behave. Not like that oldest Patterson boy."

"Jason. His mother transferred him out of my class the first year I taught here."

"Yeah. I heard something about that." She shrugged. "It happens."

"Not to me, it doesn't. At least not since Jason Patterson. I'm here because I want to make a difference. Otherwise, I'd still be a chemist, making serious money."

She planted her hands on her hips. "Spare me the greater-good lecture, Stevens. You better figure out how you're going to work with her and fast. No PTO sponsorship, no Sea World trip. It's as simple as that."

"I am *not* letting that woman ruin sixth grade for these kids. They've worked hard. Car washes. Bake sales. Sold candy out the wazoo. All the PTO needs to do is come up with the money that was promised."

She tilted her head to the side, tapping her chin with her index finger. "I hear Jason Patterson plays point for the basketball team."

"So?"

She smiled mysteriously and grabbed an insulated cup. For a woman who'd been in such a hurry, she took her time pouring her coffee. Returning the pot to the burner, she said, "It means Emily Patterson probably has a soft spot for the sports programs. And if your Sea World trip doesn't work out, maybe the PTO will spring for that new sports equipment I've been requesting forever."

Then she punched him playfully on the shoulder and headed out the door, whistling cheerfully.

The vultures were already circling.

EMILY'S STOMACH CHURNED as she approached the cafeteria, which had recently been renamed the multipurpose room. Straightening her spine, she pasted on a confident smile.

"You'll do fine." Nancy, her best friend in the world, patted her arm.

"You think? Some of the parents act like I'm something they scraped off the bottom of their shoes. That Tiffany Bigelow was the worst. Not that I want to speak ill of the dead."

"Since when? She wasn't nice when she was alive, so why should you pretend now?"

"I don't know. I don't know why I'm doing this, either."

"Because you love children and you don't want to see all the programs go down the tubes this year, just because of Tiffany's hard heart."

Emily chuckled in spite of herself. She whispered behind her hand. "I was a little surprised she even *had* a heart."

"You're not the only one. Her über-volunteer act didn't fool me. I'll never forgive the woman for telling Ana I adopted her from Russia because they wouldn't give me an American baby."

"I would have gladly scratched her eyes out for you."

Nancy slid her arm through Emily's. "I know. And I'm here to return the favor tonight. It's finally my chance to be there for you."

Emily swallowed the lump in her throat. "Thanks, friend."

"You're very welcome. Now, let's go show them who the next PTO president is going to be. The woman who will change things around here for all the parents and children who don't have a voice. The anti-Tiffanys and their kids."

Nodding, Emily adjusted the neckline of her blouse.

Nancy tipped her head. "The gray's lovely. But I'm glad you didn't go with the turtleneck. It didn't suit you."

"You don't think this is too, um, revealing?"

"No. You're absolutely beautiful just the way you are. Besides, the black camisole makes it downright respectable."

Emily tucked her hair behind her ear. Though she loved Nancy like a sister, her friend's cheerleader looks precluded her from ever really understanding what it was like to be slightly overweight and unsure. Or from totally understanding the reasons behind Emily's tendency to overcompensate by talking a little louder and allowing R-rated jokes to slip out at inopportune times.

No, when Nancy spoke, she was always classy and intelligent. People listened.

When Emily spoke, people rolled their eyes.

The multipurpose room door loomed.

Nancy patted Emily's arm again. "Okay, time to go in there and show them what you've got. You're smart, you're capable and children love you. You will be the best PTO president Elmwood Elementary has ever seen."

Emily raised her chin. Taking a deep breath, she flung open the door and strode inside.

It felt like all eyes were upon her.

The principal smiled, though it looked forced. She had to be remembering the mousetrap incident. "And here is Emily Patterson, who has so graciously stepped forward to take over the job of PTO president. Emily, please come sit here by the podium." She gestured to a row of seats.

It was a long walk to the front of the room, or so it seemed to Emily, who wished she'd lost that last fifteen pounds. And it wouldn't hurt if she had a few impressive initials after her name, like B.A. or Ph.D. But she was just plain Emily Patterson and that would have to do.

She headed toward the chair the principal indicated. She almost froze when she realized who sat in the next chair. Patrick Stevens.

He nodded tersely and shifted in his seat, his body language saying he didn't want to be within a mile of her.

Fine. She didn't particularly want to be near him, either.

Emily sat, her back ramrod-straight.

"Now," the principal said, "voting is just a formality, since we only have one candidate for the position." She smiled brightly at the handful of parents assembled. "All those in favor of Emily Patterson taking over as PTO president for the remainder of the school year, please raise your hand."

Most of the hands shot up immediately. None of the busy parents wanted the job themselves, and normally, Emily would have been right there beside them. But this was too important.

"Good. It's approved." The principal beamed.

There was a rustle as the parents lowered their arms.

Emily was aware that Patrick Stevens, beside her, didn't move a muscle. Because he hadn't raised his hand to vote.

She steeled herself not to let it get to her. Two years ago, she'd apologized for the mousetrap. She'd also made Jason apologize and work cafeteria cleanup for a week as penance. But it had been obvious Stevens had had it in for Jason, so she'd eventually asked to have her son moved to a different class.

Since then, she'd managed to avoid Patrick Stevens. Until now.

"I'm sure we'll all do our best to help Emily transition into the position." The principal gave the science teacher a pointed look. "I'll give her Mrs. Bigelow's files, and Mr. Stevens will be working closely with her regarding fund-raising for the sixth-grade Sea World trip. This is bound to be the most successful year yet."

Emily would have believed the principal, except for the nervous twitch under her right eye.

PATRICK STARED at his planning guide. It didn't give him any answers. Only told him a quiz was long overdue.

Removing a file folder from his desk, he flipped through his notes and the information on Sea World. The kids would be completely blown away by the experience. And maybe, just maybe, he could ignite that flame of scientific enthusiasm in one or two of them. He wanted to make this happen for Ari and Kat. He *needed* to make this happen.

And there was only one way to do that.

He picked up the phone and dialed. "Ms. Patterson, this is Patrick Stevens. I'd like to meet with you as soon as possible to discuss the Sea World trip. And make sure all the information Mrs. Bigelow had is there."

"Of course, I want my files to be complete…" she answered.

Patrick exhaled with relief.

But his relief was short-lived when Emily continued. "…so I can properly weigh all the requests for PTO funds."

"But Tiffany agreed to pay at least half the Florida expenses if the students could raise the initial deposits."

"Hm. I'm looking at her notes, and there's no indication she agreed to that."

Patrick gripped the phone. He could almost see the disappointment in Ari's eyes when he told the class they wouldn't see Shamu or the Shark Encounter as planned.

Calling on his very limited schmoozing skills, he managed to keep his voice even. "Do you think we could meet at the coffee shop on Cedar tomorrow after school, say four o'clock?" He had a better chance of convincing her in person.

"I don't get off work till five. I can meet you briefly about five fifteen. Then, I need to get home to my kids."

"Great. That'll be fine." He didn't have anyone he had to get home to. Other than his salamander, Newt Gingrich, tarantula, Hairy S. Truman, and boa constrictor, Arnold. But being predominantly nocturnal, they probably wouldn't even notice he was late.

CHAPTER TWO

EMILY WAS EARLY. She folded her hands and rested them on top of the file folder. Her latte was off to the side, untouched. She couldn't summon her usual gusto for sweets.

Her boss, Olivia, had allowed Emily to skip her second break in favor of leaving early. Voice mail could pick up the phones at the Luxury Lingerie office for the last fifteen minutes of the workday.

Glancing at the file folder, she tried to gather her thoughts. None of it made sense. Not Tiffany's notes, not the numbers, nothing.

The bell above the door tinkled as Patrick Stevens entered and placed his order. Tall, dark-haired and serious, he was everything a single woman of forty should want. Unfortunately, Emily's tastes strayed more toward the unreliable. What was it about her that was attracted to the worst kind of man?

She was surprised when Patrick approached, two bottles of water hanging from his fingers, while he balanced a plate with two double choco-late chunk cookies. It was a sight that might have endeared him to her, if he weren't such a pompous ass. And if she had an appetite. For cookies, that is.

"I hope you don't mind. I took the liberty of ordering an extra cookie and water bottle...."

"No, I don't mind." It was kind of sweet. But she didn't like sweets these days, she reminded herself.

Emily gestured toward the opposite chair.

While he deposited the food and drinks, she pretended to read Tiffany's notes. Instead, she found herself watching him from beneath her lashes. He had beautiful hands. Not feminine beautiful. Strong, masculine, survey-every-inch-of-a-woman's-body beautiful. They hinted at slow, skillful lovemaking.

The small, white scar at the tip of his middle finger stopped her errant thoughts.

Had he acquired a sense of humor about the mouse-trap incident?

She was afraid to ask.

Shaking her head, Emily forced her thoughts to the practical. This was her opportunity to show everyone she was more than a brash woman who couldn't control her kids. "I'm glad you suggested meeting. I've read Tiffany's notes backward and forward and I can't seem to make sense of them. I thought maybe you'd have more luck."

He handed her a water and removed the cap from his own. "Sorry, didn't realize you'd already ordered. You can save it for later. It's important to stay hydrated."

Ah. This was the Patrick Stevens she remembered. She sincerely doubted he'd acquired a sense of humor about anything.

"Yes. Thank you."

She slid the file folder across the table. "See what you think."

He opened the folder. Flipping through the pages, he frowned. "Most of this looks like doodling." Turning the file sideways, he said. "And this looks like it might be her grocery list."

"That's what I thought. Kinda weird, because Tiffany always seemed to be taking notes with her PDA. I figured she was so anal, everything would be prioritized and printed up."

"She did seem very organized. And you're right, there's nothing in here about the Florida field trip. Are you sure this was all you were given?"

"Of course I'm sure." Did he think she was so scatterbrained, she might have misplaced a whole sheaf of papers containing Tiffany Bigelow's rounded script?

Two could play at that game. "Didn't you keep any notes?"

"Yes, they're in my backpack somewhere." He shoved a piece of cookie in his mouth, wiped his hands on a napkin and rummaged through his pack.

He reminded Emily of a chipmunk. But his hazel eyes were too serious for such a mischievous creature. He might be cute, if he'd lighten up.

"Here it is." He triumphantly produced a wire-bound pad of paper, suitable for taking notes in class.

He paged through until he found the appropriate section.

Sliding it across the table, he pointed to a row of figures.

"Those are the projected costs, minus the monies we've brought in through various fundraising projects of our own."

"Yes, I think I remember hearing about a car wash?" Emily had tried to block out any information pertaining to Patrick Stevens. Apparently, she'd failed. "And a bake sale?"

He nodded, grinning. "Yeah, the kids are pretty industrious once they get their hearts set on something."

"Yes, they are." Emily swallowed hard, then glanced away, unable to meet his earnest gaze.

His obvious affection for his students stung. Why couldn't he have been that way with Jason? It might have made a world of difference to the boy. Instead, her son had been rejected by yet another male authority figure. She'd sometimes wondered if Jason's pranks had been a bid for attention, a clumsy way to connect with this reserved man.

Instead, Patrick Stevens had been cold and unyielding. And Emily's heart had broken as she'd watched Jason build a wall around his emotions. Her once fun-loving, affectionate son had grown sarcastic and rude. Prepubescent hormones were one explanation. But Emily thought his attitude was probably more the result of one disappointment too many coming from a father figure.

Of course, Emily shouldn't blame the teacher. Loving his students wasn't in his contract. Nor trying to understand them.

"Ms. Patterson?"

Emily flushed. "I'm sorry, did you say something?"

"I pointed out the figure we'll need from the PTO funds. Tiffany didn't seem to think it would be a problem."

Emily's eyes widened. "That's a lot of money. I've seen the PTO budget and I can't help but wonder why Tiffany agreed to this."

"She mentioned having some special fund-raising project in the works for the spring that would make it possible."

"What kind of special project?"

"That's just it. I have no idea. She wouldn't say. Just said it was big."

"I'll talk to Principal Ross. Maybe she knew about it. Something that big would need to be planned well in advance."

"Time is critical, Ms. Patterson. The hotel and bus companies are pressing for deposits. We have enough from our own fund-raising, but I don't want to make a nonrefundable deposit if there's a chance the PTO won't come through on what's been promised. I need to know right away."

"Mr. Stevens, obviously I can't commit to something I know nothing about. I'll talk to the principal, see if she knows where the rest of Tiffany's notes might be. In the meantime, Principal Ross is putting my name on the PTO account. I can't access the bank statements until then."

"Can't Ross access them?"

Emily shook her head. She was starting to get a bad feeling about this. "There was some mix-up at the bank and Principal Ross was removed as a cosigner. After the treasurer moved to Texas in November, Tiffany was the only one with access."

Patrick cursed under his breath. He seemed to swear a lot for a dispassionate guy.

EMILY SET A STACK of paper plates in the center of the large picnic table she used for a kitchen dinette set. Nancy's husband, Beau, was working tonight, so she and Ana were staying for dinner.

"So maybe Tiffany was playing fast and loose with the PTO funds?" Nancy's eyes sparkled with interest as she folded paper napkins and arranged them with plastic cutlery. "I knew there was something about that woman."

"I didn't say that. We won't know anything until one of us can access the account. Principal Ross said she'd go to the bank tomorrow and straighten it out."

"But still, it's a little strange, don't you think? Only Tiffany's name as signatory on the account?"

"Shh. I don't want to start any rumors." Emily nodded meaningfully toward the family room, where her two younger boys, Mark and Ryan, played hide-and-seek with Nancy's daughter, Ana.

Jason had basketball practice and Jeremy was playing at a neighbor's house.

Nancy sighed. "My bad. I guess I was hoping to dig up some dirt on the woman. She was just trying too hard to be perfect. And was downright mean, to boot."

"I hope all of this turns out to be an honest mistake. The whole PTO thing is getting more complicated by the minute. Patrick Stevens is pressing me to release funds for the sixth-grade trip to Sea World."

"You obviously need all the facts before you can do something like that. What's his hurry?"

"He has good reason." Emily put out a large bucket of the Colonel's chicken, along with containers of coleslaw and baked beans. "Hotel and transportation deposits need to be made. But there's nothing I can do."

"This is more than you bargained for, huh?" Nancy's voice was warm with concern.

"You don't know the half of it. The PE teacher gave me some brochures for sports equipment. The art teacher mentioned how desperately we need art supplies. And the music instructor showed me how old and worn-out the band instruments are."

"Sounds like a lot of pressure, Em."

"It is. And there's a part of me that thinks the money Tiffany supposedly promised for the Florida trip could be put to better uses."

"It's a tough call, no doubt about it. But if you find Tiffany's notes and she already promised the money, you'll be hard-pressed to back out now."

"That's just it. I'll be damned if I do and damned if I don't. It might be best if Tiffany's notes aren't found. Then I can at least do what my conscience says is right."

Nancy squeezed her arm. "Let's look on the bright side. Maybe her fabulous spring fundraiser will bring in so much money, you'll be able to please everyone."

Emily nodded. "Maybe."

But as a single mom on a tight budget, she knew all too well there was rarely enough money to go around and someone always ended up mad. And it was starting to look like Patrick Stevens might be the angry one if the PTO budget was tight.

PATRICK ARRIVED at school well before the first bell. It had become a tradition.

And sure enough, he saw two figures huddled in the doorway, their thin coats probably affording very little warmth. It had been a mild winter for upstate New York, but mornings were still chilly. "Hey Ari, Kat. You look like you could use some hot chocolate."

The two kids turned, nodding.

"The usual spot?" he asked.

They nodded again, following him to a bench near the doors.

Though Patrick walked slowly, he still reached the bench before them. He turned and waited.

Ari's gait was erratic, one foot turned inward. His twin sister, Kat, slowed her pace to match his.

Patrick swallowed hard as he remembered another boy with a less pronounced pigeon-toed gait. A boy who had once run, laughed and played, but was developmentally little more than a toddler now.

He pushed the thought away. He couldn't take that trip down memory lane.

When they'd settled themselves on the bench, Patrick withdrew a thermos from his backpack. He would have preferred a strong cup of coffee, but this ritual was for Ari and Kat.

He poured the steaming mixture into three cups.

The children waited patiently while he handed them each a foam cup.

The expressions in their huge, dark eyes were unreadable. Someone's stomach growled.

"I hope you guys will help me out." He withdrew a packet from his backpack. "I have these muffins that will go stale if someone doesn't eat them. I thought maybe you two could help."

"Yes, Mr. Stevens, we'll help." Kat spoke for both of them as she often did.

"Good." He handed them each a banana-oat muffin, wishing it was a four-course hot breakfast. Their parents were immigrants, both working sixteen-hour days to make ends meet. Sometimes, he suspected there wasn't enough food in the house.

Patrick sipped his hot cocoa, wondering if the kids thought it strange they didn't go inside where it was warm. But they never asked, so he was spared explaining that it wasn't prudent for a teacher to show a special interest in a child behind closed doors. He could understand the practical reasons, but it still saddened him.

Instead, they sat, shivering, right in front of the school, where they were appropriately supervised by anyone who might drive or walk by.

"I read...the book," Ari said. His speech was a bit slow because of cerebral palsy, but his mind was sharp. He'd been mainstreamed several years back and had done fine. Of course, he also had his own personal guardian angel in the form of Kat.

"What did you think of the book, Ari?"

"Dolphins are smart and nice," he enunciated slowly.

"Yes, they're good animals. There are lots of true stories of dolphins keeping humans from drowning." Funny, how he could say the word *drowning* without even flinching. Progress perhaps?

Ari's eyes were bright with excitement. "I… will…swim with the dolphins. At Sea World."

The thought made Patrick's stomach churn.

"Sure, we'll see the dolphins. I think you can even pet them from a boat."

"No." His reply was emphatic. "Swim."

Anything but that.

For the first time he could remember, Patrick ignored Ari. "What about you, Kat, did you read the book?"

"Yes."

"Do you want to see the dolphins and penguins?"

She hesitated, as if afraid to believe in something that would turn out to be a fairy tale. "I'll go if Ari goes."

"Good. You guys worked really hard at the car wash."

There was no way in hell he'd allow this trip to die. He'd promised all the sixth-graders, but most importantly, he'd promised Ari and Kat.

Emily Patterson would just have to do the right thing.

EMILY SIGHED when she hung up the phone, eyeing her overflowing In basket. Now she knew why it was mostly stay-at-home moms who were

PTO presidents. She was in the unenviable position of having to ask to leave early two days in a row.

She found her boss in her office. "Olivia, the principal from the school called and wants to meet with me."

Olivia gave her a pitying look. She probably assumed it was about Jason again.

Emily's conscience twinged, but she didn't correct her. She didn't want her job jeopardized because of her PTO position.

Fortunately, Olivia was understanding. "Voice mail can pick up the phones. And you said you'd work through your lunch hour tomorrow?"

"Yes, I will. Thanks a bunch, Olivia."

Her boss nodded. "Go."

Emily grabbed her purse, forwarded the phones and left in a matter of minutes. She was breathless when she reached Principal Ross's office, following Patrick through the door.

"Good, you're both here," the principal said. "Please close the door."

Emily's heart sank.

"Please, sit." The woman sat behind her desk and nodded toward two chairs.

Patrick pulled out one of the chairs slightly and gestured for her to sit down.

His courtesy flustered her.

But she sat.

And so did he, in the chair next to her. They were practically knee-to-knee in the small office.

Principal Ross cleared her throat. "What I have to say is rather difficult. I expect it to stay in this room. Not to be repeated to anyone."

"Of course," Patrick said.

"Yes, of course," Emily murmured, aware that she'd probably already shared too much with Nancy. But Nancy was discreet and wouldn't repeat the information.

"I spent several hours at the bank today. The PTO account was in complete disarray. But the gist is, there's only a few dollars left."

Patrick stiffened. "There's got to be some mistake."

"I'm sorry, there's no mistake. The branch manager checked and rechecked the figures while I was there. I'm afraid I'll have no choice but to contact the police."

"Do you have any idea where the money went?" Emily asked.

Marilyn Ross's mouth turned down at the corners. For a moment, Emily was afraid she might cry.

"I guess I can go ahead and tell you. There were several sizeable cash withdrawals made over the past three months. During the time that Tiffany Bigelow was sole signatory."

Patrick swore under his breath.

Emily silently agreed.

"So I'm in the unenviable position of heaping more grief on the Bigelow family."

"What effect will this have on the Sea World trip and all the other requests for PTO assistance?" Emily asked.

"The account is frozen. Tiffany had been very excited about a spectacular new connection she'd made for a fund-raising activity, but she didn't share the details. I'm afraid I was distracted by…other priorities and didn't give it the attention I should have."

"Tiffany always took notes." Patrick leaned forward. "I've been thinking she might have files on her home computer."

"The thought crossed my mind, too. But the police will be involved very soon and I don't think we'll be in a position to ask favors from Tiffany's husband. I sincerely doubt he'll let us anywhere near her computer."

Patrick hesitated, glancing at his watch. "It's late. Surely, you don't intend to call the police tonight."

The principal sighed. "No, to be honest I just want to go home and have a glass of wine. This has been one heck of a day."

"Since there's nothing more we can do today, why don't we sleep on it and maybe there will be an obvious solution tomorrow morning?" Patrick's face was bland, innocent.

But Emily could almost feel electricity rolling off him. He might have sincere hazel eyes, but he was up to something.

"Yes. Let's call it a day. I'll update both of you within the next day or so. Remember, this goes no further than this room."

Emily murmured agreement, aware of Patrick's hand on her elbow as they left the office.

"Can I talk to you outside?" he asked, his mouth close to her ear.

"Of course." Of course…she should run like hell. Because the reliable Mr. Stevens was putting out some decidedly dangerous vibes.

"Where's your car?" he asked as they left the building.

She nodded in the direction of her minivan. "Over there."

He was silent as they walked to her car.

Emily punched the button on her keyless entry tag. The lock opened, but she hesitated.

Patrick's gaze was intent. "I need to ask you to do something for me."

With some men, she would have figured he was propositioning her. The ones who hadn't figured out that, although she enjoyed an off-color joke and liked to pretend she was worldly-wise, she kept her sex life toward the nonexistent end of the spectrum. She'd learned the consequences of loving too soon, too easily.

But she suspected Patrick had something else in mind. And that intrigued her.

"What?"

"I need access to Tiffany's computer."

"You heard Principal Ross. There's no way we'll get near that computer."

"There's one way. We go tonight, together, and ask Brad Bigelow. We tell him we're very sorry to bother him, but we need Tiffany's PTO files."

"I'm not going to pester her family while they're grieving."

Patrick sighed, running a hand through his hair. "It *is* kind of ghoulish. But we'll be very tactful, very respectful. And we might discover some simple answer for the missing money. We could end up saving her family more grief."

Emily contemplated his argument. They might actually be helping Tiffany's family. It was a stretch, though. "Why do I have to be there?"

"People trust you. You're very open and always say what you think."

Emily chuckled, a hoarse, desperate sound. And here she'd thought nobody listened to a word she said. "I'm trustworthy, so you want me to lie to a man who suddenly lost his wife and the mother of his children and must be out of his mind with grief."

"Yes." He frowned. "I guess that's exactly what I'm asking."

"I'm sorry. I don't think it's a good idea. Let the police handle it."

"That's exactly what I intend to do. But you heard Ross. Once the police are involved that computer will be tied up for years. It won't harm anyone if we copy her PTO files." He leaned closer, his gaze earnest. "Please?"

"It means that much to you, this Florida trip?"

"Absolutely."

"Are you going to tell me why?"

He glanced away. "I'm not going to disappoint those kids." His voice was low.

Emily was touched. And wary. This was not the Patrick Stevens she'd met two years ago. "Okay. But I'll need to get home first to feed my kids and supervise their homework. Should we call Brad?"

"No. Let's not give him any advance warning."

"I can meet you at eight. We'll need the Bigelow's address. I think they live on Cedar...."

"I've got their address in here." He patted his backpack.

Emily had to wonder why he seemed so

prepared, as if he'd known he would need the information. She also had to wonder if maybe there was another reason he was so anxious to get his hands on Tiffany's files.

CHAPTER THREE

"YOU'RE SURE I shouldn't follow you to the Bigelows' house?" Emily asked Patrick when they met later that evening. She'd parked under a light in the coffee house parking lot.

Patrick leaned against a Lexus SUV. "Better if we arrive together—a united front. It'll seem more natural, like we're working closely on the project. I'll drive, if you don't mind."

"I don't mind." Might as well use his gas.

He walked around to the other side of the SUV and opened the passenger door for her.

More unexpected gallantry.

Bemused, Emily sank into the cushy leather passenger seat as Patrick settled himself in the driver's seat.

"Nice," she said.

"It's from my other life. Before teaching, when I made a living wage."

Glancing around the luxurious interior, Emily

said, "I have the feeling you and I have very different ideas of what a living wage is."

He laughed, backing the car out of the space. "It was nice while it lasted. The money, that is."

"What did you do?"

"I was a chemist with Porter Chemical."

"I imagine that was interesting."

"No, you don't."

Emily was taken aback for a second. Then she chuckled. "You're right. It sounds pretty boring to me. But I imagine it's interesting to the serious, scientific types."

"Is that how I strike you?" He sounded pleased.

"Yes."

"There are worse things than being serious."

"But there's such a thing as being too serious."

He glanced at her before pulling out onto Cedar. "It's a balance I guess I haven't achieved."

"Why'd you decide to stay on at the school permanently?"

He shrugged. "It fit. You ever have an experience like that, where things just seemed right?"

"Yeah, both of my marriages." The words slipped out before she could stop them.

"You've been married twice?"

Nodding, she said, "And each time I thought it was forever."

A few minutes later, Patrick parked the SUV

in front of a ranch-style home with an immaculate front yard. He let the motor idle.

Turning to her, his gaze was solemn. "You're very real, Emily. You don't play games. I admire that in a person."

This side of him rattled her. He'd said he admired her, loudmouthed Emily, mother of Jason-who-sets-mouse-traps-in-teachers'-desks.

Thanking him seemed over the top, so she opted for a smile of gratitude.

"Let's go." He reached into the backseat to retrieve his backpack, which brought him entirely too close.

Emily opened the door and stepped out before he got the idea he needed to open the door for her. Or an even weirder idea, like kissing her.

And, yet, she was disappointed when she was no longer cocooned in the car with him. It was as if they'd been in an alternate reality, where they could talk like any other two people.

He cupped her elbow as they walked to the front door. "You mind doing the talking?"

"Since I'm the trustworthy one, I guess I'd better."

He chuckled, the sound coming entirely too close for comfort in the dark. "See, you say what you're thinking."

"That's not always a good thing."

"Probably not. But at least a guy knows where he stands with you."

Emily opened her mouth to respond, but closed it. Instead, she knocked on the Bigelows' door.

A blond girl who looked to be about nine opened the door.

"Hi, honey, is your father home?" Emily asked.

The girl nodded and disappeared, leaving the door ajar.

At Emily's house, one of her kids would have simply bellowed her name from the doorway. She wondered if this was how well-mannered children answered the door.

A man came to the door. Tall, blond and muscular, he looked just like Emily expected— high school homecoming court royalty, only aged fifteen years.

"May I help you?"

"I'm so sorry to bother you, Mr. Bigelow. I'm Emily Patterson and I've taken over as PTO president at Elmwood. And this is Patrick Stevens, PTO adviser." It wasn't a lie, really. He'd given her quite a bit of advice in the past couple days. "Please accept our condolences on your loss."

"Thank you."

When they didn't move to leave, Mr. Bigelow

frowned. "What can I do for you? I already gave Tiffany's files to Mrs. Ross."

"I know and I'm so sorry to intrude at a time like this. But I need to look at the PTO notes Tiffany kept on her PC. They're probably more complete than the file I was given."

"Now's not a good time. My daughters and I were on our way out."

Patrick stepped forward. "We can copy the files onto a disk. It'll only take a moment."

"Come to think of it, Tiffany might have it on disk already. Let me check." He didn't invite them in, simply shut the door with the promise of returning in a minute.

Emily looked at Patrick.

He shrugged.

They waited what seemed more like five hours, but was probably about five minutes.

"Yep, here it is." Bigelow leaned out the door and handed Emily a floppy disk. "Marked PTO. You can have it. Hope it helps. Bye."

"Thank you. And I'm very sorry—"

The door shut in her face before Emily could apologize again for disturbing him.

"Come on." Patrick nodded toward the car.

When they'd walked several yards, Emily mused, "Did it seem as if he wanted to get rid of us?"

"He was in a hurry. We caught him on his way out the door."

"Yes...but, still, he seemed a little odd."

Patrick stopped walking. "Grief will do that to a person." His voice was low.

Somehow, Emily got the impression he was speaking from experience. "Yes, it will."

He started walking again.

She resisted the urge to ask him who he grieved for. "I'll let you know if there's anything interesting on the disk."

He was silent for a moment, until they reached the SUV, where he again opened the passenger door for her. "How about if I let *you* know if there's anything interesting on the disk?"

"Absolutely not. I didn't pester that poor man only to get secondhand information from you."

"I'm not letting that disk out of my sight. At least not until I make a copy. My place isn't too far from here. We can stop, make a copy and I'll drop you off at your car."

Emily glanced at her watch and groaned. "It's almost nine o'clock and Jason probably didn't put the kids to bed on time. How about if I make a copy and drop it off at school tomorrow?"

"No way."

"You're the one who said I was trustworthy." She raised her chin.

"I said you *seemed* trustworthy."

"Thanks a bunch."

He stepped closer. "Look, I've got a lot riding on this Sea World trip."

His proximity flustered her. Emily would have agreed to nearly anything to get him to back off. "Fine. Why don't you drop me off at my van, then follow me to my house. I'll make you a copy of the disk."

The dome light cast a weak yellow glow over her shoulder, revealing only his profile. But there was enough light for Emily to see him wince, as if he'd rather do anything than be in her home. Maybe it should have struck her as funny, but instead, it made her sad.

"Or the offer's still open—I can drop off a copy at school first thing tomorrow morning. Those are your choices."

Shaking his head, he went around to the driver's side and got in. "I'll follow you home." His voice was resigned, as if he faced impending death.

"Patrick, I promise Jason will be on his very best behavior."

He mumbled something under his breath that sounded an awful lot like, "That's what I'm afraid of."

EMILY PARKED and waited for Patrick to set the SUV alarm.

She prayed, silently, that the house would be somewhat presentable.

Patrick approached, eyeing the front of her home. "Nice. With all those planting beds, you must be quite a gardener."

Shrugging, Emily said, "I should have tulips coming up soon if the weather holds. And I'll add a few annuals, but nothing fancy, I'm afraid." She fit the key in the lock, her mouth dry. She felt very, very vulnerable inviting Patrick Stevens into her home.

The sight that greeted her made her want to turn tail and run. To Patrick Stevens, it would seem like the inmates were running the asylum. And a chaotic asylum at that.

"Come in." Her voice was weak.

Of course, it could have been because she was drowned out by the cacophony of blaring TV, a barking dog, yowling cats and screaming children.

Emily wished the ground would swallow her whole.

When it didn't, she squared her shoulders and entered the fray. She caught Mark by the arm as he raced past her. "Whoa." Then she snagged Ryan by the neck of his superhero pajamas. "What's going on here. Where's Jason?"

Both boys laughed uproariously, as if she'd entered the comedy hall of fame. Their red fruit-drink mustaches made them look like slightly insane clowns.

She gripped Mark's arm a little tighter. "I said, where is Jason?" she asked between clenched teeth.

The boys apparently scented danger through their sugar-induced high and settled down immediately.

Ryan pointed toward the family room. "Watchin' TV."

Emily frowned. She'd blocked the Playboy Channel, so she was pretty sure it wasn't a porn problem. Marching around the corner, she realized maybe the porn channel would have been the lesser of two evils.

"Ja-son." It came out high-pitched.

But Jason didn't seem to hear. Neither did his girlfriend, Cassie.

Truth be told, Emily couldn't tell where Jason left off and Cassie began, they were so intertwined. Fortunately, both seemed to be fully clothed. And there were two feet touching the floor. Cassie's by the looks of them.

"Cassie." It was whispered, almost a hiss. And perfectly pitched to get through the haze of lust hanging in the room.

Cassie shot to a sitting position, adjusting her clothes. "Um, Mrs. Patterson, hi."

"Time for you to go, Cass."

"Yes, ma'am." She threw a geometry book in her backpack and scrambled for the door.

"Jason, I've been very clear that friends aren't allowed over when I'm not home. I would suggest you go up to your room and we'll discuss this later." Certain death was promised in her tone, and Jason for once heeded the warning.

His eyes widened when he glanced past her and saw his nemesis, Patrick Stevens, standing in their living room.

Jason vaulted the coffee table and took the stairs two at a time.

"I haven't seen him move that fast in months." Emily released a shaky breath.

"Last time I saw him move that fast was after there was a small explosion in the boys' restroom." Patrick's tone was dry. He shook his head mournfully, as if to say, "What did I expect?"

Emily wanted to sit down in the middle of the floor and cry.

But there was still one child left unaccounted for.

"Where's Jeremy?"

"Upstairs. Reading."

Jeremy, the good child. At least she'd been

blessed with one kid who seemed to have both feet on the ground. Literally, and figuratively speaking.

"What's Clifford barking about?" she asked.

Both boys shrugged.

"He was howlin' earlier," Mark offered.

Oh, no. "What did you feed him? He only howls when he's about to—"

Emily slapped a hand over her mouth. She advanced on the black Lab, grasping him by the collar and marching him out the door.

That left only the two cats barreling through the house as if possessed.

"Catnip?" She didn't really need to ask.

The boys nodded and giggled.

"You two say good-night to Mr. Stevens, go brush your teeth and get to bed. And I better see clean teeth, not just wet toothbrushes. I'm on to that trick."

The boys stepped in front of Patrick, gazing upward with awe. "G'night, Mr. Stevens."

"Good night, boys," came his strangled reply.

Emily wouldn't have been surprised if Patrick had run from the house screaming.

But instead, his eyes sparkled, as if he were having a hard time containing laughter.

And for some reason that made Emily mad.

"Mark, Ryan, bed. Now."

They trotted up the stairs, the picture of obedience.

Then Emily turned her attention to Patrick, who grinned.

"You think it's funny? You think you could do better? I might just leave right now. As the only adult, you're honor bound to watch them until I get back." She'd made up the rule, but it sounded good.

And evidently Patrick took her at her word, because he became very serious. The Patrick she was accustomed to.

"Yes, ma'am."

If he saluted, she'd have to kill him.

Fortunately, he didn't.

PATRICK WAS VERY AWARE of Emily's presence as she peered over his shoulder at the computer screen.

"Nothing there," she said. "Next page?"

"You're sure you read that?"

"I can speed read."

Evidently, he must've allowed his shock to show.

"What? Lots of people speed read."

"Yes, I'm sure you're right."

"Or are you just surprised I know how to read the words with more than one syllable?"

Patrick winced. She was dead on.

"Why is it that men assume I must be stupid? Just because I'm, um, full-figured and tell a joke here and there."

He eyed her cautiously over his shoulder. She made him nervous, standing so close, her breath warm on his ear. If he turned a fraction more, he'd have a tantalizing view of the lace playing hide-and-seek with her cleavage.

"Voluptuous and irreverent."

"What?"

"That's how I think of you."

"Oh."

Emily remained silent after that.

He hoped she knew he meant it as a compliment. And hoped she *didn't* realize how totally distracting the combination was.

Closing his eyes, he tried to summon the image of Ari and Kat, laughing at the antics of dolphins.

It worked. Emily's curves were no longer an issue. Patrick was a man with a mission.

The documents flew by, a journal-like testimonial to how overscheduled Tiffany Bigelow had been.

Along about page four, Patrick started to sweat. Tiffany had apparently been unwilling or unable to refuse a single request for funds. A little mental math told him she'd promised more money than the PTO was likely to raise in four years, let alone four months.

His heart sank. He no longer wanted to think about Ari and Kat at Sea World. Because, instead, all he saw was the sad acceptance in their dark eyes. And the I-knew-it-was-too-good-to-be-true slump to Kat's shoulders. Worse would be Ari's devastation, because he'd believed Patrick's promises with his whole being.

Emily's home, a place that had initially seemed chaotic yet warm, now started to close in on him. He needed to escape, to think. To figure out some way to make this work.

Clearing his throat, he asked, "A blank disk?"

Emily didn't respond.

When he turned, he realized she'd been too shocked to speak. Her eyes were wide and unseeing, her lips trembled.

"I said, do you have a blank disk?" His voice came out harsher than he intended.

She leaned over his shoulder to open the cabinet door.

He barely noticed how close those voluptuous curves were. All he could comprehend was that he was royally screwed.

Emily handed him a floppy disk.

She was silent as he copied the disk, then accepted her copy with a murmured thank-you.

She walked him to the door, saying a quiet goodbye.

And when he stopped in the doorway and turned, she didn't try to conceal the sadness in her deep brown eyes. "I'm sorry, Patrick. It looks like there are going to be a lot of disappointed people. It'll be a free-for-all for any funds we locate."

"Yeah, well, you do what you have to do." He raised his hand in a silent goodbye.

CHAPTER FOUR

EMILY TIPTOED into Ryan's room and watched him sleep. This was what mattered. Not how much money was missing from the PTO fund and not how many teachers would probably hate her guts.

She recalled Patrick's frown when he'd suggested she do what she needed to do. It had almost sounded like a threat, except for the tinge of sadness in his voice.

She brushed hair off Ryan's forehead. He appeared so sweet and angelic when asleep. Faint traces of his red fruit-drink mustache were the only evidence of his night of six-year-old debauchery.

Smiling, she counted her blessings. Her children were precious and she wouldn't trade them for anything. Not even a spotless, peaceful house.

Tiptoeing from his room, she stopped outside Jason's door. A thin strip of light shone beneath.

Emily threw back her shoulders and prepared to do battle, when all she really wanted was a hot bath and eight hours of uninterrupted sleep.

She tapped softly and entered, allowing Jason enough time to cover up for modesty if he wasn't dressed, but not enough time to hide serious mischief—like bomb-making or drugs. Sighing, Emily knew she would have been shocked to find Jason doing something illegal or dangerous. But then again, it was often the parents who were the last to know.

Her gaze swept the room till she located her son slouching on the bed. Fortunately, he was dressed and there were no signs of a felony in progress.

Emily suppressed an urge to grab him by his shirtfront and shake some sense into him. Instead, she perched on the edge of his bed. "We have a rule, Jase, because I think it's important. You broke that rule tonight."

"We were only studying."

Emily mentally counted to ten. Not only was he lying, but by doing so, he implied she was too stupid to comprehend what she'd seen. "What? You were studying Cassie's tonsils with your tongue?"

"Mom!"

"I thought I could trust you." His betrayal hurt. She depended on him to take care of the smaller children.

"Really, we were studying. But we started kissing like two seconds before you got home and—"

"Even if I believed that, it means you weren't watching your brothers during those few seconds. That's all it takes for a child to drown or start a fire. I expect you to act responsibly when you're in charge of your brothers."

"Mark and Ryan are fine."

"No thanks to you. Which brings me to my second point. A teenage girl and boy home alone together is not a good thing. I don't care how trustworthy you are—and I like Cassie—but things get out of hand really quickly. I think it's about time for us to have a refresher talk about pregnancy and STDs."

His face blanched. "Please, Mom, not *that*. Can't you just ground me?"

The irony made Emily want to smile. She was so incredibly uncool and embarrassing to her kids. But a smart mother used it to her advantage. "It's late. I'll spare you the safe sex discussion tonight. But we *will* discuss it. And until then, you're grounded."

Relief flashed in Jason's blue eyes, so reminiscent of his father's. Oh, how she loved this headstrong child. And how it terrified her that he might do something stupid to derail his life. "Choices, Jase. Every choice you make has the possibility of changing your life, good or bad."

Jason's eyes started to glaze over. She could

tell he'd escaped to whatever alternate reality he inhabited when she lectured. Sighing, he said, "I'm tired, Mom."

"Yes, so am I." Bone tired from nonstop problems and decision-making. "We'll talk tomorrow morning."

"Uh-huh."

"Jason?"

"Huh?"

"I love you."

His frown deepened as if she'd used some horrible curse. She hoped, underneath his tough exterior, that he still enjoyed hearing his mom tell him she loved him. Because she intended to keep at it indefinitely. Some days, that was all she had to give.

When no response was forthcoming, Emily turned to leave.

"Mom?"

She stopped, her hand on the knob. "Yes?" Maybe he'd say those four little words she longed to hear.

I love you, Mom. She could almost see him as a pudgy toddler, handing her a wilted dandelion. What a sweet, sweet child he'd been. Until puberty.

Jason frowned. "What was *he* doing here?"

"Hm?" For a moment she'd forgotten their

visitor. "Mr. Stevens stopped by to copy a disk containing PTO records."

"He's not coming back, is he?"

"Not that I know of. Why do you ask?"

"Um, you're not, like, dating him or anything, are you?"

The horror in Jason's voice made Emily laugh. The boy had a vivid imagination. "No, Jason, I'm not dating him."

"WHAT AM I GOING TO DO, Nancy?" Emily almost forgot her problems as she took a bite of double cheeseburger. A large order of french fries beckoned, promising to make her forget her doubts. Two days had gone by since they'd retrieved the disk and Emily was no closer to figuring out a solution.

Nancy speared lettuce and marinated chicken, pausing to say, "I wish I had an easy answer, but I don't. Looks to me like you have two choices. One, throw up your hands and declare the school year a disaster. Because of Tiffany's duplicity, nobody would blame you."

Emily shifted in her seat. She didn't want to admit defeat.

"Or, two, you start organizing fund-raising campaigns like crazy. It'll be hard, but at least you can salvage a few of the smaller programs."

"Yes, you're right. I may be a lot of things, but I'm not a quitter. I'll need some help, though."

"You can count on me." Nancy sipped her iced tea. Blotting her lips with her napkin, she said, "I bet there's fund-raising information on the Internet."

"I'll do some surfing tonight. I'd like to ask one of the previous presidents for some ideas, if I can do it without spilling the beans about Tiffany. Remember, not a word to anyone."

"Cross my heart. You mentioned Patrick Stevens was at your house?"

"Just to copy the disk."

"Sure. The disk."

"It's the truth." Emily's cheeks warmed. "Why is everyone reading more into this than there really is?"

"Where there's smoke, there's fire." Nancy leaned forward, her eyes sparkling. "Are you blushing? In the three years we've been friends, I've never seen you blush."

"You're imagining things. Patrick can't stand me. And I'm not too thrilled about him, either." Emily felt a twinge of doubt. "But he did say I'm irreverent and voluptuous."

Nancy grinned. "Aha! I was right. And that's the perfect description—irreverent and voluptuous."

"Have you forgotten the whole thing with Jason? Even if he asked me out, do you think I'd really be interested in a man who was so cold to my son?"

"No, I guess not." She reached across the table to pat Emily's hand. "Sorry, Em, I just want you to find someone special like Beau."

"They broke the mold with that Texan."

"Yes, they certainly did. But we can find you someone just as good in his own way."

Emily raised her hand, palm outward. "No more fix-ups. I love you like a sister, but no more blind dates."

"Too bad it didn't work out with Luke Andrews. He's so nice and steady, owns his own business."

"He's a very nice man. But boring with a capital *B*. I thought if I had to hear about hardware or plumbing supplies one more minute, I was gonna scream."

"And I guess Patrick Stevens falls into the boring category, too. Those scientific types usually are. I had a chemistry professor once who talked with this nasal monotone. Put me to sleep every time."

Emily thought about it for a minute. "Patrick is sanctimonious, bordering on pompous, but he has moments of almost being a real person."

"Real is good. And he is attractive in an intense way."

"Why are we even having this discussion?" Emily knew she needed to nip this in the bud or her friend would be in all-out matchmaking mode. "I've decided dating isn't for me. My children are my focus."

"Aw, Em, I hate to see you give up on having that happily-ever-after. If it can happen to me, it can happen to anyone."

Emily suppressed a twinge of envy. "I've never seen a couple that fits together like you and Beau. It's like you two were made for each other."

"But I didn't always think that way, remember? As I recall, a very good friend encouraged me to give him a chance."

"Beau's a good man. He just took a few wrong turns on his way to finding you."

"Maybe Patrick's taken a few wrong turns, too. Maybe he regrets the whole episode with Jason as much as you do."

"He hasn't said anything. He even saw Jason the other night. Although it probably looked to him as if my kids were raised by wolves." Rolling her eyes, she described their arrival.

Nancy laughed till she had tears in her eyes. "Oh, Em, but that's the beauty of your home. It's never boring and there's always lots of love and laughter."

Emily grumbled. "Just once, I'd like people to

think of me like they thought of Tiffany Bigelow. How together and smart I am."

"You *are* together and smart."

"Till I stick my foot in my mouth. Like with that edible panty distributor who always hounded me for a date. He asked what he could do to increase our order, and I suggested they develop an edible panty that didn't taste like the fruit chewy snacks I put in my kids' lunches. I don't care how much men like the things, women aren't going to feel sexy if they associate the aroma with sack lunches."

Nancy sputtered and set down her soda. "You had a valid point."

"Probably, but the guy never asked me to dinner again. Why couldn't I just come up with something cute and classy?"

"You actually did the man a favor. You gave him solid feedback on how crummy his product was. Unless, of course, he's so wrapped up in his work, so to speak, he identified his product with his, um, equipment."

Emily rolled her eyes. "Oh, great, now I've probably left the man impotent for life, when all I was trying to do was help."

Nancy leaned back in her chair and laughed. "See, Em, you make me laugh. We just need to find a man who understands your sense of humor and isn't intimidated."

"Like such a man exists."

"How about Parents Flying Solo? Any new guys there?"

"No, though I have to admit, I haven't made many meetings lately. I've been too busy. Besides, it's not the same now that you and Beau aren't there anymore. Did you hear who was elected president?"

Nancy shook her head.

Emily updated her on the latest happenings at the parenting support group. The next half hour flew by as they moved on to other topics, chatting about their children and Nancy's real estate business.

Emily was still smiling when she returned to work.

Her smile faded when she saw two police officers in the waiting area.

Olivia immediately came out of her office as if she'd been watching for Emily's arrival. Good thing she hadn't taken a long lunch.

"Emily, these officers are here to see you." Olivia frowned, her eyes warm with concern. "I'll be in my office if you need me."

Emily's stomach tensed with dread.

The older officer introduced them and got straight to the point. "A report has been filed about certain irregularities in the Elmwood Elementary School PTO account. I spoke with Brad Bigelow this morning. He indicates you went by his house last night and asked for a computer file?"

"Um, yes. I've taken over as PTO president and I hoped the, um, disk might clarify some questions."

"Principal Ross filed a report this morning about the missing funds. Kind of coincidental that you spoke with her yesterday and retrieved the disk last night. Interfering with an investigation is serious business, ma'am."

"But there wasn't an investigation yet."

He nodded. "Technically, you're right. But you were aware there would be. There could be a question of whether you tampered with the disk."

"I did *not* tamper with it." But her conscience twinged. Should she tell them she'd made copies of the disk? No. Tampering meant changing or destroying—copying hadn't changed the original one bit. "I was hoping there might be information that would clear all this up and the police wouldn't have to be involved."

The officer held her gaze. "How closely did you work with Mrs. Bigelow?"

Emily forced herself not to blink, not to glance away. "I might have said hello to her at a PTO meeting, but for the most part, she didn't think I was quite up to her standards."

The officer's eyes twinkled for a moment and he almost cracked a smile. "Yes, I understand she could be very, um, particular."

Emily glanced at his badge. Officer G. Kirk. Jason played basketball with a Kirk. That must be his son. And she recalled hearing that his wife had had words with Tiffany over a school slogan contest or something. Nodody's ideas had ever been as good as Tiffany's.

"The word I had in mind started with a *B,* but I guess particular will work," Emily commented dryly.

Officer Kirk coughed. "Do you have the disk with you?"

"Yes. In my purse." She rummaged through her large bag and produced the disk. "Do you need some sort of affidavit that I haven't changed anything on it?"

"If you'd handwrite a quick note, that would be helpful. We might need something more formal later."

"Sure." She pulled out a yellow note pad and quickly wrote the note. Tearing off the sheet, she handed it to him. "I'm sorry, officer, I didn't intend to interfere with your investigation."

"It looks like there was no harm done." He

sealed the disk and her note in separate bags. "Thank you for your time."

"You're welcome."

Emily breathed a sigh of relief when the door shut behind him. Only then did she realize her knees were shaking. She'd put herself and her children at risk listening to Patrick Stevens.

It was hard to concentrate the next few hours, but somehow she managed. Finally, Olivia left for a meeting.

Picking up the phone, Emily dialed the number for Elmwood Elementary. She knew it by heart after having kids enrolled there so long. She punched in Patrick's room number and was surprised when he picked up.

"Don't you have classes to teach?" she demanded.

"My students are in Art. And this is?"

"Emily Patterson. The woman who went out on a limb for you. The same woman police interviewed at her place of employment because she did a favor for you."

"You're kidding. What did they want?"

"And you're supposed to be a genius. The disk, Einstein."

"Actually, I'm only highly intelligent. My IQ is a few points shy of genius level."

"Quit playing games, Stevens. They asked me if I tampered with the disk."

"You didn't. I imagine you gave up the disk voluntarily. No harm, no foul."

"Easy for you to say. I don't know about you, but I need my job. If I'm unemployed, my kids are homeless with nothing to eat. It's a little more severe than just missing a Lexus payment."

"You're right, Emily." His voice lowered. "I shouldn't have dragged you into this. I'm sorry."

His apology surprised her. Neither of her ex-husbands had ever admitted being wrong. Even Larry, when she'd caught him riding a two-bit cocktail waitress at the Lazy Eight Motel.

Of course, Larry had explained how it had all been Emily's fault because she'd gained weight after Ryan's birth. After all, he could hardly be held accountable when his wife was a fat cow, too tired to make love with her husband.

Though Emily had promptly kicked his sorry butt out of the house, a tiny part of her wondered if he'd been right. She'd even gone so far as to suggest marriage counseling. Thank goodness he'd refused, or she might still be trying to fix a hopeless relationship.

"Emily, are you there?"

"Yes, um, the other line's ringing," she lied.

"I've got to go. Just leave me out of any future schemes, okay, Einstein?"

PATRICK JUGGLED pizza boxes and a plastic sack of two-liter bottles of soda. Somehow he managed to press the doorbell at Emily's house with his elbow.

His gut told him this was a lame idea. But his conscience told him he'd gotten Emily in a lot of trouble and pizza was the least he could do.

Waiting expectantly, he hunkered down in his jacket. Clear skies, a trace of snow on the ground, it was going to be a cold night.

Finally, the door opened a crack.

Patrick bit back a groan. It figured. "Jason, hi, is your mother home?"

"She's in the shower."

The boy's answer left Patrick nonplussed. He hadn't thought she would have rushed in the door from work and jumped into the shower. "Oh. I, um, brought pizza."

"Yeah, I can see." The door widened a bit and Jason crossed his arms over his chest, leaning against the wall. "She doesn't want your *pizza*." He looked Patrick up and down, his smirk leaving no doubt it was more than food he referred to.

Patrick might have been amused if he hadn't had a history with the kid. As it was, he reminded himself he was the level-headed adult and should respond as such. "Can you let her know I'm here?"

"Like I said, she's in the shower."

"You can't call through the bathroom door?"

"Nope. She sings in the shower. Real loud. And off-key."

The visual made Patrick smile. He decided to take the bull by the horns, so to speak. "Okay, how about if I come in and wait?"

"No way. One of Mom's rules. No guests while she's in the shower."

Recalling Jason's interrupted wrestling match with his girlfriend the other night, Patrick realized the rule was probably prudent.

"Okay. I'll wait out here, then."

"She takes a *really* long shower." Jason nodded toward the boxes Patrick held. "And hates pizza."

"Oh." Maybe this hadn't been such a good idea. He was tempted to turn and leave. But remembering how much trouble he'd caused for Emily, he knew he had to try. "I'll just wait out here on the steps, then."

Jason shrugged. "Suit yourself."

The door slammed in Patrick's face.

Patrick surveyed the front porch. It was tidy, but bare. No comfy glider where he could park his rear. So he sat on the front step, the cold seeping through his Dockers almost immediately.

Ten minutes later, he hoped maybe Jason had been exaggerating.

Fifteen minutes later, he realized the pizza was stone-cold and he'd lost all sensation in his nose. His stomach rumbled. He figured the pizza couldn't possibly get any colder and placed the boxes on the steps. He stood, rubbing his arms to warm them.

Twenty-five minutes later, Patrick rang the bell again.

"What?" Jason's tone was belligerent when he opened the door.

"Surely, your mother is out of the shower now?"

"Nope. Told you she took a long shower. Why don't you just leave."

Why indeed? Because it had become a contest of wills. He would see Emily tonight if it killed him. And, if the temperature dropped any more rapidly, that was a very real possibility.

"I c-can wait." He clamped his mouth shut to stop his teeth from chattering.

"Yeah, sure you can." As the door swung shut, Patrick could have sworn he heard Jason call him a loser.

His pulse pounded. He had the urge to yank the

door off the hinges and give the kid a piece of his mind. But he was here on a peacekeeping mission and yelling at Jason would hardly break the ice with Emily. He merely needed to harness his anger. Shrugging, he figured anger was probably a good thing—it'd keep his blood pumping *and* keep him from freezing to death.

He jogged in place, slapping his arms to increase circulation, for what seemed like hours. Patrick was about to concede defeat when headlights sliced through the night and Emily's van pulled into the driveway.

"That little SOB," Patrick swore through clenched teeth.

CHAPTER FIVE

EMILY PULLED INTO the driveway, wishing for the zillionth time the garage was uncluttered enough to actually house the car. A glance toward the dark porch confirmed that Jason hadn't had the forethought to turn on the light for her. Sighing, she turned off the engine. It had been one heck of a long day.

She went around to the back of the van and opened the hatch. Grabbing several grocery sacks, she headed for the door.

"Need some help?" A male voice startled her. Peering into the gloom on the porch, she thought she detected a familiar form.

"Patrick, what are you doing here?"

"P-pizza. Peace offering. I'm sorry I got you in trouble." The poor man appeared to be shivering. And his attempt at making things right made her view him a little more kindly.

"You didn't have to go to all this trouble."

"Yes, I did. Let me help you." He took the groceries from her hands.

Ah, score more points for the science teacher. Emily was rapidly getting over being miffed at him for dragging her into the disk caper. "You look half-frozen. Why in the world didn't you go inside?"

"Um, Jason said you were in the shower. No guests allowed while you're in the shower."

Emily slapped her hand over her mouth and groaned. "And you've been out here how long?"

He didn't meet her eyes. "A few minutes."

She got the impression it had been a lot longer than a few minutes. "I think Jason was being a little too concerned with the rules tonight." She should be dancing a jig because he remembered them at all. But Jason's selective enforcement suggested his adherence had been out of spite, not obedience.

"Which rule is that?" Patrick asked.

"The one where I asked the boys to tell people I'm in the shower when they're here and I'm not. That way, some whacked-out stranger doesn't know they're home alone."

"Whacked-out stranger. Thanks a lot."

"Not you. A hypothetical stranger."

"Ah. So Jason was only following instructions?"

"I'm sure that's what his defense will be." She opened the door with her key. "Come on in, if you don't mind being subject to World War III. Jason and I need to discuss a few things."

"I could stay out here till you're done."

"No way. You already look chilled to the bone. Besides, why should I have all the fun?"

"Fun?"

"Oh, yes. Two can play at this game. Watch and learn."

His smile was bemused. "Lead on, oh great one."

She stepped into the entryway and called, "I'm home."

Jason came around the corner as if he'd been waiting. His eyes narrowed as he saw her companion. "Hi, Mom."

"Hello, hon. Would you go get the rest of the groceries?"

"Um, sure." He sidled past her as if he scented danger. He'd probably expected yelling and accusations. Heck, he'd probably *hoped* for yelling and accusations. The child seemed to thrive on chaos.

But she had way more in her arsenal than that. Emily turned to Patrick and winked.

He tilted his head to the side, but didn't comment. Instead, he said, "I'll go grab the pizza before raccoons haul it off. Luckily, pizza nukes fine."

Emily touched his arm. "Patrick, it really was

thoughtful. And I'm sorry Jason treated you so badly."

"No problem."

But his tense shrug told her it *was* a problem. And that made Emily sad. Jason would pay for mistreating her friend, and he would pay dearly.

The thought stopped Emily short. Patrick, a friend. Who'd have thought? Nancy and a few of the girls from work had been her only real friends for years. As for boyfriends, they usually took off once they met her kids, or realized she wasn't quite the good-time gal they assumed. Yes, there was more to the science geek than met the eye.

Emily hummed a little tune as she took the groceries to the kitchen and started putting them away, taking time to give Mark and Ryan big hugs when they clambered in from the back yard.

"Emily?" she heard coming from the entryway.

"In here, Patrick."

Patrick and Jason apparently reached the kitchen door at the same time, plowing through, shoulder to shoulder. Neither seemed inclined to yield to the other.

"Jason, Patrick is a guest in our home. You allow him to come in first."

Her son averted his face. "Yes, ma'am."

She handed a stack of paper plates to Mark.

"Would you please set the table, honey? Ryan, you can put out cups and utensils."

Both boys accepted their duties with enthusiastic whoops.

Patrick smiled at their eagerness. The same smile she'd noticed when he talked of his students.

"Jason, would you please start a fire?" Emily retrieved the long stick matches from the highest cupboard. "In the fireplace," she amended quickly, remembering Jason's penchant for finding loopholes.

"We don't need a fire, Mom. Remember, we don't have that much wood."

"We have enough. Poor Patrick is frozen half to death."

She could feel Jason tense, preparing himself for battle. "It's not my fault he stood out there in the cold. I just did what you said about not having people in when you're gone."

"Of course you did, dear." She patted his cheek lovingly.

Jason's eyes widened. "Um, yeah, I did. I'll go light that fire. In the fireplace."

"Thank you, honey."

Mark and Ryan froze, then tiptoed around her, as if they sensed something was up. Maybe the second endearment had been laying it on too thick.

"Is Jeremy in his room?"

The boys nodded.

"Would you please go get him?"

Nodding in unison, they ran to the base of the stairs and hollered, "Jeremy."

Emily rolled her eyes. "I could have done that."

After she reheated pizza, everyone filled their plates and found a seat at the table. Emily made polite chitchat for a few minutes before she went for the jugular. "Oh, Jason, the school newsletter says they're looking for chaperones for the dance Friday night."

Jason's eyes widened in horror. "No way, Mom."

Patrick tilted his head to the side, as if watching a foreign film and trying to decipher the subtext. And there was subtext galore.

Jason was a smart kid, and she would bet her last dollar he knew what his punishment would be. He just wasn't quite sure how it would be administered.

"I've already decided to volunteer, so no arguing. I want to make sure I get to know each and every one of your teachers."

"But, that's what the parent/teacher open house is for." Jason's voice was an octave higher than usual.

"Yes, you're right. But I obviously haven't

spent enough time at my children's schools. Because you apparently thought I wouldn't want Mr. Stevens in my home. Using your very best judgment, you decided Mr. Stevens was a complete stranger after spending nearly a month in his class."

"No, I didn't think that."

"Oh? Then why did you leave him standing on the front porch when you knew darn well I wouldn't be home for half an hour?"

"I told him to go."

Emily started to burn. Jason's insolence was worse than she'd suspected. As if, after his prank with the mousetrap, Patrick didn't already think she was the worst mother on the planet. "I beg your pardon? You told him to go?"

"I, um, suggested that you would be in the shower for a long time and he might want to, um, leave."

"It sounds to me as if you were rude to Mr. Stevens."

Patrick shifted in his seat. "I wouldn't go so far as to say he was rude."

She shot him a look. "Then you're too kind, Patrick. But I intend to make sure there aren't any misunderstandings in the future about who constitutes a stranger." Turning to her son, she said, "I will make it a point to meet each and every teacher at the dance and introduce myself as your mother. I will also introduce myself to any of your friends I haven't met yet and get better acquainted with the ones I do know."

The color drained from Jason's face. "You can't."

"I can and I will. Furthermore, you were rude to Mr. Stevens and owe him an apology."

"Sorry," Jason mumbled.

"Apology accepted." Patrick's voice was low.

She glanced at Mark and Ryan, who were more subdued than normal. Regretting casting a pall over the meal, Emily smiled brightly. "Now, let's enjoy our pizza."

But then an idea occurred to her. One she just couldn't let pass. "Patrick, it was very sweet of you to bring dinner tonight. Do you think you might consider being my co-chaperone at the dance Friday evening?"

Patrick chewed his pizza and swallowed hard. "Dance?" His voice held a note of panic.

"Why, yes. That way Jason will have the chance to get to know you." And understand her choice of friends was not subject to his manipulation. Particularly her male friends.

"I think we're pretty well-acquainted, now, don't you, Jason?" Patrick asked.

"Yeah. We sure are, Mr. Stevens." Jason

nodded so rapidly Emily was afraid he'd give himself whiplash.

Patrick's response was much less enthusiastic than she had hoped, but she didn't intend to let that stop her. "And Patrick, I understand Linda Price will be there. She's president of the high school PTO and was close friends with Tiffany Bigelow."

"Oh, I didn't know."

"I'm looking forward to the opportunity of chatting with her regarding Tiffany's record-keeping procedures." Emily willed him to understand her doublespeak. "She might know where we could find additional, um, materials."

"Materials. Yes, well that does sound, um, promising."

"And even if she doesn't have any information, I understand she is an absolute pro at fund-raising. Something you might consider in light of recent developments. I know I've been giving it a lot of thought."

Patrick nodded. "Absolutely. In that case, I accept your invitation. What time's the dance start?"

"Eight o'clock. I'll pick you up at seven-fifteen. That way I'll have time to drop off the little kids at my friend Nancy's house, then swing by and pick up Cassie."

Jason groaned. "We were gonna double-date with Vince and his girlfriend."

"Now, see, didn't this turn out nice?" Emily smiled brightly. "You can double-date with your dear old mom and Mr. Stevens. What could be better than that?"

What indeed?

PATRICK DISCONNECTED from the Internet. Emily would be there shortly and he hadn't found any solutions in his investment portfolio. He'd considered funding the trip himself, anonymously, of course. It would be worth every penny to watch Ari and Kat experience a whole new world.

But a quick glance at his portfolio had quashed that idea. He had a substantial sum set aside, but it would take more than a substantial sum to care for Roger once his mom and dad were gone. They made do with a couple of part-time home health aides and were great caring for his brother. Unfortunately, it was a full-time job for both of his parents, instead of the easy retirement they deserved. He worried sometimes they were working themselves to an early grave, but both claimed to enjoy having Roger living in their home.

Patrick ran a hand through his hair. Giving up on the Florida trip wasn't an option, either, at least in his mind. Maybe they'd luck out and Tiffany's friend would tell them where Tiffany had secreted the PTO money.

The doorbell rang. Glancing at his watch, he nodded. Emily was right on time.

When he opened the door, he wasn't surprised to see Jason hanging back, expression sullen, holding the hand of a pretty teen. The infamous Cassie. But it was Emily who nearly took his breath away. She wore a suede skirt, boots and had her soft brown hair pulled back from her face. All suitable chaperone attire. But she also wore an itty-bitty, low-cut T-shirt that accentuated every lovely inch of her chest. What looked like a hand-crocheted vest went over the top to give the impression of modesty. But all it did was encourage him to visualize what she looked like sans T-shirt, with only the crocheted vest playing peekaboo with her breasts.

He cleared his throat. "Come in. I have to feed Newt before I go."

"Newt?"

"My salamander. Let me dump a few crickets in his tank."

"Live crickets?"

"Yes."

Emily made a face. She wandered around his living room, studying his awards, stopping at the lone family photo. "Your mom and dad?"

His stomach clenched. "Yes."

"You're an only child?" It was an assumption many people made. Maybe because Patrick was serious and introverted. It hadn't always been that way though.

"No. My brother isn't in the picture." *In so many ways*.

"Are you the oldest?"

"Yes." Chronologically and mentally. Because there was no way Roger would ever be able to approach Patrick's near-genius. But Patrick thought he would give his very life if Roger had the opportunity to show him up. Sibling rivalry had no place in the dynamics of their relationship. At least not in the past twenty-five years.

"Are you two close?"

"Yes. Roger's my best buddy." At least that's what he told his brother every time he visited. It never failed to elicit a smile, sometimes marred by a spasm, other times accompanied by a trickle of saliva. But Roger's smile touched a place in Patrick's heart no other could reach. Not that many had tried. Most people were content to accept Patrick's reserve at face value.

But Emily wasn't most people. She studied his face. "I bet he looked up to you as a child."

Patrick smiled, remembering the kid brother

he couldn't seem to shake. "Yes, he followed me everywhere."

He turned at Cassie's sharply indrawn breath. "Is that real?" the girl asked, pointing to Arnold.

"Yes. That's Ahhnold." He approximated an Austrian accent. "And this guy over here is Hairy S. Truman."

"All Republicans," Emily observed dryly. "A political statement?"

"No, just my warped sense of humor. It started with Hairy, for obvious reasons. Newt, as a play on words, because newts are a part of the sala-mander family."

"That's really tight, Mr. Stevens," Jason said.

Cassie withdrew her hand from Jason's and stepped back. "I think it's gross. What does the snake eat?"

Patrick's first instinct was to tell her the whole gory truth and gross her out. *Live rats. Arnold squeezes them to death before swallow-ing them whole.*

But tricks never led to anything good. He decided to provide Jason with a mature role model. "Rodents."

Patrick was proud of his self-restraint when Emily repressed a shudder.

Fortunately, Cassie didn't seem to realize the term *rodents* wasn't the name brand of a processed pet food that came from a sealed bag. She said, "Whatever."

"I'm ready." He made sure all the enclosures were secure, leaving on the heat lamps. "Let's go."

Patrick was tempted to call shotgun as they approached the van, so like a family expedition. But he realized Jason wanted nothing more than to sit in the backseat with his girlfriend, sneaking a kiss when he thought Emily wasn't looking in the rearview mirror.

The kids had made it pretty clear they didn't appreciate being chaperoned. Yes, in bringing Patrick to the dance, Emily had elevated age-appropriate punishment to an art form. He knew from experience peer pressure and the threat of embarrassment worked wonders with the teen set. Patrick had no doubt he would be immediately invited in to the Patterson household if he visited again, day or night, whether Emily were at home or three states away. She'd certainly made her point.

Emily pressed the lock release on her key tag. "Are you sure you're okay with me driving?"

"Positive."

The drive to the high school went quickly. Jason and Cassie exited the van before Emily shut off the engine.

She rolled down her window. "See you inside,"

Emily called out to them in an overly loud voice, enunciating clearly.

They pretended not to hear her.

Patrick went around to the driver's side, but he was too late to hold the door for her. For some reason, that rankled. Though Emily could obviously take care of herself, he felt compelled to do things for her. He had a pretty good idea pampering was toward the bottom of her list.

"You're an evil woman, Emily Patterson." He couldn't quite keep the admiration from his voice.

She grinned, lowering her voice to a Mae West growl. "When I'm good, I'm very good. But when I'm bad, I'm even better."

His imagination was off and running with visions of her wearing the crocheted vest and very little else. His groin responded. "I'm sure you are."

And Emily, brave, irreverent Emily, blushed.

Down, boy. He reminded himself she was someone's mother, for God's sake. *Four* little someones' mother. The thought was an effective mood killer. "I mean, I'm sure you are very good at your job. Where did you say you work?" Lame save, but better than nothing.

Emily glanced away. "Luxury Lingerie. And I guess I'm a pretty darn good administrative assistant."

They waited for a car to go by before crossing the parking lot. Patrick cupped Emily's elbow in a friendly, don't-want-you-to-get-run-over gesture. "How long have you been there?"

"Twelve years. Since right after Walt left. Walt was my first husband."

Her long-term job surprised him. For some reason, his initial impression had been that she was flighty. But then again, they hadn't met under the best circumstances. "You worked after the younger boys were born?"

"I didn't have much choice. Larry couldn't keep a job—Larry was my second husband. And when he left, he cleaned out what little I had in the bank."

Patrick shook his head. "I don't get it."

"Get what?"

"I don't get women letting men take advantage of them like that."

Emily stopped in the middle of the sidewalk. She put her hands on her hips. "I made a mistake."

"I could have told you that. I mean, why would such a beautiful, courageous, intelligent woman allow any man to treat her that way?"

She folded her arms over her chest. Her voice was soft when she said, "You're not going to get laid tonight, Patrick, so save the BS." Then she turned and stalked toward the gym.

He stood for a moment, wondering what he'd said wrong. Compliments were a good thing, weren't they? Apparently Emily didn't think so.

He couldn't help but admire the steel in her spine. Then he noticed the luscious curve of her hips. Was he, on some subconscious level, trying to get laid?

Shaking his head, he lengthened his stride to catch up. He grasped her elbow. "Emily."

She stopped. Her eyes sparkled under the outdoor lighting, whether from tears or anger, he wasn't sure. "What?"

Patrick tried to articulate what he didn't really understand himself. "It wasn't BS. I won't lie, I find you very attractive. But I have no desire to start a relationship with you. It just wouldn't work. I simply describe you the way I see you."

"That's a hell of a way to mess with my mind. Insult me one second, then the next say one of the sweetest things a man has ever said to me. You swear you're on the up-and-up, but tell me you're not interested in a relationship. What exactly are you doing here, Patrick?"

He swallowed hard. "Research?"

"Research this." She made a rude gesture and stalked through the double doors.

Patrick's mouth dropped open.

And then he laughed. He'd never met a woman

so unpredictable and refreshingly honest. Now, if he could just figure out exactly how he'd ticked her off so badly.

CHAPTER SIX

EMILY STEPPED THROUGH the doors and felt as if she'd stepped into a time warp. There was something about a school gym that transcended space and time. It was as if she'd entered her own high school gym in the mideighties. The only thing missing was the big hair.

The odor of stale athletic socks and sweaty bodies lingered in the air, despite the elaborate decorations. Festoons of crepe paper and balloons, confetti on the refreshment table, disco balls reflecting the light. And on the dais, a DJ and sound system.

"Hey, wait up." Patrick appeared at her elbow.

Inviting him had been a mistake. How could she have known he'd turn all goofy on her? First, his compliments had made her mad. How could he think she'd fall for that crap? But then she'd understood he'd been absolutely sincere.

Her chest grew tight. His sincerity had caused her to, for a very short time, figure she might stand a ghost of a chance with a man who saw her not as a brassy, burnt-out mom, but as the kind of woman she desperately wanted to be.

Patrick grasped her forearm. "What gives? You suggested I come tonight to research fund-raising alternatives and see if we could get some information from Linda Price. And yet, somehow I've offended you."

You offered me a glimpse of what could be, then yanked it away in a nanosecond.

"Look, Patrick, you're right. I gave those reasons when I invited you. Somehow, I lost sight of why we were here. I'm sorry."

He frowned, apparently processing her statement through that analytical mind of his. For a highly intelligent man, he sure was clueless at times.

Taking a deep breath, she decided to be as forthright as he seemed to think she was. "From the way you were talking, I thought maybe you considered tonight a date."

Hesitating, he said, "And you thought I was reading more into it than I should?"

"No. I was bothered because then a second later, I found out tonight was nothing more than research to you and I was…disappointed. So it was my expectations that were wrong."

His eyes widened. He opened his mouth, but nothing came out.

Emily's cheeks grew warm. She was not about to stand around and wait for the extended silence to get more embarrassing. "I'll go introduce myself to the teachers."

Spying a face she recognized from newsletter photos, Emily headed for the woman still hanging streamers.

"You must be Linda Price." Emily craned her neck to see the woman's face. "I'm Emily Patterson. Jason Patterson's mom."

The woman efficiently pulled sections of tape from the dispenser she wore on her wrist, clasping a piece between her teeth. "Hm."

"Would you like some help?"

"No, I've got it," she lisped.

Emily felt invisible, just like she had at the Elmwood functions on many occasions. As if she didn't fit in. Added to Patrick's near-rejection, she figured the evening was going to be a long one.

But she had a mission to complete, and complete it she would. "You're busy. Maybe we can chat later?"

Linda mumbled noncommittally.

Shrugging, Emily turned and bumped into Patrick.

He grasped her arms to steady her. "Seems like all I do is chase you tonight. I didn't think our conversation was over."

Emily couldn't force herself to look up and meet his gaze. Instead, she glanced over his shoulder. "Patrick, everything I said before was a mistake."

"Hey, I never had a girl ask me to a dance. This is all new. Can we start over? Maybe mix a little PTO business with a dance or two and see where it takes us?"

Glancing up, Emily couldn't help but smile. He had that sincere Boy Scout expression of his. How could she refuse?

"Okay. That sounds like a good plan. Looks like most of the chaperones have arrived. Let's go work the crowd."

They passed Jason and Cassie as they navigated the room. Jason pretended he didn't see them and Cassie gave a nervous wave.

"Man, I thought I was past all that high school social stuff, but I feel like I definitely don't fit in," Patrick said.

Emily eyed him intently. Her curiosity got the better of her. He was an attractive man once he loosened up a bit. "Get bullied because of the science club thing?"

Patrick shook his head. "No. And as a matter of fact, I wasn't a real active member. Signed up for science club just because it would look good on my transcripts. Mostly, I worked my butt off at the local burger place and studied like crazy."

"Hm. I have a hard time imagining you slinging burgers."

"Imagine away. My folks had a lot of expenses, and I didn't want to add to their worries. So I saved up and bought my own car, paid for gas, insurance and maintenance."

"Ah, ever practical."

"What about you? Where'd you fit in?"

Emily thought about it for a moment. "I pretty much had a club of my own. The Ordinary Remington Sister."

"As opposed to?"

"The beautiful Remington sister, Lisa, and the pretty, perky, brilliant Remington sister, Ramona."

"I can't believe you ever considered yourself ordinary. You are an extraordinary woman."

Emily made a stopping motion with her hand. "No. Let's set some ground rules straight for tonight. No more flattery. It confuses me and makes me uncomfortable."

Patrick frowned. "I'm sorry. I didn't intend to make you uncomfortable. I wouldn't say it if I didn't think it was true."

"Thank you. It's really sweet. But I can't handle it, okay?"

"Okay."

"I see Jason with a group of his friends. If you'll excuse me, I'll go say hello. I need to make good on my threat. After this, I'll leave him alone to enjoy himself and we can do some PTO recon."

Patrick grinned. "I think he's learned his lesson. I doubt he'd turn me away from your door now even if I sprouted fangs."

"Exactly," Emily said over her shoulder, as she headed off to complete her mission. She spoke for a few minutes with Jason and his friends, then chatted with teachers and another set of parents who'd been brave enough to volunteer.

She nearly forgot Patrick for a moment. Glancing around, she spotted him near the punch bowl, in earnest conversation with the basketball coach.

She joined him, nodding to the coach. "Coach Evers."

"Ms. Patterson, good to see you. I was telling Patrick here about Jason's jump shot. And how he really pulls the team together."

"That's wonderful to hear, Coach."

Patrick handed her a foam cup filled with punch. "Yes, and Coach Evers also shared some fund-raising tips with me."

The lights dimmed, the music rose to a near-deafening level. Couples streamed toward the dance floor.

Linda Price hurried toward them. "Coach, there's a light out over there. Would you be a real sweetie and change the bulb for me? We don't want any dark corners." She flashed dimples that probably had been successful leverage in convincing every man in her life to assist her.

And Coach was no different. Nodding, he said, "Sure thing. Nice meeting you, Stevens. See you at the game, Ms. Patterson," he hollered to be heard above the pulsating hip-hop beat.

Linda looked at Emily. "Patterson?" she mouthed.

Emily nodded.

Jerking her head in the direction of the girls' restroom, Linda motioned for Emily to follow.

Emily looked at Patrick and shrugged.

He motioned for her to go.

Linda stopped in a relatively quiet alcove outside the restrooms. "You're Jason's mom?"

"Yes, I introduced myself earlier, but you were busy." Too busy to be polite.

"Oh, um, sorry. I've been a little distracted. Normally, Tiffany Bigelow and I worked as a team. Pretty much had dance preparation down pat. So, now, it's rather…sad."

Emily felt a little sorry for the other woman. "You were good friends, weren't you?"

Linda nodded. "Yes, we've known each other since high school. Were cheerleaders together."

"I'm sure her death was quite a blow." Emily touched her arm.

"Yes, it was." Linda tucked a strand of her golden hair behind her ear. "Now, I thought you and I could trade off checking the girls' restroom, say every half hour. Make sure there's no smoking or drug use. Or couples using the stalls for, um, privacy."

Emily gulped, figuring her eyes had to be the size of silver dollars. "At a school dance?"

"Yes, sometimes the kids get a little carried away. I'll take the half hour check and you can check on the hour."

"Okay."

Linda's cell phone rang. Her face softened when she looked at the readout. She flicked open the earpiece. "Hi. I'm working the dance right now. Meet me at eleven?"

Envy washed over Emily in biting waves. Linda Price was married to her high school sweetie and still got misty-eyed when he called, even after years of marriage.

Emily walked a few paces away to give her privacy. All she heard was a whisper, followed by flirtatious laughter.

A second later, Linda clicked her phone shut and returned. "Sorry about that. Now, I better go check on lighting and refreshments. Thanks for helping out with bathroom detail."

"No problem. But one thing first, Linda? I've taken over as Elmwood PTO president and I'm not sure I have all Tiffany's notes. Did she ever discuss her big spring fund-raiser?"

Linda smiled, her dimples belying the flash of fear in her eyes. Or had Emily imagined its presence?

"Oh, no, Emily. Tiffany said her plans were tip-top secret, even from me."

"Did she have any files or notes you knew about? I received a wire-bound notebook and a floppy disk. That's it."

"No, I don't know a thing. Tiffany kept a pretty tight lid on her ideas. It's a shame what Principal Ross is putting the Bigelow family through. They should be allowed to grieve in peace, not have to worry about a criminal investigation."

Emily paused before answering, unsure how much she should admit to knowing. She went for a noncommittal, "It's a very difficult time for the Bigelows, I'm sure."

Linda's smile tightened. "Yes, I'm sure. I absolutely must do a sweep of the dance floor, see that everything's perfect."

"Yes. And I'll check the bathrooms on the hour."

"Thanks." Linda hustled off, leaving Emily slightly disconcerted.

It wasn't until a few minutes later, she realized why. She needed to talk to Patrick and fast.

Scanning the darkened room, she spied him standing to the side of the stage near the amplifier.

She touched his arm. "We need to talk."

He smiled quizzically.

"We need to talk," she yelled.

The tune changed to a slow song. Unfortunately, the DJ didn't lower the decibel level.

Grasping Patrick's hand, she hauled him toward the dance floor. "Let's dance."

He shrugged.

When they reached the edge of the dance floor, he tugged her toward a less packed corner and pulled her into his arms.

Oh, my.

Emily trailed one hand around his neck.

Patrick took her other hand in his and applied pressure to the small of her back.

He could dance.

All coherent thought fled as she gazed up at him.

He smiled and pulled her closer.

Oh, my They fit together nicely. And it had been so long since she'd been held by a man.

Focus, focus.

Emily wracked her brain, trying to remember why she'd needed to talk to him. She was vaguely aware of Jason and Cassie dancing a few feet away. They were so close, a sheet of plastic wrap wouldn't have fit between them.

The mother in her recalled the safe sex talk that was long overdue.

The woman in her wished she and Patrick were that close.

The PTO president in her noticed Linda flit by and remembered her mission.

"Patrick, I talked to Linda about Tiffany Bigelow," she whispered next to his ear. For such an intellectual guy, he certainly wore a manly, outdoorsy cologne. It smelled delicious, inviting her closer.

He bent his head, his mouth close to her ear. For a moment, she thought he might nibble her lobe. "Any news about the missing money?"

"No. And she claims not to know anything about Tiffany's records. But the weird part is, she knows Principal Ross filed charges. And it was supposed to be kept secret."

Emily felt Patrick's muscles bunch beneath her fingers as he shrugged. "Small-town gossip?"

"That's the thing. I haven't heard word one going around town. And I've been very careful not to say anything."

"I certainly haven't said anything. That would be totally unprofessional."

"So how did she find out?"

"The police probably talked to her for the same reason you did."

Someone jostled them and Emily glanced over Patrick's shoulder to meet her son's glare.

Patrick maneuvered them farther away without checking to see who had bumped into them. Good. He had enough cause to dislike Jason without adding another transgression. And for some reason, it was becoming more and more important to her that he like Jason.

The song ended and she started to pull away.

But Patrick didn't release her. He held her gaze, his eyes warm with interest. "Another dance? To see where this might lead?"

Nodding, Emily was vaguely aware of Jason leading Cassie off the dance floor.

Then she simply lost herself in the joy of being held by an attractive man. A man who thought she was courageous, intelligent and beautiful.

"NOT NOW, Cassie." Jason shrugged off Cassie's attempt to pull him toward a secluded corner where the second lightbulb of the evening had mysteriously burnt out.

Instead, he stood off to the side, arms crossed, watching his mother make the biggest mistake of her life.

She was falling for Mr. Stevens and he'd be damned if he'd stand by and let it happen.

He'd just been a little boy when his dad had left. He recalled a time when it had just been Mom and him and Jeremy. Then he remembered his mom bringing home Larry, a man she looked at an awful lot like she was looking at Stevens now. Her face all soft, smiling, gazing into his eyes as if she wanted to be kissed.

Jason's blood ran cold as Stevens bent his head.

No way. Not here. Not now.

It had taken them too long to get things back to normal after Larry-the-jerk left, leaving two half brothers for Mom to feed and Jason to babysit. Not that Jason didn't love the little ankle biters. But there was no way he'd allow Mr. Stevens to worm into their lives and break Mom's heart, probably adding a couple more half brothers to the mix. And who would be there when he left Mom brokenhearted?

Jason. Like always.

There had to be some way to stop it.

Then he remembered the stink bombs in his pocket.

Jason made his way to the boys' restroom, but saw Coach Evers go inside.

Glancing toward the door with the girl silhouette, he recalled the first time he'd run inside the girls' bathroom on a dare. It hadn't been that hard. And maybe, just maybe, he would luck out and no one would be inside.

CHAPTER SEVEN

PATRICK RELUCTANTLY RELEASED Emily. "I enjoyed dancing with you."

She gazed up at him, her big, dark eyes widening. "Yes," she breathed. "Me, too."

It would be easy to pretend this was a real date and there was no fund-raising research involved. To hold her close, revel in the feel of her body pressed close to his, steal a few kisses on the dance floor. So why couldn't he seem to get beyond a relatively chaste slow dance?

Because Emily and her ready-made family scared the living daylights out of him. She was a package deal and he'd do well to remember that.

Sighing, he released her hand.

Emily glanced at her watch. "Damn. I'm late to check the restrooms. I'll be back in a minute."

Patrick watched her walk away, his gaze drawn to the sway of her hips. For a tall woman, she was surprisingly graceful, like some heathen princess strolling barefoot among her subjects.

His imagination took flight, replacing her suede skirt with one made of grass, her T-shirt and peekaboo vest replaced with a bikini top. And to complete the effect, a fragrant blossom tucked behind her ear, set off by the silky brown hair cascading down her back.

He watched as she opened the door to the girls' restroom. Emily recoiled, covering her mouth with her hand. Something was very wrong.

Patrick sprinted through the crowd. The odor hit him at about the same time someone yelled, "Stink bomb." The cry was echoed from at least two other areas of the gym. Although he backed a step, there was no relief from the noxious fumes.

Grabbing a paper napkin from the refreshment table, he covered his nose and mouth, breathing through his mouth. His stomach rebelled at the putrid odor. But Patrick's training kicked in and he started herding teens toward the exit, keeping his voice calm. "Walk outside, everyone, calmly and quietly."

All the while, he searched for Emily out of the corner of his eye. She'd disappeared into the crowd, blending with a group of students.

The fire alarm sounded, underscoring the need to get everyone out of the building. Fortunately, the students were accustomed to fire drills and did exactly as they were told.

Coach Evers stopped him. "Good job, Stevens. Make sure everyone stays orderly and assembles out front. I'll clear the building."

"This won't activate the sprinkler system, will it?"

Coach Evers shook his head. "Not unless there's smoke. Let's hope the little jerks don't set off smoke bombs, too."

"I'll keep an eye out for anything suspicious."

"Thanks, bud." He clapped Patrick on the shoulder. "Let's get these kids out of here."

Patrick gestured for a few stragglers to join the others. Less than five minutes later, he stood on the front lawn, trying to keep order.

Linda Price trotted up, coughing, her eyes red and swollen. Although she was a terrific organizer, she seemed at a complete loss in a crisis. "What are we going to do? It'll take days to air out the gym."

"I imagine we'll wait for the fire department to assess the situation. Who's the faculty member in charge?"

"Coach Evers. And I don't see him anywhere."

"He's clearing the building."

Sirens grew louder as two fire engines pulled into the parking lot. Firemen jumped out of the truck and headed for the building.

The conversation level around them rose. A hoot

of laughter erupted nearby. The change in venue apparently hadn't dampened the students' fun. Soon, though, the cold would cut through the excitement, and they'd have some uncomfortable kids.

Worried, Patrick walked through the throng, looking for Emily. Finally he found her. "There you are. Are you all right?"

She nodded, her eyes shadowed with concern. "I found Jason and Cassie. I told them to stick together and wait for us near the flagpole."

"Good idea. I have no idea what the protocol is under this situation."

"There's Coach Evers." She nodded toward where the coach conversed with one of the firemen, slapped him on the back and headed their way.

"He doesn't seem too panicked, so I assume it's not hazardous. Just very rank."

"I hope it's not dangerous. I'd never forgive myself if something happened to any of these kids on my watch." She rubbed her arms, shivering.

Patrick wrapped an arm around her shoulders. "They're fine. Nobody was hurt."

His heart constricted when she leaned into him for a split second. He liked being there for her. Way too much.

But she recovered quickly as the coach approached, her back stiffening. "Coach Evers, please tell me what's going on."

"The initial stink bomb was set off in the girls' restroom. Two others were set off at the opposite end of the gym, probably shortly after the first stink bomb was discovered. There's no way the dance can continue—the principal's on his way over to send everyone home. You and Stevens did a terrific job keeping everyone calm. Thanks."

"That's what we're here for," Emily said.

Patrick felt his blood pressure rise. "The dance is ruined for a whole bunch of kids because of a stupid prank. Thank God the little idiot didn't set off a smoke bomb instead. The sprinklers could have engaged and the damage would have been extensive."

"You're right," Evers said. "These kids are all impulse. Don't stop to think of the ramifications."

The principal arrived and instructed the teens to call home and let their parents know they were all right and that the dance would be ending early.

When he finished, the principal approached Emily and Patrick. He extended his hand and introduced himself, saying, "Thanks for thinking on your feet tonight. Something like this could have easily gotten out of hand if the adults hadn't kept clear heads. We're damn lucky there wasn't a stampede for the door. Who knows what would have happened then? Anyway, if you folks could hang around for a few more minutes till we get most of these kids dispersed?"

Emily glanced at Patrick. He nodded slightly. "Sure, we'll stay," she said.

"If there are any stragglers who can't reach parents, Coach Evers and I will wait with them in the library. I better find Mrs. Price. Thanks again."

Shortly after he left, Jason and Cassie appeared. "What'd the principal say, Mom?"

"Stink bomb in the girls' restroom, and two more in the gym itself. A silly prank, but we were very fortunate people didn't panic. Someone could have gotten seriously hurt. As it is, it'll take days to air out the gym. You may not have basketball practice next week."

Jason's eyes widened. "Aw, that really sucks."

"Yes, it does." Patrick's tone was sharper than he intended, but kids simply didn't comprehend the severity. "But it would have been much worse if people stampeded for the door. People have died under similar circumstances."

Jason looked down at his sneakers. "Wow, I never would have thought of that. Um, Mom, can Cassie and I go wait by the car?"

The crisp Elmwood air stung as Patrick

inhaled deeply. Silly prank. Who knew better than he how seriously someone could get hurt as a result of a "harmless" prank. But, fortunately, not here, not tonight.

Emily glanced around. "It looks like the kids are heading out pretty quickly. You and Cassie get in the car and start the heater. I'll meet you at the car in five minutes. No monkey business, mister."

"Okay." Jason clasped Cassie's hand and they walked slowly toward the parking lot.

Something wasn't right. Patrick thought Jason was just a little too compliant. Then he remembered the cherry bomb incident in sixth grade. Surely Jason hadn't been stupid enough to try a similar prank at a high school dance?

His stomach tightened as he recalled standing out on the Patterson's front porch in the aching cold. And the mousetrap in his desk drawer. He'd like to think Jason had matured past that point, but he had to wonder.

The drive to Patrick's house was unusually subdued.

Emily parked and opened her door.

"Hey, no need for you to go out in the cold." He brushed a strand of hair from her cheek. "Go home and get warmed up by the fire. It's been an intense evening." He turned toward the backseat. "You, too, Jason, Cassie."

Jason grumbled something indecipherable, then very clearly, "See ya, Mr. Stevens. Don't let us keep you." His eyes held a challenge.

Patrick hesitated, unsure of dating protocol. Unsure whether this qualified as a date, and if so, if it were acceptable to seek a kiss good-night with his date's teenage son sitting nearby.

He opted for planting a quick kiss on Emily's cheek. He touched her arm and said, "Thanks. Stink bombs notwithstanding, I had fun and I didn't expect to."

"More fun than research?" Her eyes sparkled with mischief.

"Definitely. Besides, we were able to combine research and dancing quite nicely. Coach Evers gave me a couple ideas. Too bad Linda didn't have any information on Tiffany's fund-raising."

"Come on, Mom." Jason leaned across the console, ostensibly to change the radio station, but effectively using his body as a barrier between Patrick and Emily.

Patrick grasped Jason's forearm and pushed back his shirt sleeve. "What's this?"

"I dunno."

"Jason, hon, you're bleeding." Emily frowned.

"Looks like you scraped it on something. Broken glass or plastic?"

Jason paled. "I smelled what I thought was

gas, so I pulled the fire alarm. I must've scraped it on the broken glass."

"You set off the fire alarm, Jason?" Emily asked.

"Yes, Mom, but that's it, I swear. All I did was pull the alarm. Isn't that what we're supposed to do when there's a fire or an emergency, like the whole building's gonna explode?" He raised his chin. "Sheesh, I get in trouble for doing the right thing."

Emily's gaze wavered.

Patrick wanted to tell her Jason was probably lying through his teeth to save his sorry hide. But he didn't think she'd enjoy hearing that from him. He kept silent.

"We'll discuss this later. I only hope you had nothing to do with the stink bomb."

"I told you, all I did was set off the alarm. You don't believe me? Your own son?" Jason's voice quavered.

Was it a convincing act or had Patrick misjudged Jason?

Emily glanced from Jason to Patrick, as if hoping Patrick would rescue her. But he couldn't.

Finally, she turned to Jason. "I believe you."

Triumph shone in Jason's eyes as he held Patrick's gaze. He might as well have proclaimed flesh and blood won out every time.

THE NEXT DAY at a matinee movie, Emily and Nancy waited outside the restroom stall for Nancy's daughter, Ana, to use the facilities. At four years old, Ana refused any help, but tended to take twice the time Emily's boys had at the same age.

Fortunately, most of the movies were in session, so the place was deserted. Beau, Mark and Ryan were saving their seats before the movie began.

"So you danced with Patrick, huh? Dish." Nancy's eyes sparkled with anticipation.

"Yes. It was…nice."

"Did you ever decide if it was a date?"

"No. I got the feeling he wanted to kiss me on the dance floor, but with several hundred teens acting as chaperones, who could tell?"

"No kidding. And somehow I get the impression Jason wouldn't be too wild about the idea. I asked him how the double date went and he said something like it would have been okay if Mr. Stevens hadn't been there."

Emily sighed. "There's friction. I don't know if it's the history between them or if Jason would hate any man I dated."

"My guess is it's going to take a while with Jason. Any man would have to earn his trust, probably Patrick more so than most." Nancy bent down and checked under the stall. "You okay, Ana?"

"Yes, Mom."

"We'll miss the beginning of the movie if you don't hurry. And Daddy will probably eat all the popcorn."

"I'll hurry."

"Good girl." Nancy smiled and winked. "Our version of sibling rivalry. I swear Ana can eat more than a grown man."

"Maybe she remembers the orphanage and competing for food?"

"I'm not sure. I was warned about hoarding behavior, but it's never been a problem. As far as I know, they always had enough to eat at Pechory. Not a lot of the modern niceties, but it was a clean, caring place for the kids."

"Well, Beau is like a kid himself at times, so you're probably on target with the sibling rivalry." Emily chuckled. "You got one of the good guys, Nancy."

"Don't I know it. I thank God every day. I'm not going to be content till we find you a special man, too."

"With my track record, it could be a while."

"Look at Beau's history. He was married three times before he married me and we couldn't be happier. He'd pretty much tackled his demons by the time I met him. And we work hard at our relationship."

"Hard work doesn't scare me." Emily checked her makeup in the mirror. Removing a tube of lip gloss from her purse, she applied a thin layer. "But I've found both people in a marriage need to be willing. One person can't prop up the whole shebang. And some people, like Larry, shouldn't have gotten married at all. I'm never going into another relationship thinking I can fix a man if I just love him enough."

"Hm. We'll just have to find someone fabulous for you. Someone so perfect, he doesn't need fixing. I had high hopes for Patrick Stevens, but then again, I had high hopes for Luke Andrews and he bored you to tears."

"Mom, I need tissue," Ana called from inside the stall.

Nancy went into an open stall and procured a handful of tissue, passing it under the door. "Here you go, sweetie."

Emily felt a tiny pang of envy. She loved her four boys more than life itself, but it was small female rituals like these she would never be able to share with them. Shopping was another. "You're sure Beau doesn't mind keeping an eye on Mark and Ryan?"

"Positive. I bet he's just absorbing all that testosterone. He complains about being adrift in the estrogen ocean at times."

Emily laughed. "I guess it's all relative, then. I was just envying you your relationship with Ana and wishing I had a daughter."

"Well, it could still happen."

"Bite your tongue. Four children is plenty. All a man has to do is look at me and I get pregnant." Emily shuddered. The wistful gleam in her friend's eyes made her immediately contrite. "I'm sorry, hon, that was really thoughtless. Any news on the fertility front?"

Nancy shook her head. "No. Beau and I have two beautiful daughters between us and though we'd love to have a child together, it might not be in the cards."

"How's Rachel doing at NYU? I'm so impressed she was able to graduate from high school a year early."

"She's fabulous." Nancy sighed. "We miss her, though. I wish she'd picked a closer university."

The stall door clicked open and Ana emerged, her blue eyes bright with interest.

"Don't forget to wash your hands," Nancy instructed.

"I won't." Ana complied. "Hurry, Mom, we'll miss the start of the movie."

Nancy rolled her eyes and shrugged.

They rushed through the multitheater complex. As they approached the entrance to their theater, Emily felt a shock of recognition as a man approached. "Patrick."

"Emily. Um, great to see you."

She glanced quickly beyond him and was relieved to see he was alone. Not that she would have been jealous if he'd had a date. Well, maybe a little. "Are you seeing the polar bear movie?"

He grinned sheepishly. "Yep. You caught me. I love any kind of animal documentary. Since I couldn't rent a kid to come with me, I'm here solo."

Nancy extended her hand. "I'm Nancy Stanton, you must be Patrick. I've heard a lot about you."

Emily elbowed her in the ribs, but Nancy just smiled innocently.

Patrick juggled popcorn and soda to take Nancy's hand. "Nice to meet you."

"Why don't you join us? My husband, Beau, is saving seats along with Emily's boys, Mark and Ryan."

He hesitated. "I'm not sure—"

"Of course you're sitting with us." Nancy laughed her tinkling, cheerleader, of-course-everyone-likes-me laugh.

Patrick tilted his head to the side, apparently mesmerized by her luminous smile.

If she didn't love her like a sister, Emily could have happily gouged out her best friend's eyes.

"Thank you. I'll join you, then, if Emily doesn't mind?" Patrick glanced at her.

What was she supposed to say? Besides, her pulse leapt at the idea of spending more time with him.

"Sure. That's great." And she sounded like a great big clod after Nancy's effortless display.

Patrick opened the door for them. "After you, ladies."

Nancy nodded ever so slightly and winked so only Emily could see the gesture. Patrick obviously had her stamp of approval.

Fortunately, the lights were still on when they entered the theater. Beau waved, apparently afraid they couldn't find the tall Texan by sheer height alone.

When they reached the row of seats, it took quite a bit of maneuvering to get Ana on one side of Beau and Nancy on the other. Then came Mark, Ryan and Emily, leaving Patrick on the end.

Nancy, ever the social butterfly, remembered her manners while Emily was still recovering her equilibrium.

"Patrick, this is my husband, Beau. Beau, this is Patrick Stevens, Emily's…friend."

Beau stood and the men shook hands over the kids' heads. "Stevens, good to meet you. Any friend of Emily's is a friend of ours. As a matter of fact, she's like a member of our family." Beau's smile was tight and warning crackled in the air.

Emily could have kissed him. The big galoot thought he needed to protect her. The gesture warmed her heart. It meant she belonged.

The lights dimmed and Patrick sat next to her. His shoulder bumped hers as he settled in. Longing coursed through her. Not a sexual thing, though there certainly was that undercurrent. No, longing for this to be an every Saturday ritual she could count on, to give stability and joy to an otherwise topsy-turvy life.

"Jason and Jeremy aren't here?" Patrick whispered as the preview began to roll.

"No. Jeremy's at a friend's house and Jason went hiking with Cassie's family."

Patrick offered his popcorn.

Emily declined, instead doing battle with her sons' quick hands darting in and out of the supersize tub she'd bought. Ana wasn't the only child present who could eat more than a grown man.

Shortly after the movie began, Emily relaxed and simply enjoyed the polar bears' onscreen antics, the laughter of her children and an occasional chuckle from Patrick. Contentment, so fleeting in her hectic, single-mom life, stole over her, making her wish she could bottle the moment.

Was it the product of being with her children and good friends, or was Patrick's presence the catalyst?

The thought discomfitted Emily, because she'd learned long ago not to base her happiness on a man. She shrugged off the thought and decided to enjoy the outing no matter what.

All too soon, the movie ended and the credits rolled. Emily stood as the kids gathered up their empty food wrappers, popcorn bucket and soft drink cups.

Patrick stretched as the lights came up, and they waited for patrons to pass in order to exit their row. Emily glanced toward the other side of the theater and her gaze locked with Linda Price's.

Linda quickly glanced away, prodding her daughter toward the other exit. Following close behind was Brad Bigelow and his daughter—the same girl who'd answered the door at his house.

Emily mentally sorted through possible con-clusions and was ashamed of herself. So what if Linda Price and Brad Bigelow took their children to the movies together? It was probably just a nice gesture to give Brad and his daughter a bit of normalcy in the midst of recovering from Tiffany's death.

But then Brad placed his palm on the small of Linda's back and warning bells went off in Emily's mind.

"Go, Mom." Mark prodded her.

She realized Patrick stood in the aisle, holding off the crowd for her.

"I'm sorry," she murmured, glancing to where she'd seen Brad and Linda. But they were gone, swallowed up by the sea of moviegoers.

"We gotta go," Mark and Ryan whined in unison.

"I knew those jumbo sodas were a mistake," Emily commented.

"I'll take them," Beau offered. "We'll meet you in the main lobby."

"Thanks, Beau, you're a sweetie."

"Always." He smiled and winked, taking a boy by each hand.

When they reached the lobby, she grasped Patrick's arm. "I just saw Linda Price here with Brad Bigelow."

"Small world."

Nancy tilted her head. "I saw them, too. With their younger children."

Patrick frowned. "It *is* a family movie."

"I mean, it looked like they were together, together," Emily said. Turning to Nancy, she asked, "Did you notice how he touched her?"

Patrick crossed his arms and leaned back. "What's your point?"

"Brad's hand was hovering between the I-think-you're-special zone and the I-want-to-get-horizontal-with-you zone. Definitely not in the friend area."

"Ah." Nancy nodded. "I think you're right. I wonder if this started after Tiffany died? Linda's married, isn't she? Or maybe I heard something about her being separated?"

"Wait a minute, you two. Don't tell me you've decided Brad and Linda are having an affair based on one possibly benign gesture?"

Nancy nodded. "Exactly. My intuition tells me it was far from benign."

Patrick rolled his eyes. "Oh, brother."

"Don't discount intuition. It can be amazingly accurate." Emily raised her chin. "The question is, does their relationship have anything to do with Linda's death and the missing PTO money?"

CHAPTER EIGHT

PATRICK LAUGHED in disbelief. He felt as if he'd been dropped somewhere in the vicinity of Oz. "You're not serious, are you? Thinking a harmless outing between Brad and Linda has something to do with the missing PTO money."

Emily linked her arm with Nancy's and said, "We're saying it's something to consider."

Mark and Ryan raced up, saving Patrick from any more convoluted reasoning. Beau followed close behind. He seemed like an okay guy, but Patrick detected a little resentment simmering.

"You ladies ready to go?" Beau asked, turning to Patrick and extending his hand. "Patrick, it was good meeting you. See you around some time."

"Good meeting you, too." Patrick met the challenge in the other man's stare. He'd been dismissed, and damn, if it didn't rankle. Not that he had any intention of doing more than saying goodbye to Emily.

"Emily, Mark, Ryan, take it easy." He nodded toward Nancy. "Nice to meet you, Nancy."

Nancy's eyes sparkled. She reminded him a bit of Emily in her zest for life. "Patrick, we're having a barbecue later and you simply must come."

Patrick opened his mouth to politely decline, but Nancy just kept talking as if his attendance was a foregone conclusion. "Emily can give you our address and directions. Or maybe you can just leave your car at Emily's and ride with her. Let's see, it's two o'clock now. Why don't you guys come any time after three. The steaks will go on the grill at five. See you then. Bye."

"I, um, we…" Emily stammered into thin air, because Nancy had whisked her family away and only the four of them remained.

Patrick was torn and indecision wasn't normally a problem for him. "I really shouldn't."

Emily hesitated. "I apologize for Nancy putting you on the spot, Patrick."

He couldn't help but grin. "She doesn't allow for defeat, does she?"

"No. Not when entertaining is involved. And apparently, she really wants you to attend the barbecue. You might as well give in. Otherwise, she'll hunt you down and, in that very nice cheerleader way of hers, she'll drag you to their home."

Patrick had to admit he didn't want to go back to his apartment. That was one of the reasons he'd opted for a movie. A guy could only take so much television and his own company, reptiles, amphibians and spiders notwithstanding. "Since you put it that way, I guess I'll go."

Emily glanced at her watch. "Why don't we meet at my house, in say, an hour?"

"That'll work. I don't want to arrive empty-handed. I'd like to stop and get a bottle of wine."

Nodding, Emily said, "Fine. Although Beau's not much of a wine drinker. I guess it's a Texas thing."

"Long-neck beer?"

"Yes, though they're hard to find in this area."

"I think I know a specialty store. I'll be at your house in an hour." For two people who weren't dating, they sure were having a lot of outings that seemed like dates.

According to Patrick's watch, he arrived at Emily's house forty-five minutes later. He made his way through a gauntlet of BMX-style bikes, skateboards and Roller Blades parked in the walkway.

He rang the bell and was relieved when Emily answered the door almost immediately. He wasn't eager to be face-to-face with Jason again, especially not while requesting admittance to the Patterson home.

"Great, you're here," Emily said, holding a rectangular baking pan covered with foil. Over her shoulder, she hollered, "Mark, Ryan, let's go."

The two boys raced out of the house with the Labrador close on their heels. Emily snagged the dog's collar. "Oh, no you don't, Clifford." The Lab hung his head in disappointment as she herded him back through the entryway. She shut the door with an emphatic thunk and locked it.

Patrick suppressed a smile. "What about Jeremy and Jason?"

"Still MIA. Jason's having dinner and watching movies over at Cassie's. Jeremy's spending the night at his friend's house."

Patrick grinned. Suddenly, the barbecue seemed a lot more promising. Certainly less tense without Jason.

"Why don't I drive, then?" He eyed the two boys, figuring they couldn't make too much of a mess in ten minutes. "We can all fit in the SUV."

"Sure. Boys, we're going in Patrick's car."

Mark and Ryan jumped up and down with excitement.

Patrick smiled at their enthusiasm. They were great kids. Too bad he couldn't say the same for Jason.

EMILY PLACED THE BROWNIES on the table next to an astonishing array of side dishes and condiments. "I should have known you'd have a five-course meal."

Nancy laughed. "You know me too well. But nobody bakes brownies like you do. Beau and Ana have been eagerly awaiting them."

"I had to develop a specialty in defense of my Martha Stewart friend." She surveyed the table. "It's beautiful. You never cease to amaze me."

Nancy hugged her. "Just like you never cease to amaze me. I'm in awe at how you juggle so many balls in the air and never drop one."

Emily glanced out the kitchen window. "It's turned out to be the perfect day for a barbecue. Almost like spring. Mark and Ryan sure didn't waste any time finding the trampoline. I hope they don't bounce Ana right off."

"Beau'll make sure they're careful." Nancy moved to the window, standing beside Emily. "Looks like he's showing Patrick his landscaping projects and the new barbecue. They seem to be getting along fine."

Emily smiled. "Yes, the Lone Star beer seemed to go a long way toward thawing Beau's attitude."

"What do you mean? He likes Patrick."

"He just seemed, well, a little reserved for Beau, the man who never met a stranger."

"He's protective, Em. Kind of like a big brother. He doesn't want to see you hurt."

"And yet, you, more of a sister than my flesh-and-blood sisters, are throwing me at the man."

"I am *not* throwing you at him."

"Let's see, inviting him to sit with us at the movies."

"He seemed a little lonely."

"He was perfectly content to see the movie by himself. And then the barbecue?"

"I'm hospitable."

"You're matchmaking."

Nancy laughed. "Only returning the favor. I have you to thank for pushing Beau in my direction."

"You two were meant for each other."

"And maybe you and Patrick were meant for each other."

Emily swallowed hard, suddenly terrified. Because normally she would have laughed off the idea. "Nance, I'm not sure I'm ready for a relationship again."

"Sometimes you don't know if you're ready."

Emily watched Patrick through the window. For a science geek, he adapted socially with an ease that Emily envied.

"You only had one child, Nancy. A woman with four children is a lot harder for a man to accept. Especially since Patrick and Jason have never gotten along."

"Why don't we just have a good time this afternoon and not worry about the rest?"

Emily nodded. "You're right. It's a beautiful, sunny afternoon. Let's go join the fun." She linked her arm through Nancy's and they went outside.

Emily was surprised to find Patrick and Beau tossing the football with the kids. She stood back and watched, her heart in her throat.

It was hard to tell who enjoyed the game more, the kids or the men.

Patrick glanced in her direction. "Come on, ladies. Join us. We can have a game of touch football."

Emily looked at Nancy.

Nancy shrugged and laughed. "You bet. Girls against boys?"

"No, way. I want you on my team." Beau wrapped an arm around her shoulders. "How about you and me and Ana against Patrick and the Pattersons?"

"You're on," Patrick said. He waved Emily over. "Come here, we need to huddle and set strategy."

Emily touched Ana's shoulder. "Honey, you're on your mommy and daddy's team."

The little girl crossed her arms over her chest, apparently ready to mutiny. She adored Mark and Ryan and followed them like a puppy.

Emily bent down and whispered, "They'll chase you when you run with the ball."

Ana's eyes brightened. As Emily suspected, even four-year-old girls liked to be chased by boys. She nodded and joined her parents.

"Okay, guys, what's the plan?" Emily wedged herself between Mark and Ryan in the huddle, so she wouldn't be too close to Patrick.

"How do you throw?" Patrick asked her.

"Pretty darn well, thank you. But I'm a better receiver. One of the advantages of being tall."

Patrick grinned. "One of many advantages." His eyes were warm as he appraised her.

Emily rolled her eyes. But she enjoyed the flattery.

Patrick outlined a simple play, gave the boys their jobs rushing and generally creating confusion.

Mark hiked the ball to Patrick. Emily dodged around Nancy and headed for the goal line. She turned in time to see Patrick let loose with an impressive spiral. It landed in her outstretched arms and she tucked it to her chest. Turning, she crossed the goal line only moments ahead of Beau.

"Touchdown," Mark and Ryan yelled.

Patrick gave Emily a high five. "Nice catch."

"Good pass."

We make a good team.

Emily pushed the thought aside. She'd been a single mom so long, teamwork with another adult seemed foreign.

While the Stantons huddled and discussed strategy, Patrick motioned the boys over, his voice low. "Remember Ana's just a little girl. Go easy on her."

"Well, duh," Mark said.

"Ana's almost like a little sister to them, without the sibling rivalry," Emily translated. "They're pretty protective of her."

"Good."

Nancy hiked the football to Beau, then sprinted for the end zone. Beau faked a pass, then handed off to Ana. "Run, Ana, run."

The boys could have easily blocked the little girl. But Mark tripped and fell to the ground. Then Ryan had a similar accident.

Ana ran, legs churning, tongue protruding with concentration. When she reached the end zone, everyone cheered, "Touchdown."

Ana raised the football with both hands, smiling broadly. "I did it," she squealed.

"You sure did," Patrick said, nodding his approval to Mark and Ryan.

They ran a few more plays, each of which resulted in one of the children making a touchdown. Then Beau pleaded fatigue. "I'm gonna have to retire my cleats and put on my barbecue apron. The steaks in the fridge?" he asked Nancy.

She nodded. "Yes, they're ready to go."

Emily didn't want to be left alone to make polite chitchat with Patrick. "I can go get them. Then help out in the kitchen if Nancy will let me."

"There's absolutely nothing left to do," Nancy said. "You grab a beer or soft drink and have a seat."

"Both of you have a seat, then, and I'll shuttle the steaks out. It's the least I can do," Patrick said.

"Will you guys quit trying to out-nice each other? We could starve." Beau eyed the setting sun. "I'll get a fire going in the fire pit. It's going to get nippy here pretty soon."

"Good idea. And Patrick, I'll gladly accept your gracious offer to help," Nancy said.

Once Patrick headed for the house, Nancy started moving patio chairs to surround the stone fire pit. "Maybe we can pop some popcorn after supper—the old-fashioned way."

Emily helped Nancy move the chairs, then selected a seat. Contentment stole over her. Good friends, good conversation, more precious to her than any Saturday night on the town.

Beau soon had the fire crackling.

Patrick returned carrying a platter. "This what you need?" He handed the platter to Beau.

"Yep."

"Anything else I can do to help?"

"I've got it. Just sit down by the fire and relax."

Patrick moved beside Emily's chair. "Where're the kids?"

"Playing hide-and-seek over on the other side of the yard. It's quiet, so it must be the seeking part of the game."

"What about later? Are you okay with them being around the fire? That mesh cover isn't much protection if a kid knocks into it or falls on it."

His concern surprised her. "They've been around the fire pit before and are very aware of the danger. So is Ana."

"I'm just wondering, well, with the trampoline and the fire pit and all. Seems like a lot of hazards." He sat in the chair next to her.

Emily shifted in her seat. She felt a little like he'd just accused her best friends of being bad parents. "Beau and Nancy are very safety conscious. And the kids are always well-supervised. For someone who doesn't have kids you sure are super concerned about safety issues."

"You don't have to be a parent to realize that all it takes is a few seconds and lives can be changed forever." He stared into the fire. "Accidents happen."

"Blame it on me, Patrick," Beau said from the barbecue area a few feet away. "It's the redneck in me, I guess. I was raised around open fires and swimming holes and managed to survive."

"You were fortunate," Patrick murmured. His eyes were shadowed.

Emily wanted to ask him why he'd become so cautious, but didn't feel she knew him well enough.

Nancy came to the rescue. "Yes, you *were* fortunate, William Beauregard Stanton the third. And you know as well as I do, you were the first person to teach Ana the proper way to use the trampoline and how to be safe around the fire. And if I remember correctly, you vetoed the swimming pool idea until she's older."

"Damn right I vetoed it. I'd never forgive myself if she got hurt or drowned. But we've got to allow her to be a kid, too. We can't wrap her in cotton her whole life."

Emily could feel Patrick stiffen next to her. She glanced at him and he frowned. He cleared his throat. "It's a balance, I guess."

"Exactly." Nancy leaned forward. "Did Emily

let you taste the brownies? Her brownies are to die for."

Emily rolled her eyes at her friend's less than tactful change of subject and attempt to sell her as a domestic goddess. With any other man, she might have been tempted to make an off-color joke about his tasting her goodies, but with Patrick she was embarrassed. "They came from a box, Nance. It's not brain surgery."

"I'm sure they're terrific," Patrick murmured, but he seemed distracted. That distraction continued for the rest of the conversation and through a portion of supper. Only when Nancy broke out the Pictionary game did he snap out of it.

Everyone pitched in to clean up the supper mess, then they had a rousing game, girls against guys.

Before Emily knew it, Ana was rubbing her eyes and Mark and Ryan were winding down. Glancing at her watch, she said, "Oh my gosh, it's almost eleven. I need to get these kids home."

She and Patrick thanked Nancy and Beau, then herded the boys to the SUV.

Emily leaned back in the plush leather seat and sighed. She could get used to the luxury of having a guy like Patrick around. Someone to talk and laugh with, someone to share the hard work and worries of parenthood.

All too soon, they pulled into Emily's drive.

And lo and behold, Jason had remembered to turn on the porch light.

Patrick turned to her. "I had fun tonight. You've got nice friends and a couple of terrific kids."

Emily tried to ignore the fact that only two out of her four children had thus far met with his approval.

"I had a good time, too. Nancy and Beau are the best. And you hold your own pretty well in Pictionary, Mr. Stevens."

Patrick eyed her intently. "So do you, Ms. Patterson." He leaned over and touched his lips to hers.

A loud "Ew" from the backseat told her one of the boys had seen the kiss.

Patrick withdrew, his eyes alight with amusement. "They don't miss much, do they?"

"No, unfortunately they don't."

"I'll walk you to the door."

As he helped her out of the car, the boys raced up the porch steps.

Patrick touched her arm. "I meant to talk to you about the Sea World trip, but tonight didn't seem like a good time."

Emily said, "You boys go on ahead. I'll be there in a minute."

"Would you consider meeting with me tomorrow afternoon, so we can discuss it? Maybe kick around some fund-raising ideas? I still intend to make this trip a reality." His voice was low, intent.

"Patrick, I admire your dedication, really I do. But I'm not sure there's anything we can do."

"Just meet with me, okay? If not tomorrow, maybe stop by school on your way to work? I'm usually there early. Besides, there's someone I want you to meet." His eyes were warm and pleading.

Emily was intrigued, in spite of the knowledge that there was no way Patrick would be able to make the Sea World trip a reality at this late a date.

The porch light went out and they were enveloped in darkness. Then the light came on again.

"Yes, I guess I can swing by Monday morning."

"Great. Seven-fifteen?"

The door opened, and Jason stood in the doorway, arms crossed, frowning. He looked every inch the furious father.

Emily's heart ached that he'd taken on the heavy load of man of the house at an early age. But a part of her also rebelled at the thought of anyone, let alone her teenage son, directing her social life.

"Yes, seven-fifteen will be perfect." She kissed Patrick on the cheek and smiled.

He cupped her face with his hand, bending closer.

Jason's voice boomed uncomfortably close. "It's almost midnight, Mom. I started to worry...."

Patrick made a low sound of frustration. He stepped back, his arm dropping to his side. "I'll see you Monday, then."

"Yes. Good night."

Emily followed her son in the door, but turned and watched Patrick stroll down the steps. Sighing, she closed the door and leaned against it. Why did dating at forty have to be so much more complex than it had been at twenty?

CHAPTER NINE

EMILY STARED at the computer screen on Sunday evening, taking advantage of a quiet moment. Mark and Ryan were in bed and Jason and Jeremy were doing homework.

She'd found numerous sites dedicated to fund-raising, but it seemed most of the larger events were booked months in advance. If only they could recover the nearly fifteen thousand dollars that had disappeared under Tiffany's leadership.

Sighing, Emily realized the matter was in the police's hands. Despite that, Principal Ross indicated it was unlikely the money would ever be found. The principal had had no choice but to advise the teachers and PTO officers that some irregularities had been noted in the PTO fund and an audit might be required. Requests for funds would be considered on a very limited basis.

On a whim, Emily Googled Tiffany Bigelow. There was a reference to her status as PTO president on the Elmwood Elementary site. There was a photo of her at her church bazaar, which she'd helped organize. And there was a photo of her attending the Elmwood Heart Ball the previous spring, smiling brightly, arm-in-arm with her husband, Brad. The caption indicated she was a staunch supporter of the cardiac wing at the hospital.

Emily felt a twinge of guilt researching the poor, dead woman. Apparently her charitable efforts had gone much further than simply Elmwood PTO president.

Then Emily found a URL for a casino in Atlantic City. Clicking on the link, she was surprised to see that Tiffany had been a winner at the dollar slots shortly before her death. Interesting. The accompanying photo gave the impression the PTO president seemed right at home on the casino floor.

Although why that surprised Emily, she shouldn't know. She'd been to Atlantic City once and thoroughly enjoyed the sheer energy of the place. The hustle, bustle, the lights, all the different people.

Emily's search engine showed two more entries for Tiffany and Atlantic City. Probably the same trip.

"Mom, I need the computer to type my social

studies paper." Jeremy's hand was warm on her shoulder.

She turned and gave him a big hug. Sometimes she feared her more studious son got lost in the noisy shuffle that was the Patterson household. "It's kind of late, don't you think?"

"It's due tomorrow."

Emily tipped her head to the side. "You don't normally wait until the last minute. What gives?"

Jeremy adjusted his glasses. "Um, I was tutoring another student with math."

"I love that you help other kids, honey, but I don't want your own studies to suffer. Who were you tutoring?"

"Madison Smith."

"Ah. The cute girl who's had a crush on you forever?"

"Mom." He rolled his eyes.

"It's the truth. And you're getting to that age where boys are interested in girls. It's nothing to be embarrassed about."

"It's not like that." He sighed heavily. "Can I use the computer when you're done?"

Emily closed her browser. "Sure. Just don't be too long."

"I won't." He hesitated. "Mom?"

"Hm?"

"Why were you looking up Mrs. Bigelow?"

"Just PTO stuff."

"The kids say the police were at her house asking a bunch of questions."

"I hate that people are gossiping, Jeremy. I imagine her family's hurting enough already." Emily regretted checking up on the woman. Still, the references to Atlantic City bothered her.

EMILY PULLED INTO the Elmwood Elementary School parking lot promptly at seven-fifteen the next morning. Patrick's SUV was already there.

She wrapped her sweater around her as she trudged toward the front door.

"You made it," Patrick called out from a bench near the front door.

Emily was surprised to see two dark-haired children sitting with him.

"Hi," she said.

"Emily, these are two of my students, Ari and his sister, Kat. Kids, this is Ms. Patterson."

"Hello, Ms. Patterson." Kat offered her gloved hand in a very adult manner.

Emily was impressed as she shook the girl's hand.

"Hello, Ms....Patterson," Ari said more slowly. He obviously had some sort of disability.

Emily shook his hand, too. The children both had lovely manners.

"Ari, Kat, why don't you two scoot to the other side." Patrick indicated the other side of the bench. "So Ms. Patterson can sit here with me. We have a few things to discuss."

The children gathered up muffins, cups and napkins and slid them to the other side of the table.

"We have a breakfast tradition, of sorts. Since I'm a single guy, I usually have muffins and fruit in danger of going bad if someone doesn't help me eat them. Sometimes Ari and Kat join me for breakfast al fresco."

Emily sat next to him. "Sounds like a win-win situation."

"It is. And Ari and Kat are kind enough to help me out."

"Very nice. Isn't it a little cold out for a picnic though?" Her breath plumed in the morning air.

"I like to think of it as invigorating." Patrick nodded to the box of muffins. "Help yourself."

She noticed Patrick always seemed to be trying to feed people, from their first coffee-shop meeting to now. "No, thank you, I had breakfast at home. But you guys go right ahead."

Kat and Ari had been waiting patiently. Once they had permission, they practically inhaled their muffins. The sight tore at Emily's heart.

Although they'd certainly had some lean times

around their house, her kids had never gone hungry. And, God willing, they never would. She considered herself fortunate.

"I did some surfing on the Web last night." Emily pulled her scarf around her chin. "It looks like most of the large fund-raising activities need to be booked months in advance. There's a local candy manufacturer I intend to contact to see if maybe we can still organize a candy sale, though."

Patrick nodded. "That'll work. Coach Evers mentioned something like that. Wrong time of the year for wrapping paper and gifts. Unless they have spring and summer items."

"It's something to think about. I'm afraid the parents might all be tapped out from the holiday wrapping paper drive. The PTO secretary indicated that particular fund-raiser was successful. Too bad we don't, um, have access to those funds." She danced around the subject, tilting her head toward Ari and Kat.

"Yes, it is too bad."

"I was thinking we might try some of the more traditional ideas, like you did earlier in the year. Car washes, bake sales. Did you try a white elephant sale?"

"No. How would that work?"

"We'd ask folks to clean out their garages and donate the stuff they don't want anymore."

Patrick nodded. "I'm not sure if that will get us to Sea World, but I'm sure willing to try."

"See dolphins," Ari said slowly, his brown eyes alight with excitement.

"And whales," Kat added.

"Yes, the kids are very excited about the project. It's the kind of experience that some of the children will never have otherwise." Patrick's mouth thinned.

Emily touched his arm. "I can see why this trip means so much to you. I'd like to help in any way I can."

He held her gaze. "Thanks, Em. I appreciate it."

It seemed as if he wanted to say more, but the children were discussing the merits of whales and dolphins and a car pulled into the parking lot.

Principal Ross got out of her car and walked up the front steps. "Good morning."

They all exchanged greetings.

"I'm glad you're here, Emily." She rummaged in her briefcase. "These fund-raising flyers arrived for Tiffany. Also a letter responding to some sort of inquiry from Tiffany. Looks a little too good to be true. Double your money in one event."

Emily accepted the materials. "I'll look them over. Patrick and I were meeting this morning to brainstorm ways we could raise the funds for the San Diego trip."

The principal glanced at Ari and Kat, who were quietly munching on muffins. "We'll need to meet soon to discuss all the proposals. If we work hard, we might be able to salvage a few of the smaller projects…."

"How about if Emily and I brainstorm and meet with you, say, Thursday, to come up with a plan?" Patrick asked.

"Sounds reasonable. Enjoy your breakfast." She nodded and unlocked one of the front doors. "Kat, Ari, when the office staff gets here, maybe they'll have a project you can help with."

"Yes, ma'am." Kat's nose was red and she looked cold. "We'd like to help."

"Good." The principal disappeared behind the tinted glass doors.

Patrick said, "Once the office staff gets here, then there's enough supervision for Kat and Ari to hang out inside and get out of the cold."

Emily wondered at his statement. They seemed like such nice, well-behaved children. Then she realized the supervision was probably needed for legal reasons, not for keeping the children out of trouble. It made her a little sad to know that people who wanted only the best for kids had to be so careful showing it. But then again, as a mother, she shuddered to think what could happen if a pedophile slipped through the background checks and found a way to spend time alone with children.

Her estimation of Patrick rose. He obviously cared about Ari and Kat, but walked a complex tightrope in order to help them.

Glancing at her watch, Emily sighed. "I've gotta run. I'll call you later and we can maybe get together before we meet with Principal Ross and work on a battle plan?"

"Yes, sounds like a good idea. You know how to reach me here. Have I given you my home phone, too?" Patrick's question was casual, but Emily's pulse quickened.

"No, I don't believe you have."

He pulled a sheet of notebook paper from his backpack and scrawled his name and number. "Give me a call and we'll set up a time."

Emily accepted the paper, feeling they'd crossed an invisible line. Then she felt silly, as if having his home phone number were any big deal. "Sure, I'll call you."

PATRICK PULLED THE LASAGNA from the oven just as the phone rang. He burned himself in his haste to put it down.

He grabbed the phone with one hand and

answered, while turning on the cold water tap at the same time. He held his burned hand under the running water.

"Hi, Patrick, this is Emily. Did I catch you at a bad time?"

"No. Just doing a little cooking." He winced at his exaggeration. Women liked men who cooked, didn't they? But, his lasagna had come straight from a red box in the frozen food section. Why bother using his culinary skills for one?

"Did you still want to get together before we meet with Ross on Thursday?"

"Yes. I'm still hoping to find some brilliant answer to our problem."

Emily's sigh was evident, even across the phone lines. "I sure would, too. But the more I look at things, the more confused I get."

"Is there something new?"

"I called the company that sent the letter to Tiffany. It was kind of a strange conversation. At first, the woman said Tiffany needed to make a second deposit. I explained that Tiffany had died and I was taking over. Then it sunk in that she'd said *second* deposit. There might be money out there we can recover."

Patrick felt a spark of hope. "How much money?"

"That's the thing. I don't know. The woman

said she had another call and hung up on me. I've called back several times and all I get is voice mail."

"Does sound kind of suspicious."

"The other thing is that this company is based out of Atlantic City."

"What's so unusual about that?"

"I Googled Tiffany's name and apparently she'd made several trips to Atlantic City in the months before her death. One picture showed her at a casino winning a slots jackpot."

"Hm. Alone, I'd say it's nothing. But with this company in Atlantic City, too, it's starting to look a little coincidental. Tell ya what, I have a friend in security at Porter Chemical Company. You'd be amazed at the stuff he can access on his computer. I'll give him a call and see what he can find out. Maybe you can come over here Wednesday evening and I can go over his findings with you? That way we wouldn't have to worry about your kids overhearing anything potentially negative about Tiffany."

"That'd be a good idea. Jeremy says there are already rumors flying among the kids at the junior high. We'll need to make it early evening. I'm still not too sure about leaving Jason in charge of the little boys for long stretches. Especially after the last fiasco."

Patrick chuckled, recalling his first impression of the Patterson household—chaos, pure and simple. Oddly, it was a chaos that appealed to him at times when he was alone in his quiet apartment. "How about seven? Plan on an hour or an hour and a half, can you do that?"

"That'll work."

"Good." They said goodbye and Patrick replaced the receiver.

He glanced at the sink, wondering why on earth the faucet was running full blast. Then his hand started to sting and he remembered his burn.

Funny, how Emily Patterson could make him forget his pain.

EMILY SMOOTHED HER HAIR as she approached Patrick's door. Glancing down at her black slacks, crocheted sweater and black leather jacket, she wondered if perhaps jeans would have been better.

Probably. But she'd been in constant motion since she'd gotten home from work and hadn't had a chance to change. At least that's what she told herself. Truth was, she wanted to look nice.

Not for Patrick, though. She wouldn't, *couldn't* go that far. Nor would she admit he was kind of growing on her.

She rang the bell and waited a few seconds before the door opened.

Patrick opened the door wide. "Come on in."

He looked pretty cute in jeans, sneakers and an MIT sweatshirt. Now, she really felt overdressed.

"You want a soda or something? I think I might have a beer in the fridge somewhere."

Emily flushed. Did she look like the kind of woman who slugged down beer at every social gathering? Then she berated herself for being too sensitive. "Water's fine."

"The stuff's in here." He led the way to his den, where he had a lovely cherrywood computer desk, but the bookshelves looked as if they might be thrift-store rejects.

His computer appeared to be new and powerful. At least a lot newer than Emily's two old workhorses.

Patrick pulled over a chair. "You can sit here." He sat at the padded leather computer chair. "I'll show you some of the references I was able to come up with on my own."

Emily sat gingerly on the chair, scooting closer to the computer. Coincidentally, closer to Patrick, too.

"You're right, it looks like Tiffany spent a lot of time in Atlantic City recently." He clicked on a link. "Is this the picture you were talking about?"

"Yes."

"There's also a reference at another casino and Tiffany participating in a ladies' poker tournament."

"Poker? Tiffany?"

"Yes. Apparently she was pretty adept at hiding her emotions, among other things. She made it to the semifinals."

"But this doesn't have anything to do with the PTO funds, does it?" Emily's eyes widened. "Unless you think the PTO funds financed her trips."

"That's why I asked you to bring the bank statements. We can cross-reference the dates with ATM withdrawals. Not that it will probably do us any good."

"Was your friend able to find anything out?"

"Yes, he was able to dig a little deeper. The Bigelows are like most people, living paycheck to paycheck. There was a fifty-thousand dollar life insurance policy on Tiffany. Considering she left behind two kids who will need to go to college, that's not a lot these days."

"Poor Brad. He sure has his hands full. If Linda's marriage was already over, I'd almost say he deserved a little happiness."

Patrick raised his hands, shaking his head. "We're not even gonna go there. Pure speculation."

"You don't believe me, but that's okay. It probably had absolutely nothing to do with the PTO fiasco and that family's been through enough. Besides, it's none of my business."

"Good, we agree. My friend was able to find out a little about that company you called the other day. They do, in fact, offer casino type packets as fund-raisers. Set up the games, give prizes instead of money. It's all perfectly legal in most states, including New York."

"I wonder if that was her big fund-raiser? A casino night?" Emily was impressed. "If she could have pulled it off, it would have been huge. Getting people to gamble legally, with the proceeds going to charity."

"Yes, this is probably the big event she alluded to. But, my friend indicates the owner has been investigated for fraud in the past. Makes me wonder if the whole thing is a cover for something more."

Emily absorbed his statement. "Doesn't that seem a little too, well, gangster-ish?"

"You could be right," Patrick said. "I'm probably grasping at straws, hoping to find a way to pull my rear out of the fire. I really don't want to disappoint all those sixth graders."

"Whether it's all on the up-and-up, it sounded to me like the company might owe us a refund on a deposit Tiffany made. And at this point, we can use every penny we can get. The problem is, they won't return my calls."

"That's why I called earlier today."

"What did they say?"

"I got the same runaround you did. As soon as I mentioned Elmwood Elementary and Tiffany Bigelow, the woman had an urgent call and hung up on me. After that, I got voice mail."

Emily tapped her pen on her pad of paper. "So what do we do? If I were getting this kind of runaround at work, I'd probably fax a letter asking them to get in touch with me."

"Sounds reasonable."

"I'll do that first thing tomorrow morning. I'll word it in a very nonthreatening manner, very general."

"That's probably the best step. But I wouldn't count on getting a response."

Emily shook her head. "No, I'd be surprised if we did. But at least we'll be covered and have proof that we tried if something comes up later. And there's always the off chance they'll start co-operating."

"Always the optimist, huh?" Patrick's voice was warm.

"Some days, that's all that gets me through." She smiled.

He leaned closer and brushed a strand of hair off her cheek. "You're pretty amazing."

Emily shifted. He was close, too close. And she wanted to lean into him, a warning sign if there ever was one. "You're doing that flattering thing again."

"I know. And I think maybe you better just get used to it."

For once in her life, she didn't have a smart-aleck comeback. She simply froze as he bent forward and touched his lips to hers.

Then he leaned back in his chair and the kiss was over before she knew what happened. "I better not do that, or you might not agree to go to Atlantic City with me."

"Atlantic City?" she squeaked.

"Yes. When that company fails to respond to your fax, I intend to spend a weekend in Atlantic City and find out exactly what was going on down there. If there's a dime of PTO money owed us, I intend to find it. And since you're the one who can get people to open up, you're the logical person to go with me."

CHAPTER TEN

PATRICK SWALLOWED HARD, avoiding Emily's startled gaze. Where had that invitation come from? One minute, he'd been thinking aloud about a spur-of-the-moment trip to Atlantic City, even though he wasn't a spur-of-the-moment guy. Then, in the next breath, he'd invited Emily along. This was *not* like him.

The thing was, the idea of a road trip appealed to him. It had been so long since he'd done anything spontaneous. And he really wanted Emily to go with him. Not just because she was straight-talking and people opened up to her. But because she was fun and smart and always kept him on his toes.

"I mean, if you think you can get someone to watch the kids on such short notice."

"What sort of travel arrangements are we talking about?" She threw up her hands. "Why am I even asking? There's no way I'll go to Atlantic City with you. One, I doubt I could get a sitter at the last moment, two, it might just be a scheme on your part to get laid, three, I probably can't afford it, and four, Principal Ross would probably have a coronary."

"That's why we don't tell her."

"We're meeting with her tomorrow morning."

"Just let me take the lead. And as for your other objections, we'll book separate rooms at separate ends of the casino if you'd like—I'm sure I can get rooms dirt-cheap. And I bet Nancy and Beau might be persuaded to watch the kids. We can use up some of my frequent flyer miles and won't have to waste time driving. You'll be gone twenty-four, maybe thirty-six hours." The more he thought about it, the more Patrick liked the idea.

"The fund-raising company will be closed." There was a hint of doubt in Emily's voice, as if she really wanted to be convinced she could take this trip.

"From what I hear, no business involving customer service in Atlantic City closes for very long. Certainly, they'll be open on Saturday at the very least. And if we show up on their doorstep, it will be a lot harder for them to dodge us."

"I don't know."

"And we can snoop around the casinos where Tiffany seemed to be a bit of a regular. See if we might scare up some information."

"What, like show her picture around like the cops on TV? I think you're a little overeager to play detective, Patrick."

He shrugged and grinned. "It's the scientist in me. I hate not having answers. I dig and dig until I find them. But I wouldn't stoop to something as obvious as showing Tiffany's picture around. A few casual questions maybe."

Emily rolled her eyes. "Oh, brother. I don't even know why I'm listening to you."

"Because you want to know the truth, too. And you think there might be money out there belonging to the students at Elmwood Elementary. Students like Ari and Kat. And Mark and Ryan, too."

Emily hesitated, frowning.

Sensing victory at hand, he pressed his point. "Those kids don't deserve to be disappointed. I know you don't want that any more than I do. So you might as well give in gracefully and agree to be my partner in crime, so to speak."

"Here's what I'm willing to do." She crossed her arms over her chest. "When we meet with Principal Ross tomorrow morning, we won't know for sure about going to Atlantic City, so there's no reason to mention the possibility. As soon as I get to work, I'll fax a letter to the company. And if they don't respond by end of business tomorrow, I'll ask Nancy if she and Beau would watch the kids for me."

"Fair enough."

"And like you said, we'll have *two* rooms."

Patrick tried not to be disappointed. He hadn't expected anything else, had he? Smothering a smile, he had to admit he would have been pleasantly surprised if Emily had agreed to share a room and consequently a bed.

But then again, sleeping with Emily could get complicated fast and he wasn't sure if he wanted that kind of complication in his life.

"Of course, two rooms. Just let me know as soon as you can on Thursday so I can book the flights."

"I will." Emily rose from the chair and moved a few feet away. "But Patrick, there's something I need to know."

"Shoot."

"I've figured the compliments are just your way of trying to make me feel good. But what about the kiss?"

Patrick swallowed hard. He'd hoped they could gloss over that. "I'm not sure, Em. It just seemed…" He shrugged. "Right."

"You keep me off balance, Patrick, and I don't like that."

"I'm sorry. Sometimes it just seems very

natural to be with you and it seemed natural to kiss you."

Emily's back stiffened. "The deal is, you're sending mixed messages. I'm the mother of four children. I can't just go with the flow and see where things take me. If I'm to date someone, it has to be deliberate, after looking at all sides of the situation. It's not just me a man dates. There are six of us. The man, me and my kids. As a mother, I *have* to look down the road. Anticipate problems."

Her words bothered him. Because she was right and that meant he'd been an unthinking jerk. "I'm sorry. I didn't look at it from your perspective. I've only dated one woman who had a child, a baby in fact, and the relationship didn't go far enough for it to be an issue."

"We aren't dating, Patrick. So far, we've been together mostly as a matter of chance, not choice. That's why I want to enter into this Atlantic City thing with my eyes wide open. If we go, we have to go as friends, nothing more. That means no spur-of-the-moment kisses, no lavish compliments or flirting."

To Patrick, that took some of the fun out of the trip. But he could see her point. He raised his hands in defeat. "Okay. Just friends. No kisses, no matter how innocent. And I'll try to keep the flattery to a minimum. Deal?"

Frowning, she eyed his outstretched hand. For a woman who had won the first round, she didn't seem happy. Sighing, she said, "Deal."

After she left, he returned to his den. He'd noticed Emily looking at his diplomas on the wall. Fortunately, her inspection hadn't made it to the far wall, where he had a few family photos arranged.

One, his favorite, showed him and Roger, grinning for the camera, by Shamu's enclosure. He'd been about eleven, Roger about nine. It was the summer before the accident, the last summer they'd been whole and happy.

Patrick turned off the light switch and left his past behind. He was very glad Emily hadn't noticed the photo. Because beneath that voluptuous exterior, she had the inquiring mind of a scientist, and he doubted she would have quit digging until she'd pulled the whole sad story out of him.

EMILY SLID INTO THE BOOTH at her favorite Italian restaurant, breathless. She budgeted carefully for her lunches with Nancy and always looked forward to them.

Nancy smiled in greeting. "How's your day so far?"

"Work itself is okay. It's the PTO stuff that's got me on pins and needles."

Opening her menu, Nancy raised an eyebrow. "You've really taken to the position. I, for one, would probably find it boring."

"You can't tell a soul." Emily leaned forward. "This is just between you and me."

Nancy lowered her menu, her eyes bright with interest. "Of course. I promise. What's going on?"

Emily glanced around. Nobody was seated close enough to overhear their conversation. "Patrick and I have found some interesting leads." Then she explained.

"Wow. Tiffany and poker. Who'd have thought?"

"The great part is that there might be some money we can recover from the casino company."

"That would be wonderful. How much would a deposit for something like that be?"

"I have no idea. They didn't post any rates or deposit information on their Web site. All very vague."

"This just keeps getting more and more interesting. I wonder if Brad knew?"

Emily was tempted to confide in her friend about Tiffany's finances, but couldn't bring herself to do it. For some reason, she felt a little protective of the dead woman's reputation. Maybe it came from a lifetime of feeling like everyone talked behind her back, implying she wasn't very bright and was way too brash.

Shrugging, she said, "I kind of feel sorry for the man. Here I thought Tiffany was damn near perfect. Turns out she might have been as human as the rest of us. Too bad she wasn't nicer to us when she was alive."

"I guess she might have been overcompensating for some insecurities of her own. Funny, other people's lives look so good from the outside…."

"I've never thought of it that way before. I've always felt I was different. Like everyone knew I didn't fit in."

"Em, you fit in just fine. You're way too hard on yourself. It looks like Patrick thinks you fit in. You've spent a lot of time with him lately."

"Mostly engineered by you."

"Didn't you say you met with him at his apartment last night? Sounds to me like he's making excuses to see you."

"He just wanted to share what his security friend found out and show me some stuff on the computer."

"Come on, Em, he could do that at the school, using one of their computers. Or at the public library. Or he could just tell you over the phone, with no show-and-tell involved."

Emily opened her mouth, then clamped it shut.

She couldn't meet Nancy's gaze. Not with terms like *show-and-tell* floating around. It brought to mind an entirely different visual, one much less innocent than the chaste kiss they'd shared at Patrick's place.

Nancy reached for the bread basket, then paused, her eyes narrowing. "There's something you're not telling me. 'Fess up, something happened, didn't it?"

Clearing her throat, Emily said, "He kissed me." The admission came out in a tiny, very un-Emily-like voice.

"I knew it." Nancy grinned from ear to ear. "He's got the hots for you."

"It wasn't like that. It was one of the most innocent kisses I've had since I was thirteen."

"There's nothing wrong with innocent kisses. As long as the intent was there."

"What intent?"

"To get to know you better. To explore the possibility of romance. The possibility of starting a relationship." Nancy selected a bread stick and placed it on her plate. "What did you do?"

"I just kind of sat there, stunned. It was over before I knew it."

"So you didn't gag or retch or anything?"

"No! Patrick's a good-looking guy, in that serious, scientific way. A nice guy, too, I think."

"I agree."

Emily took a deep breath. "That's why I'm thinking of going to Atlantic City with him." There. She'd said it.

Nancy coughed, grabbing her soft drink. After a long slurp, her face returned to her normal color. "I must have misheard you. One second you're talking about an innocent kiss and the next you're heading to Atlantic City with the man."

"You heard me just fine." Emily raised her chin. "The trip would be purely for research purposes."

"Oh, is that what they're calling it these days?" Nancy waggled her eyebrows.

Normally, Emily would have been right there with an off-color joke. But for some reason, the trip to Atlantic City wasn't something she wanted to joke about.

"I'm serious. The thing is, if the fund-raising company doesn't return my calls or fax, we may need to go to Atlantic City."

"I see." Nancy tore her bread stick into several pieces. "That's quite a leap from innocent kiss to a trip to Atlantic City. I may have to revise my earlier opinion of Patrick."

"No, I made it perfectly clear there would be no sex involved. He agreed to two rooms."

Nancy reached across the table and patted her

hand. "Oh, Em, I'd love for you to have a nice, romantic weekend in Atlantic City with great sex and all the bells and whistles. But I guess I'm a little protective where you're concerned. I don't want to see your heart get broken."

"Like I said, it would be just as friends, nothing romantic. And it won't happen at all if I hear from the casino company today. So far, they've been dodging both me and Patrick. I'd love to find out they owe the school a hefty refund."

"I've heard of those organized casino events for charity. Probably quite an undertaking, but I bet we would have raked in the money."

Nodding, Emily said, "And there's another thing. I'd need to ask a huge favor."

"What's that?"

"Would you consider watching the boys? It would only be for like twenty-four hours. Thirty-six at the most," Emily assured her.

"Of course, we'd love to." Nancy frowned. "I'm not sure how Beau will take to the idea of Patrick whisking you away for the weekend, though. He's downright protective of you—must come from having a teenage daughter."

"I'll leave it to your power of persuasion. The man is putty in your hands, Nance."

Her friend grinned. "Yes, he is. Consider yourself footloose and fancy-free for the weekend."

EMILY GLANCED at the clock. The business day had ended five minutes ago and still no response from the casino gaming company.

Footloose and fancy-free for the weekend. Nancy's words came back to her. Had she ever been footloose and fancy-free? Maybe in the years before children. But now, she was all talk and no action. There were too many other lives at stake and she refused to risk her children's sense of security. Her marriage to Larry had been hard on Jason and Jeremy, the divorce even harder. Mark and Ryan had been toddlers and barely remembered their dad. No, she wouldn't repeat that mistake.

Emily's hands trembled as she picked up the phone and called Patrick. He answered on the second ring.

"Patrick, this is Emily. How'd the meeting go with Principal Ross?"

"Not bad. She would have preferred you had been there, too, but she understood that you couldn't take the time off work. Besides, there wasn't much more you could have done. I told her we were trying to track down a company that might have been holding a deposit for Elmwood Elementary."

"What did she say?"

"She wasn't very hopeful. There were apparently no checks to this company showing in the account reconciliation. It appears Tiffany did a lot of work on a cash basis. ATM withdrawals mostly."

"Very convenient."

"Yes, and definitely against protocol. But Principal Ross was out on sick leave during that time—surgery. And the treasurer moved to Texas. So Tiffany pretty much had a free hand."

Emily sighed. "What a mess."

"Yes. And I'm getting the impression Ross just wants it to go away. It doesn't make her look good, that's for sure. I've always known her to be a pretty straight shooter. Otherwise, even I'd start to wonder."

"If she was out for surgery, there wasn't a whole lot she could do."

"Did you hear from the casino company?"

"No. I sent the fax first thing this morning, too, just like we discussed."

"Looks like we're going to Atlantic City, then." His voice was very enthusiastic. "Did you talk to Nancy?"

"Yes, and she said they'd be happy to watch the kids. So, um, I guess you can make those airline reservations." Her stomach sank. Her heart pounded. She wasn't ready for this.

"Are you okay? You sound funny."

"I'm fine." No, she wasn't fine. But she wasn't a coward, either. "Just remember, two rooms. We're going as friends."

"I remember. I'll make the reservations and give you a call. Are you at home?"

"No, work. I should be home in about half an hour."

"Good. I'll call you a little later this evening. This trip will be worth it, you'll see."

Emily hoped she did see. Because right now her stomach was doing flip-flops.

CHAPTER ELEVEN

SIGHING, EMILY PICKED UP a pair of dirty gym socks—one dangling from Jason's desk chair, the other wadded in a ball on top of the desk.

She had a simple dinner in the oven and was trying to get a load of laundry done before Patrick called. Truth be told, she was harnessing nervous energy.

How in the world was she going to tell the kids she was going to Atlantic City for the weekend? And with a man, no less?

Straightening her spine, she decided the truth was the best option. She'd always tried to be honest with her children. This was a business trip of sorts. End of story.

But the butterflies in her stomach told her otherwise. She wanted it to be more than platonic. That was the problem. And she couldn't allow herself to act like a carefree teen, have a wonderful weekend fling and be done with it. Those days were long gone.

Spying another sock wedged next to the monitor, she grabbed the offending garment, accidentally knocking a few sheets of paper to the floor.

She picked them up, only glancing at the content. Then she looked closer. It was from some sort of teen anarchist Web site. And it appeared to be a blueprint for mischief-making devices, like stink bombs.

Emily's heart sank.

Jason. Haven't you learned anything?

He'd made such improvements since he'd entered high school, and she'd hoped his days of pranks were over.

Glancing at the next page, she wondered if he'd actually produced any of the items. Then an awful thought occurred to her. The stink bomb at the dance. Surely, Jason wouldn't have done something that stupid, would he?

She folded the papers and tucked them away in her pocket.

What in the world was she going to do? Not for the first time, she wished she and Walt had one of those friendly give-and-take type divorces, where she could call him and discuss Jason. Where they could put their heads together and come up with a game plan.

But with her family all in Florida, there was no

one. And at times like these, the lack of a father figure weighed heavily on Emily's mind. How she wished she'd been able to provide her children with the home life she'd envisioned. Both a mom and a dad to count on when times got tough.

Although far from perfect, Emily'd had that kind of home life, so where had she gotten so off course?

By making poor choices. Both her sisters were married to their college sweethearts. And her parents were still going strong after nearly fifty years. But somehow the knack for picking a decent spouse eluded Emily. She always chose men who needed fixing, men who couldn't or wouldn't be the equal partner she needed.

The phone rang and one of the boys picked up before she could get to a receiver.

"Mom," Mark bellowed up the stairs. "It's for you."

"I'll get it in my room," she called to him.

Shutting her bedroom door behind her, she picked up the receiver. "Okay, Mark, I've got it. You can hang up."

There was an audible click.

"Hello," Emily said.

"Hi, this is Patrick. Just wanted to give you the itinerary details."

Patrick. She'd almost forgotten. "I'm not sure I should go to Atlantic City."

"What do you mean? When I talked to you a couple hours ago, I thought it was decided."

"I thought so, too. But something's come up with Jason. I don't think I should be leaving the boys for the weekend." Her conscience twinged. But she really did need to be with Jason to sort all this out.

"May I ask what came up?"

Emily hesitated. Jason was already a thorn in Patrick's side and she didn't want to give him any more reason not to like her son. But it would be so nice to be able to get some outside perspective. "I found something on Jason's desk. It was, um, instructions on how to make a stink bomb. And other things. Bottle rockets, smoke bombs."

"I see."

"I haven't had a chance to talk to him about it yet. I guess there could be some explanation…."

"Emily, there's no good explanation for making those things. It's not like it's something he'd receive for a homework assignment. And bottle rockets could be downright dangerous."

"I know, you're right. I guess I was hoping I wouldn't have to deal with it. I'm just not sure what to do."

Patrick paused. "Why don't I run over there?

We can think it through together? If nothing else, sometimes it helps to talk to someone else."

"You'd do that?"

"Sure. I don't like hearing you upset like that. How about if I come over in about an hour? Will that work?"

"Or you can come over now and stay to dinner. I've got a casserole in the oven."

"Ah, a home-cooked meal. I'll be there."

"See you." Emily hung up and marveled at how easy it had been to invite him for dinner. It was starting to feel as if Patrick belonged in their home.

She gathered the laundry basket and went downstairs, feeling a little more hopeful. A little less alone.

Mark met her at the bottom of the stairs. "Who was that?" he asked, his eyes bright.

"That was Patrick—I mean Mr. Stevens. I invited him to dinner."

Mark let out a whoop and ran off, presumably to spread the news. Ryan would probably be as overjoyed as his brother. It was the older two boys who might not be as welcoming.

PATRICK HESITATED outside the Pattersons' door. He had no business being here. This was a family situation and he wasn't family. But he couldn't stand by and watch Emily struggle with this all by herself. And, as an educator, he might be able to help.

Knocking on the door, he steeled himself for Jason. But it was Emily who answered the door, her cheeks rosy, wisps of silky brown hair escaping her ponytail.

"Come on in." She nudged the black Lab out of the doorway.

Warmth enveloped him as he entered her home. And not all of it due to the central heating. Part was because of the chemistry he felt every time he was near her. And part of it was the feeling of coming home.

His heart swelled when Mark and Ryan raced into the room and greeted him enthusiastically. Ryan even gave him a quick hug. Swallowing hard, he met Emily's gaze. Her expression was unreadable.

"Supper's about ready." She headed toward the kitchen, gesturing for him to follow. "You can keep me company while I put on the finishing touches."

Clifford prodded Patrick's hand with his nose. Patrick patted him on the head. The dog's entire body moved in sync with his enthusiastically wagging tail.

Chuckling, Patrick asked Emily, "How about if I set the table?"

She smiled, nearly dazzling him with her raw sex appeal. "That's the best offer I've had all day."

The thing was, he didn't think she had any idea what an incredibly desirable woman she was. And he was pretty sure she had no idea the kind of offers he was tempted to make, like laying down his life for one of her smiles.

Shaking his head, he reminded himself he wasn't a kid, and he knew a lot better than to get involved with a woman with four children.

"Mark, Ryan, put Clifford out back and go tell your brothers supper is ready. I think Jeremy's in his room and Jason is next door at the Mitchells'."

The boys ran off to do her bidding. They really were good kids.

"Here you go." Emily handed Patrick a stack of paper plates. The silverware was a hodge-podge, too. But somehow it came together as an ensemble, more inviting than fine china.

"Oh, I almost forgot to tell you." He placed the last plate on the table. "Principal Ross wants you to lead the PTO meeting Tuesday night."

"Me?"

He glanced up. "Surely you knew that was part of the job?"

The color drained from Emily's face. "I guess

I did. But I thought with the money missing and all that Principal Ross would handle it. What am I going to say?"

"You better get together with Ross on that. She wants to review your agenda on Monday."

"Agenda?"

For such a quick wit, Emily seemed to be having problems grasping simple concepts.

"Yes, you know, the list of things you plan to cover."

"Other than the whole money problem, I haven't given it much thought. I'm really at a loss."

Patrick's heart squeezed at the indecision in her eyes. "Why don't I see if I can get a copy of the meeting minutes for the past couple months and see what they discussed. That'll give you an idea where you should pick up."

Emily's relief was palpable. "That'd be great. I'm, um, not so good at all this meeting stuff. I kind of freeze when I'm in front of a whole room of people. Or get all flustered and say the wrong thing."

"You'll do fine." He tried to infuse his words with an optimism he didn't feel. Although most of the PTO folks were great people and had only the kids' best interests at heart, a few seemed to have their own agendas and wouldn't hesitate to annihilate Emily if they sensed her fear.

Emily frowned. "Tiffany made this all seem so easy."

"She had a lot of experience. You'll do fine, too."

"Do you really think so?" She gazed up at him, her eyes wide. The woman he'd once thought fearless seemed to need his reassurance.

He brushed a strand of hair from her cheek. "Yes, I do."

She leaned closer.

He bent his head.

Mark and Ryan burst into the kitchen, interrupting what might have been more reassurance than the situation warranted.

Patrick stepped back quickly. "*Robert's Rules of Order.*"

"I beg your pardon?"

"Are you familiar with *Robert's Rules of Order?* I can loan you the book."

She planted her hands on her hips. "What in the world are you talking about, Patrick?"

"That's how the meeting is structured. How you entertain motions and vote. Things like that."

"Then I'll definitely need to borrow your book. Because I didn't even know there was such a thing."

He started to sweat. Yes, there were a couple of parents who would take great joy in humiliating Emily. And he'd be damned if he'd stand by and let it happen. "We can look at the book on our way to Atlantic City. If we can get everything squared to go, that is."

"Who's going to Atlantic City?" Jeremy asked as he entered the room.

"Hey, Jeremy."

"Hey." He barely glanced at Patrick. "Mom, I asked who's going to Atlantic City?"

Jason entered the kitchen and stopped in his tracks, eyeing Patrick as if he were a serpent. "What's he doing here?"

"I invited Patrick to dinner, Jason."

"Mom, you still haven't answered my question." Jeremy's voice was tight.

Emily glanced at Patrick, shrugging helplessly. Taking a deep breath, she said, "I have PTO business in Atlantic City this weekend. Patrick was going to go with me. But, as it is, it looks like I better stick closer to home."

Jason crossed his arms. "Yeah, right, business. Mom, how could you? Haven't you learned anything? With Larry-the-jerk it was a trip to the Poconos."

"You remember that?"

"Sure, I remember. I was a kid, but I wasn't stupid. Now it's the same thing all over again."

"It is *not* the same."

Patrick felt like a spectator to an oncoming train wreck. He wanted to rush to Emily's rescue, but knew this was between her and her son. Though he did want to hear all the gory details about Larry-the-jerk.

"Come on, Mom, he only wants one thing. Can't you see that?"

Patrick stepped forward, all thoughts of neutrality gone. "Hey, don't talk to your mother like that. She deserves your respect. We're friends, nothing more."

His conscience twinged, because a part of him really would have liked it to be more. A part that hadn't considered how a son might view his mother's romantic interests.

"Yeah, right. I've seen how you look at her. You might hide behind all the scientific crap, but you're just looking for a piece of ass." Jason raised his chin, his eyes blazing.

"Jason!" Emily exclaimed.

Patrick's pulse pounded. It took supreme effort to keep his arms at his side and not reach out to wipe that smug look off Jason's face. Who did the little brat think he was?

Patrick took a deep breath. "Look, you want to protect your mom and that's a good thing. But we're just friends."

Emily's mouth tightened. "Jason, you've

been rude to a guest in our home again. Apologize immediately."

"I won't."

"Then go to your room without supper."

"Fine." He stomped out of the room.

Emily turned her back on him and busied herself at the stove. Patrick thought he heard her sniff back tears. "Go ahead and sit down," she said over her shoulder.

He took a step toward her, his every instinct to comfort. But, sensing three sets of eyes watching him, he realized it would be foolish. He took a seat at the table.

The silence was awkward as hell.

"How was school today, guys?" he asked in an overly hearty voice.

All three boys stared at their plates, avoiding his gaze. They murmured in unison, "Okay."

With her back to him, Emily wiped her sleeve across her eyes. Turning, she pasted on a brave smile, but it started to slip the second her gaze met his.

"I'm sorry, Patrick."

"It's not your fault."

"It is." She placed a trivet on the table. "I've made some mistakes and unfortunately my kids have paid the price."

He got the impression she was giving up on

him, giving up on men. And dedicating herself to years and years of passionless living, atoning for the mistakes she'd made.

Shaking his head, he thought what a waste it would be. Because she was a woman meant to be loved. And he had a sneaking suspicion he wanted to volunteer for the job. "It doesn't change the fact that it's PTO business and we need to go there."

"You don't need me."

"But I do." His tone was firmer than he intended. "Why don't we discuss it after supper?"

Sighing, Emily nodded. She picked up a pair of pot holders and retrieved a casserole from the oven, placing the dish on the trivet in the middle of the table.

"Smells delicious." What would have been the truth five minutes earlier was now merely polite conversation. Patrick's appetite was gone.

Supper was a quiet affair, even the younger boys were subdued. It bothered Patrick that he'd introduced this strife into Emily's family. Maybe the Atlantic City trip wasn't such a good idea after all.

When they'd finished, Emily instructed the boys to clear the table. Patrick silently helped.

After Emily loaded the dishwasher, she dried her hands on a towel. "Are you boys done with your homework?"

Mark and Ryan nodded.

"You can go watch TV, then, if you'd like. Jeremy?"

Jeremy rolled his eyes.

She patted him on the shoulder. "I know, I probably don't even need to ask you. You're usually way ahead on your work."

He shrugged stiffly.

Jeremy reminded Patrick of himself when he was a few years older than the boy. After Patrick had decided his life depended on getting good grades and righting the wrong he'd done to his brother. That was when the once average student had become an honor student.

"Can I go play video games in my room?" Jeremy pulled a handheld game from the depths of his pocket.

Emily ruffled his hair. "You don't have to hide away in your room. You can play down here."

"It's too noisy. And Mark and Ryan'll bug me."

Shrugging, she said, "Okay."

Jeremy left the kitchen.

"He's a good kid," Patrick commented.

Sighing, Emily said, "I worry about him sometimes. He keeps things bottled up and spends so much time alone in his room."

"Does he have friends?"

"A few. Not many."

"A few is all it takes. He'll be fine." He hated to see Emily worry so much. He'd always thought he was sympathetic to the needs of single parents. But seeing Emily's struggle up close and personal added a whole new dimension to his understanding. It seemed like a draining, nearly impossible job.

"I guess you're right." She hung up the dish towel. "Want to go sit on the porch? That's about the only place we can talk in relative quiet."

"Sure." But he wasn't at all sure what he should say to her. His instinct was to press her into going on the trip. But seeing the effect the mere mention of the trip had on her boys, he had to wonder.

He followed her out to the porch, where she opened a door he hadn't noticed before. She pulled two folding chairs from the storage closet, handing him one.

"Boy, I wish I'd known those were here the night I brought pizza. My rear just about froze to your front steps."

Emily chuckled. "You did look a few minutes away from hypothermia. I realized you were a lot more determined a man than I originally thought. Most guys would have given up and left."

"I'm persistent. Used to drive my mom crazy when I was a kid. Once I got hold of an idea, I wouldn't let it go."

"You said your folks live in the Syracuse area?"

Nodding, he said, "Yes, a small town about half an hour outside Syracuse. It was a great place to grow up."

"How'd you end up in Elmwood?"

"It was a decent commute to my work at the chemical plant, but far enough away to have that small-town feel."

"Do you see your family often?"

"I try to get up there once a month. My brother's, um, disabled, and I like to give my folks a break. They have caregivers who come in twice a week, but that's not nearly enough."

Emily touched his arm. "How difficult for them. I'm sorry."

The concern in her eyes was almost his undoing. He rarely talked about Roger, but for some reason he felt like Emily might understand. But the habit of avoidance was too strong. "Yes, it's difficult. They don't seem to resent one minute they spend with Roger, though. How about your family? Do you see them often?"

"The kids and I usually try to spend the week between Christmas and New Year's in Florida. The boys love the ocean and seeing their cousins. It's a nice break from the snow. Then my parents and sisters come up here from time to time, usually during hurricane season."

"Sounds like you're pretty close."

"In some ways, yes."

"That's kind of cryptic."

"I always felt a little like the odd sister out." Emily pulled her sweater close, crossing her arms. "My older sister used to tell me I was adopted and there was a part of me that believed her, because I just didn't fit in like the others. But, later, I realized the family resemblance was too strong for me to be adopted."

Patrick cupped his hand under her chin. "Emily, I can't imagine you not belonging. You're so warm and generous."

Emily pressed her cheek to his palm for a second. Then she pulled away. "None of that, Patrick. It's not because I'm not tempted. It's because of my kids. I owe them a stable life, without men traipsing through it. You can see how well they reacted to my going away for the weekend."

He patted her shoulder awkwardly. "I guess I didn't really understand until I saw it with my own eyes. Not only are your kids leery of me because of who I am, but they're leery of me from past experience."

"With good reason. I've put those kids through hell. Jason and Jeremy have been through two divorces, Mark and Ryan, one." Emily's eyes filled with tears. "I won't turn their lives upside down again."

"Let's just forget about Atlantic City for right now. I can keep calling and sending e-mail to the company. Maybe even follow up by snail mail." He tried to infuse his voice with optimism but failed miserably.

"You don't really expect to hear from them, do you?"

"To be honest, no. But we might get the same reaction if we show up in person. They might blow us off completely."

"Thanks for understanding."

"No problem."

Emily pulled a folded sheet of paper from her pocket. "Would you mind looking at this? It's the stuff I found on Jason's desk."

He unfolded the paper. Frowning, he swore under his breath. "I can't believe they put this kind of stuff on the Internet where kids can get ahold of it. Aren't there parental controls?"

"Yes, but Jason figures out a way around them every time. I even change my password every couple weeks, and somehow he still knows."

"He's a smart kid. Too bad he doesn't apply it to something more useful. You're going to talk to him, aren't you?"

Emily brushed a strand of hair from her eyes. "Yes. I'm just not sure what I'll say. How do I ask him if he set off that stink bomb at the dance?"

"Exactly like that. Straight to the point."

"The thing that concerns me is that he has information about smoke bombs, too. What if it'd been a smoke bomb at the dance?" She shivered. "The sprinklers would have gone off and a lot of stuff damaged."

"Not to mention the possibility of people panicking if they thought there was fire. Someone could have been hurt." Patrick's stomach knotted at the thought. "And the bottle rockets are just as bad. Kids have been blinded and lost fingers messing around with those things."

"I better talk to him tonight."

Patrick stood, taking that as his exit cue. Or maybe he was just looking for an excuse to leave. Emily and her life were more complex than he'd ever anticipated. There was a part of him champing at the bit to get back to his bachelor apartment and enjoy the peace. "I better get going. Thanks for supper. It was terrific."

"You're welcome. And thanks for listening."

Patrick forced himself to take the porch steps at a sedate speed, when his instinct was to bolt for his SUV. "I'll talk to you later," he called over his shoulder.

"Yes, later." Emily's voice was so low, he barely heard her.

He glanced over his shoulder and realized it

was a mistake. Because Emily looked so brave and lonely standing there under the porch light. And he felt like a complete jerk for deserting her.

CHAPTER TWELVE

EMILY TOOK A DEEP BREATH and knocked on Jason's door.

"What?" came his muffled reply, his tone anything but welcoming.

"It's me, Jase." She stepped into the war zone that was his inner sanctum. Heavy metal band posters adorned the walls, while a trail of clothes, some clean, some not-so-clean, led from the doorway to bed.

Jason appeared to be absorbed in a computer game.

Emily rested her hand on his shoulder. She could feel him tense at her touch and it just about broke her heart. "Jase, we need to talk."

"I've already been punished for being rude. You said come upstairs, so I came upstairs."

"We've got two different issues going on here. Yes, I want to talk to you about the way you act around Patrick. But, first, I want you to turn the game off, so we can talk about something else that concerns me."

"In a minute. I can't save here."

"Close it anyway." Emily's tone was harsher than she intended, but it had been a long day and she was tired of Jason's tricks.

He sighed deeply and managed to save the game, despite his protest to the contrary. Swiveling in his chair, he crossed his arms. "What?"

She scooted his backpack aside and sat on his bed, handing him the folded computer papers. "I found these on your desk."

He snatched the papers away and unfolded them, frowning. "That's an invasion of privacy. You shouldn't be going through my stuff."

Emily took a deep, cleansing breath and counted to five in her head. "First of all, they were in plain view. I was simply looking for dirty socks. Second, if I thought you were thinking of doing something dangerous or illegal, I'd certainly consider going through your stuff. Deal with it."

"Hey, what happened to democracy?"

"It doesn't exist in this household. This is a benevolent dictatorship." It had been a running joke between them since he'd studied government in sixth grade. Now it didn't seem very funny.

Jason didn't seem to think so, either, because he didn't crack a smile.

"There's something I need to know, Jason. Did you plant those stink bombs at the dance?"

"Why would I do that?" He met her gaze without flinching. After a few seconds, his eyes widened innocently. A sure sign he was hiding something.

"That's what I want to know. Tell me the truth. Were you involved in any way with those stink bombs?"

His gaze strayed somewhere over her left shoulder.

"Oh, Jason. Don't you know any better?"

"It was just a joke, Mom. Not any big deal."

"You ruined the dance for hundreds of kids. And what really worries me are some of the other things on that list of yours. Bottle rockets are dangerous. And if it had been a smoke bomb at the dance, the sprinklers would have gone off and the gym been damaged. People could have panicked and gotten hurt. And, as your parent, I would have been legally responsible."

"Is that what this is about? You're worried about getting sued?"

"I'm more worried about your safety and the safety of others."

"Nobody got hurt, Mom. I wasn't dumb enough to set off a smoke bomb."

"But you did set off the stink bomb. This kind

of behavior has to stop, Jase. I've been burying my head in the sand. I'm moving the computer to my room. You'll have to use the one downstairs so I can monitor your Web surfing."

"You can't do that." His tone was outraged.

"Yes, I can. And if I even suspect you're looking at something you're not supposed to on there, you'll lose all computer privileges."

"No way."

"Absolutely."

"None of this would have happened if Mr. Stevens wasn't sticking his nose in where it doesn't belong."

"What does this have to do with Patrick?"

Jason opened his mouth as if to say something, then shut it again. "Nothin'," he mumbled.

She grasped his chin. "Look at me. What does this have to do with Patrick?"

He jerked his chin free. "He was dancing with you and looking at you all lovey-dovey. Acting like he was gonna make out with you on the dance floor."

Emily's heart plummeted. "So you set off the stink bombs. That is wrong on so many levels."

"Hey, it worked, didn't it?" Jason's bravado almost covered the spark of apprehension in his eyes.

"First of all, *you* made the choice to do something you knew was wrong. You need to take responsibility for that instead of blaming it on circumstances. Second, I'm an adult and I won't have my social life manipulated by my children."

"You haven't done such a good job of handling it yourself."

His words cut, as he knew they would. "Jason, I've made mistakes. And you will probably never know how much I regret the effect my mistakes have had on your life and your brothers'. But that doesn't give you license to control me. You are the child and I'm the adult."

"Yeah, right."

Emily itched to turn him over her knee and swat his behind. This cocky man-child was so infuriating. Somehow, she managed to keep her cool. "Whether you agree or not, that's the way it is. Now, I want you to draft a letter to your school principal and president of the student body, apologizing for the stink bomb."

"I won't do it."

Emily stood. "Oh, yes, you will. Because you have no privileges until I've reviewed your letter and watched you hand it to your principal. You will apologize in person."

"That's just mean."

She headed for the door, chin held high. "And be sure to use spell check."

Emily closed the door behind her with an emphatic click. She managed to keep the tears at bay until she reached the front porch. She sat on the top step and hugged her knees to her chest, rocking and crying silently.

JASON CRUMPLED UP the paper into a tight ball. He was such a loser. How could he have been so stupid to leave the instructions right there on his desk?

The detective shows on TV would have said he wanted to get caught. But he didn't think that was true.

At least now it was all out in the open. How much he hated his mom seeing Mr. Stevens. And how there was no way he'd stand by and watch it happen.

The thing was, his mom smiled a lot and seemed happy around Mr. Stevens. But then again, she'd smiled a lot and seemed happy around Larry-the-jerk, too, and he'd broken her heart. Jason'd only been seven or eight when Larry had left, but he still remembered his mom crying all the time and barely able to get out of bed in the morning. With two little ones to care for on top of it.

Jason had helped the best he could. And sworn he'd never let another man hurt his mom like Larry-the-jerk.

Shaking his head, he thought about how things had finally been getting back on track when Mr. Stevens had shown up, all nice and pretending he was a good guy.

Jason knew the truth, though. Mr. Stevens was nice until you started to expect something from him, then he just threw you away like a piece of trash. He'd done it to Jason and he'd do it to his mom, too.

But Jason wouldn't let him. He still had a few tricks left up his sleeve. And he'd gladly pay the consequences if it kept his mom from getting hurt again.

"WHAT'S WRONG, EM?" Nancy's voice was filled with concern.

"Here I thought I'd been covering pretty well. I didn't want to spoil our lunch." But glancing around at the colorful piñatas and festive Mexican decorations, she realized she'd only been fooling herself. Even at their traditional TGIF lunch, she felt about as festive as a grave-digger at a funeral.

"Out with it."

"It's Jason again."

"The girlfriend?" Nancy took a bite of her taco, chewing thoughtfully.

"No. In a roundabout way, it involves Patrick."

"How so?"

Emily explained about the stink bomb at the dance and Jason's excuse.

"Ah. So, since he's protecting you, that makes it all right?"

"I think in his mind it does."

"What're you going to do?"

"I made him write an apology letter for the principal and student body president. I'll take off my lunch hour on Monday to make sure he apologizes in person, too. Then there will be some sort of consequence at school. Probably cafeteria detail again. And he's lost all privileges at home."

"Sounds like you're doing all you can."

"But I'm the adult. He needs to know that I'm strong enough and intelligent enough to make my own decisions. He needs to know he can't manipulate me. Not only is it important for me as a parent, I think deep down he needs to feel secure that I can take care of myself and him."

"I think you've done a terrific job taking care of your sons. What else do you think you can do to prove yourself?"

"I'm not sure."

"Maybe it's not so much a case of proving yourself, but showing the kids you have a full life in other ways than being a mother."

Emily wasn't sure where her friend was

headed. "How do I do that? I work and do activities involving the kids and their interests."

"You could, um, go to Atlantic City after all."

"Just to spite Jason?"

"No, but to show him you won't be manipulated. Go, do your business, come home all fine and strong and he'll see his worries were for nothing."

"But, Nance, what if he's right? What if I'm such a screw-up with men that I need my teenage son to look out for me?" It hurt to even voice the thought. She could always be honest with Nancy, though.

"You made a couple of mistakes when you were young. You've learned from them and you won't make the same mistake twice."

"I wasn't that young with Larry."

"Young at heart, then. You didn't have me for a friend, either. I'd tell you if I thought Patrick was a jerk. Do I worry about you getting hurt? Yes. But I honestly think Patrick is a good guy and it's worth the risk. And, hey, you two could succeed at keeping this thing platonic. Stranger things have happened. And wouldn't that be a great learning experience for your boys? A man and a woman actually being friends just because they like each other and have something in common."

"Yes, stranger things have happened. With women who have more willpower than I do."

"You have plenty of willpower."

Emily gestured toward her hips. "Have you seen me pass up a bacon cheeseburger? I wouldn't still have fifteen pounds to go on my diet if I had willpower."

"You enjoy life. There's nothing wrong with that, in moderation. It's been a long while since you dated. I think it's time you took a chance on Patrick. At least take the trip to Atlantic City and see if there's anything there. That way, if you give it a try and it fizzles, no one will be the wiser."

"I can't believe the advice you're giving me. I need a good, stern, be-a-responsible-mother lecture, and you're telling me to run off to Atlantic City and have a fling."

"No, that's not what I'm telling you. I'm telling you that you're a mom *and* a woman. You need to take care of that woman inside. If it means a weekend in Atlantic City and ticking off your oldest son, then so be it. Em, you've got to have some fun in life, too, or you're going to burn out way before you get Mark and Ryan raised. Isn't that what you told me with Ana?"

Emily's eyes misted at the intensity in Nancy's voice. "You're a good friend, Nancy Stanton."

"Only returning the favor. Now, please tell me I should call Beau and ask him to roll out the sleeping bags for a Patterson boys' sleepover."

Emily couldn't trust herself to speak. She nodded, her heart sinking, but a spark of excitement building. Then an awful thought occurred to her. "What if Patrick's made plans?"

"Then I bet he'll rearrange them. Do you have his phone number on your cell?"

Emily nodded.

"Then call him."

Pulling her cell phone from the side pocket of her purse, Emily felt almost surreal. She called Patrick and kept the conversation short and sweet, clicking her phone shut with a finality that scared her.

Nancy tilted her head to the side. "Well?"

"He, um, was a bit surprised I changed my mind."

"And?"

"And he's sure he can get us seats on the red-eye out tonight. We'll be back Sunday afternoon, if that's okay?"

"That's absolutely perfect."

Emily hoped she was right. Because her pulse was pounding and her breathing quick and shallow. When she thought of all she had to do to get the boys ready to spend a weekend at Nancy's, she almost changed her mind.

But the thought of Jason, defiantly telling her

she wasn't capable of making good decisions, was enough to keep her from capitulating.

She would face Jason and his teenage disapproval and they would be clear, once and for all, who was the adult and who was the child.

Emily only hoped she ended up with the adult role, and not the teen.

A hysterical laugh burbled up in her throat.

This weekend would either cure or kill a lot of her doubts.

EMILY GLANCED OUT the cabin window, the engine's vibration seeping through the soles of her shoes. Excitement bubbled inside her.

She turned to Patrick. "It's been a long time since I've flown."

"Don't you fly to Florida?"

"No, too expensive for five of us. We drive."

"That's a long trip."

"You're telling me. Especially with four kids in the van."

He smiled. "I don't know. It sounds like an adventure."

"Spoken like someone who doesn't have kids."

His expression sobered and she could have kicked herself for being insensitive. "I'm sorry, that didn't come out right."

"That's okay. It's just, well, lately I've kind of

felt a lack in my life. You start staring forty in the eye and it makes you think."

"That's for sure. So you want children someday?"

"I always thought I did. But," he shrugged, "meeting the right woman's been the problem."

Emily searched for something, anything to say to make it better. "You have plenty of time. Guys can father children clear into their eighties."

"I always envisioned myself young enough to toss a baseball with my son, or help my daughter with her science fair project. Not doddering into senility."

She gave up on making it better. Instead, she changed the subject. "Did you bring that Robert's book?"

"Yeah." He pulled his backpack from beneath the seat in front and unzipped the compartment. "It's right here."

Accepting the book from him, she opened to the table of contents page and gulped. It looked extremely dry. "You're sure there aren't any *Cliffs Notes?*"

Patrick grinned. "Not that I'm aware of. I did, however, make up a page summarizing the nitty-gritty for conducting a meeting." He handed her a sheet of paper, neatly organized, complete with bulleted highlights.

She raised an eyebrow. "What, no pie chart?"

"I'm a teacher, it comes with the territory. Humor me, okay?"

"Oh, I'll humor you. I'm just not sure who is humoring whom."

"I know you've got the meeting on Monday with Ross and we're going to be busy once we land, so I thought I'd save you some time. It's as simple as that."

Emily tilted her head to the side. He seemed sincere. "Then, thank you."

"You're welcome." Patrick retrieved a file folder from his pack as the jet started to taxi. "I also brought the meeting minutes for the past couple months."

Accepting the file folder, she thumbed through the contents. Who knew a PTO meeting could be this complex?

The plane picked up speed, lifting off with a jolt.

She sucked in a breath of anticipation.

Patrick took her hand. "Are you a nervous flyer?"

"No. I *love* flying. I'm just excited."

"We're on our way." Patrick released her hand, leaning back in his seat and smiling.

"Yes, we certainly are." But a small part of her wished he'd held her hand a little longer. It had felt good to have a man willing to be strong so she could let down and be weak for once.

The cabin soon leveled off and they were in the clouds. The rest of the trip went by quickly as they discussed the ins and outs of conducting a PTO meeting and went over the key items left open from the previous meetings. They talked about Patrick's class, Kat and Ari in particular. And though they touched briefly on the other boys' school experience this year, they studiously avoided any mention of Jason.

When they approached Atlantic City, Emily couldn't help but exclaim over the lights. "It's gorgeous."

"Pretty impressive. I haven't been here in a while."

"Were you a regular? Somehow I don't see you as much of a gambler."

"I used to come with a couple of my buddies from the chemical plant. I enjoy the gaming as long as I have a set limit. Once that's gone, I'm done."

"That's very wise. I brought a few dollars to gamble and that's it." Emily tried to keep the trace of wistfulness out of her voice. What was it like to be single and have money to burn? Not have to worry about kids growing out of shoes, or that Jeremy might need braces soon?

The plane descended, the wheels touching down smoothly.

"I have a couple vouchers for chips left over from the old days. I figured we'd split them. No risk, just fun."

Emily had a sudden, sick thought. "Do you really have all these vouchers and frequent flyer miles? Or are you paying for all this so I won't feel bad?"

Patrick chuckled. "Sorry, Emily, wish I was that gallant. But I'm on a budget. I'm just sharing the freebies."

"In that case, thank you. I pay my own way."

"You won't hear any complaints from me. Fortunately, I got a great deal on the rooms, so we won't break the bank."

"Rooms plural? Good. I have to admit I'm relieved."

"Why? You think I'd pull a fast one on you? You should know me better than that by now."

Her cheeks warmed. "Yes, I should. Sorry, old habits die hard."

Patrick held her gaze. "I'm not your ex-husbands. I might not be perfect, but I wouldn't intentionally hurt you."

"Yeah, Larry said something about not wanting to hurt me when I found him in a motel room with another woman."

He made a sound of frustration low in his throat. "I don't know what to say, Em."

She patted his hand. "It's okay. There's really nothing for you to say. Just understand why I'm a bit prickly sometimes."

He nodded. "Noted."

The seat belt lights went off and Patrick stood to retrieve their carry-ons from the overhead bin. Then he whisked her to the rental car counter, where he'd already reserved a car. A red Mustang convertible of all things.

Emily chuckled with disbelief. "We'll freeze."

"Not with the heater on full blast." He grinned wickedly. "Come on, let's have some fun."

As they cruised through town, top down, heater on full blast, she had to admit he was right. Emily threw back her head and laughed, reveling in the wind ruffling her hair. "This *is* fun."

"I figured we could gamble a bit. Have one of those all-night buffet meals. Then hit the sack for a couple hours. How's that sound to you?"

It all sounded fabulous. The hitting the sack together was way too tempting. It had been too long since she'd been held by a man through the night. But she was determined it wouldn't happen this weekend. "I guess that sounds okay. You did say two rooms, didn't you?"

"Yes. Scout's honor." He held up three fingers.

"You were a Boy Scout?"

"Cub Scout for almost a year. Until they tactfully suggested to my father that it might be better if I didn't return."

"Patrick! *You* were thrown out of the Boy Scouts?"

He nodded sheepishly. "I guess I pulled one too many pranks on our campout. I think it might have been the garter snake I put in the leader's sleeping bag."

"No way."

"Yes, unfortunately, it's true."

Emily shook her head. "I have a hard time seeing it. You're so, well, serious now. I mean you have a terrific sense of humor and all, but I can't see you letting loose and pulling practical jokes."

"I grew up." There was a wistfulness in his voice, making him sound like Peter Pan pining for Neverland.

"Just because you're grown up doesn't mean you can't like a practical joke every once in a while. The kids and I have a ball on April Fool's Day. You should have seen their faces the year I told them they could have ice cream for breakfast."

"I bet they thought they were dreaming."

"They were so disappointed when I told them it was April Fool's." She glanced out the window.

"I have to confess, I did allow them some ice cream for breakfast. I figured it had milk in it, so it was nearly as good as cereal."

"You say that like it's some deep, dark confession. I think it's great you let them have a treat on one special day."

"I figured you'd think I was the worst mother on earth." She sighed. "Sometimes I'm such a pushover."

He reached across the console and squeezed her hand. "We all are, for the people we love."

Emily's eyes misted. And to think she'd originally thought Patrick was stiff and unyielding. Absently, she rubbed her thumb over the slightly raised scar on his middle finger.

"Patrick?"

"Hm?"

"Would you have ever set a mousetrap in your teacher's desk?"

There was silence for a moment. Emily peeked at his face, expecting censure. Instead, she found him smiling slowly.

"Emily, I would have most certainly placed a mousetrap in my teacher's desk if I'd thought of it. A truly inspired prank, though somewhat painful."

"So you don't think Jason is a horrible kid?"

Patrick hesitated. "It would take more than a

mousetrap in my desk for me to decide anyone was a horrible kid."

Emily's heart contracted at his careful avoidance of her question. But, she realized, he'd answered her in a way, by what he'd left unsaid.

He thought her son was a horrible kid, not because of one incident, but because of many.

CHAPTER THIRTEEN

PATRICK HAD AS MUCH FUN watching Emily as he did gambling himself. She had such an earthy effervescence. And everyone loved her. Even the dealers didn't scold her too seriously when she broke a rule, like allowing her hand to stray from the table while playing blackjack.

"They think you're pulling cards from your sleeve if they lose sight of your hand," he whispered in her ear.

She laughed. "Like I'm that coordinated."

He resisted the urge to kiss her, right there on the casino floor.

Emily seemed made for Atlantic City, where boldness and bravery were much more important than tact.

She'd blossomed since they'd left Elmwood. It wasn't hard to imagine her as a young single woman, laughing, loving, living. It wasn't hard to see why a guy had snagged her the first opportunity he got.

And it also made him understand how much responsibility she carried on her shoulders every day. He was humbled by how gracefully she carried it, never complaining, never whining.

With a jolt, he feared he could fall in love with Emily if he weren't careful. And he wondered if he even wanted to be careful.

But then he thought of Jason and the other boys and knew his obligation was to be very, very careful where their mother's heart was concerned. Because Jason had made it abundantly clear that Emily loved with her whole heart and could be destroyed by another disastrous relationship.

"Blackjack," Emily squealed, her eyes alight.

The other players at the table congratulated her and the dealer darn near cracked a smile.

"All right." Patrick squeezed her shoulder.

She accepted her chips and rose from the table, handing a chip to the dealer. "This is for you. I'm going to leave while my luck still holds."

As she stepped away from the table, the area seemed dimmer, somehow. As if a bright, beautiful supernova had burned out and left darkness behind.

He wrapped his arm around her. "I'm impressed. It takes a lot of self-control to step away from the table when you're winning."

Emily stopped, smiling slowly. "You know what? It *does* take self-control. And here I thought I didn't have any."

"You're kidding, right? It must take the control and organizational skills of a five-star general to get four kids ready for school on time and make it to work every day."

"I never thought of it that way. I always feel rushed and frazzled."

"But you get the job done. That's all that counts."

"Yes, I do, don't I?" She briefly rested her head on his shoulder. "You're a good guy, Patrick."

He cleared his throat. "I, um, try to be. Now, how about if we find one of those all-night buffets?"

She raised her head. "Great. I'm starving."

"Me, too." He kissed the top of her head, leading her toward the restaurant area. He didn't add that he was starved for her laughter, her touch. Because that would have definitely been crossing the line.

EMILY TUCKED HER ARM in Patrick's as they left the restaurant. At nearly dawn, the casino was relatively uncrowded. There was actually room to move without bumping into someone. Contentment stole through her. It had been a glorious day. She hid a yawn behind her hand.

"Time for a nap, huh?"

"Way past my bedtime. But it was fun."

"I'll walk you to your room, then hunt mine down." He compared their check-in folders. "The numbers are pretty close. Not adjoining, though. I was very clear on that point."

Emily giggled at his defensiveness. "I believe you, Patrick."

"I respect your boundaries."

"I know you do. You've always been on the up-and-up with me." And he had.

They found her room and then looked for his. Fortunately, they didn't have far to go—it was across the hall and two doors down. Definitely close enough for Emily to sneak across the hall in the middle of the night.

Shaking her head, she tried to remove the thought. It had been a wonderful day and she wanted to top it off with another dose of self-control. If she could walk away from the blackjack table while winning, she could certainly walk away from a cute and rumpled Patrick without wondering what it would be like to make love with him.

"I'll see you to your door."

"That's not necessary. It's right over there."

"What kind of gentleman would I be if I neglected my duties so close to having you home safely?"

Emily glanced down when they reached her door. It seemed too much like being escorted home after a date. Maybe that was what Patrick intended?

He certainly appeared to be considering kissing her. His gaze was warm, focusing on her lips.

She drew in a steadying breath. "Well, um, thanks. I'm here, as you can see." Pulling out her key card, she hesitated.

Patrick cupped his hand around her chin. "Good night, Em."

She held her breath, waiting.

He leaned forward and brushed her cheek with his lips. Then he walked to his room, unlocked the door and stepped inside without looking back.

Emily touched her cheek where he'd kissed her. She didn't know what to think, but she was too tired to ponder the significance.

PATRICK WAS AWAKENED by a pounding on his door. Rubbing the sleep from his eyes, he peered at the clock. Eleven. Question was, a.m. or p.m.?

He staggered to the door and opened it.

Emily sashayed in carrying two takeout sacks, an excited gleam in her eye and a lilt to her voice. "I bring food."

"Um, how long was I asleep?"

"Four, maybe five hours."

"And you're alert?"

"Sure, after colicky babies, kids sick in the middle of the night and all that stuff, I can get by on a few hours' sleep if I need to."

"It's inhuman to be this cheerful." He ran his hand through his hair.

"The casino company opens in an hour and we want to be there right away."

Shaking his head, Patrick had a hard time reconciling the perky steamroller with the Emily he'd left last night.

The Emily he'd left last night had had eyes wide with uncertainty when he'd touched her cheek. Had exhaled a soft sigh of disappointment when he didn't kiss her as he'd wanted.

But he'd known he couldn't possibly kiss her on the lips. He would have been a goner and there would be no way he could have resisted trying to seduce her.

"I hope you brought coffee."

"Sure did." She placed the sacks on the table. "We've got coffeemakers in our rooms, but the selection of coffee was piss-poor."

He grunted in response, somewhat mollified.

She stood before him, hands on hips. "I guess you're not a morning person, huh?"

"What was your first clue?"

"Besides your sparkling personality? The fact

that you're standing there in your boxers and don't seem to mind. I expected you to be more, um, modest, I guess."

Patrick glanced down, and sure enough, he was in his boxers and bare-chested. "You're right. I'm usually a little more circumspect. Excuse me and I'll throw on some jeans."

Emily's smile was wicked. "Oh, I don't mind. You've got nice legs."

He wasn't sure whether to be embarrassed or proud. He decided on the latter. "Yes, well, I play basketball with a couple other teachers."

"It shows."

Her teasing put him at a distinct disadvantage. It made his sleep-deprived brain threaten a meltdown. What was he doing? Oh, yeah, clothes. Patrick grabbed his shirt and pants off the chair and headed for the bathroom. He could feel Emily's gaze travel down his backside, thighs and calves.

Her throaty chuckle was almost his undoing.

She was toying with him. Was it payback for not kissing her last night?

Patrick dressed quickly while pondering the puzzle that was Emily. He'd been a perfect gentleman, merely following her wishes for a platonic trip. But he'd seen longing in her eyes. Knew she wanted to test the waters as much as he.

"I asked around in the coffee shop," she called to him. "Nobody seems to know much about this company. Either they're small potatoes or they're doing a good job flying under the radar."

"Or maybe they're on the level and really bad at following up on inquiries."

"They wouldn't be in business long if that was the case. Why, are you having second thoughts?"

Patrick turned off the bathroom light and returned to the main room. "No, I'm not awake enough to have second thoughts. Merely playing devil's advocate."

"You're the one who wanted to do this."

"Still do. Is this mine?" He grabbed a tall to-go cup.

"Yes. Maybe I should have gotten you the super grande size. You surprise me, Patrick. I figured you woke up instantly alert and organized, your brain going at lightning speed."

"Guess again."

Speculation gleamed in Emily's eyes. "I kind of like it. Makes you more human."

He made a noncommittal noise.

"That was darn near a grunt. I'm going to have to revise my opinion." She sighed heavily. "Here I thought you were more evolved than most men."

"And I didn't take you for being evil, but I'm revising my opinion. Now, sling one of those doughnuts over to me before I expire." He took a long swallow of coffee.

She handed him a cream-filled doughnut, helping herself to a chocolate-frosted one.

Biting into the doughnut, he could almost feel the sugar hitting his bloodstream, teaming with caffeine. "Ahh. I could get used to this."

"I figure there's probably a Krispy Kreme on every corner in Heaven."

"Amen. With a Starbucks next door."

"Absolutely. You know, we've passed a milestone in our friendship. Not only have we seen each other first thing in the morning, we've also agreed on a few sacred points like coffee and baked goods. Want to try for politics?"

"No way. Takes more caffeine than this." He gestured with his cup.

"You're not going to tell me why you named all your reptiles after Republicans?"

"Only if you tell me why you married two men who were so obviously undeserving of you."

Emily carefully placed her doughnut on a paper napkin, wiping her fingers on a second napkin. When she raised her face, her eyes blazed. "Patrick, let's get one thing straight. I thought you were a peckerhead when I first met you. I've revised my opinion in recent weeks. But that could change really quickly. Not only are you breaking our flattery pact, but you're also using backhanded flattery as a way of prying into things that are none of your business. Back off."

Patrick did just that. He backed a few steps away from her anger.

"What do you mean you thought I was a peckerhead?"

"You acted like a pompous, judgmental ass, who had no idea what real children were like. And you had the nerve to lecture me on raising my kids."

"I was merely trying to help. It was pretty obvious Jason was out of control."

"Why? Because he put a mousetrap in your desk? Something you said you might have done at the same age?"

"And the cherry bomb in the boys' restroom. And the little gambling racket he had going on at the playground at lunch."

Emily hesitated. "What gambling racket?"

"You didn't know? The kid was shooting craps. Took in a lot of lunch money, from what I heard."

"Why didn't anyone tell me?"

"Probably because nobody could catch him red-handed."

Tapping her chin with her forefinger, she said, "That would explain why he had more spending money than usual that year. He said it was birthday money from my sister, but now that I think about it, that birthday money sure lasted a long time."

"Did it run out over summer break?"

"As a matter of fact, it did. Why, that sneaky little…"

"You know, that's one of the things I admire about you, Emily. You're in your children's corners one hundred percent, but you don't refuse to admit one of your children might have made a mistake. Some parents refuse to see it, even when the evidence is right there."

"It's not easy. It's a mother's instinct to protect her child. But kids make mistakes. And it doesn't do them any good if they don't learn from their mistakes. Take responsibility and experience the consequences. At least that's what I try to do."

"You're a wonderful mother, Em." Patrick was surprised to realize he meant every word of it, and then some.

Sighing, she said, "There are days I wonder."

"Hey, this is your weekend to leave all the kid stuff behind. Let me comb my hair and brush my teeth and we'll go check out the charity casino place. I've got enough sugar and caffeine coursing through my veins to leap tall buildings with a single bound."

"Sounds good. I plan on enjoying this weekend."

A few minutes later, they left his room, equipped with the address for the company and a city map.

Patrick eyed the sky as they crossed the parking lot. "Looks like we might get some rain. I'm afraid we should probably keep the top up."

"Darn. I was looking forward to feeling the breeze in my hair."

Shrugging, he said, "Down it is. You want breeze, it's breeze you get."

"You don't mind?"

"Hey, it's kind of fun to take chances once in a while."

She looped her arm in his and it felt perfectly natural to be on vacation with her, arm in arm. And Patrick was finding he had more fun in Emily's company than he had in a long, long time.

The gaming company was only a short drive away, but Saturday traffic was heavy.

"Over there, on the right." Emily pointed to a dingy three-story building.

They pulled into the lot and parked. Patrick pushed the button to raise the top. "Doesn't look like much."

"They certainly don't have a lot in overhead, do they?"

As it turned out, the gaming business was only

one of many small businesses housed in the building. There was no one at the reception desk when they entered the cramped suite.

Emily leaned close, her voice low. "I have a hard time seeing Tiffany doing business here."

She was right. The interior wasn't any better than the exterior. The reception desk was made of cheap pressed wood, with years' worth of dings and scratches. The four mismatched chairs lining the wall appeared as if they dated back to the seventies.

There was a doorway behind the reception desk, with what looked to be another nondescript office.

"Hello," Patrick called.

A woman appeared from the back room. She was tall, thin and middle-aged, her skin sallow. "What can I do for you?" Her voice was flat.

Patrick caught Emily's eye and nodded slightly.

She stepped forward and extended her hand. "I'm Emily Patterson. I think we spoke on the phone. We're from Elmwood Elementary."

The woman frowned, as if she couldn't place the name.

"We think Tiffany Bigelow might have put down a deposit on behalf of our school."

The woman's eyes narrowed at the mention of Tiffany. "Our computers were down late in the week, so I wasn't able to locate the information you needed."

"Oh, I understand. I know when our system goes down at work, everything grinds to a halt. There's pretty much nothing we can do till they get the system up and running."

"I'm glad you understand."

Emily walked around the side of the desk and looked at the monitor. "Good. It looks like you're up now."

"Um, yes." She stiffened. "Please have a seat and I'll check that information for you."

"Thanks so much." Emily ignored her request, watching over the woman's shoulder as she worked. "I can't tell you how much we appreciate this. Especially on a Saturday."

"Certainly."

They waited while she keyed information. "Tiffany Bigelow you said?"

Patrick had the idea she knew darn well who they were talking about. "Yes."

"As a matter of fact, it looks like Ms. Bigelow cancelled the casino event several months ago. We should have refunded your deposit."

Emily's eyes lit with the mention of a refund.

Patrick felt his spirits rising, too.

"If you don't mind waiting, I can cut you a check now."

"That would be wonderful. Of course we don't mind waiting. How much is the refund?"

He held his breath, hoping for something substantial.

"Two hundred and fifty dollars."

"Oh." Emily's smile faded. "You're sure that's all?"

"Positive. Here, you can look for yourself."

The woman pointed to the screen. "See, here's the money we received. A more substantial deposit would have been due just prior to the event."

"Yes, I can see you're right. Thank you for showing me."

She shrugged slightly and rejoined Patrick.

Five minutes later, they had their check and were out the door.

Emily's shoulders slumped in disappointment. He hated to see her earlier excitement dulled.

He wrapped his arm around her and squeezed. "Hey, it's two hundred and fifty bucks more than we had before."

"I was hoping it would be so much more. Two hundred and fifty dollars won't even begin to get your class admission to Sea World, even with the money you've already collected."

"We'll just have to put our heads together and figure something out."

Emily hesitated. "Do you think their computers were really down this week?"

"No way to tell for sure, but I somehow doubt

it. If they were down, why not just tell us that instead of avoiding us? Seems like better business, to me."

"Exactly. And you know what else?"

"What?"

"There was a cross reference under Tiffany's name." Her voice rose. "It was for the Elmwood Heart Fund. And the deposit there was ten thousand dollars."

"Tiffany probably volunteered at that event, too."

"Something about it bothers me, though."

"Still?"

"Why was the Elmwood Heart Fund deposit so much more than ours?"

Patrick thought she was grasping at straws. Sure, he was disappointed, too, but they were nowhere near the Heart Fund league. "Bigger event?"

"Could be."

"But you don't think so. Honestly, Em, I think it'd probably be a waste of time to pursue this any further. It's looking like we need to focus on procuring more funding instead of chasing down blind alleys."

"You don't have to spend any more time on it. I'm going to do more checking, though."

Patrick had the uncomfortable feeling her quest was about to become his.

CHAPTER FOURTEEN

JASON SAT on the couch at the Stantons' house and pretended to watch the lame old movies with his brothers, Nancy and Beau. He even managed to chuckle at a few of Larry, Curly and Moe's stunts. But inside, he was royally pissed off.

His mother had gone to Atlantic City with Mr. Stevens. Even after he'd told her what a mistake it would be. And he was stuck here pretending everything was okay, while his mom was probably getting horizontal with Mr. Stevens.

He shuddered at the thought. Mothers weren't supposed to do those things.

How come she couldn't see that Mr. Stevens was a loser? That he'd use her for one thing and then dump her?

And to top it off, there was a big party out at the quarry and he was missing it. Cassie'd said she intended to go with her friends. He could just imagine Kirk Trainer seeing his golden opportunity to steal her away. The guy had made no secret he had the hots for Cassie.

When the movie ended, Jason tried to appear casual when he asked, "Would it be okay if I pitched a tent in the backyard tonight? I couldn't get any sleep last night with Mark and Ryan squirming all over the place and Jeremy talking in his sleep."

Nancy said, "I suppose—"

"Nope. No can do, Jason." Beau crossed his arms, staring at him. His voice brooked no argument.

But Jason had to try. "Please, Mr. Stanton? I won't bother anyone. I could really use the sleep."

"Yes, as I recall, I was very concerned about *sleep* when I was your age. Your mother would tan my hide if I allowed you to sleep outdoors and by some weird coincidence, your girlfriend somehow ended up in that tent. Or if by another weird coincidence, you sleepwalked to the local hangout."

Damn.

"I wouldn't do something like that. I promise." He widened his eyes innocently.

Mr. Stanton chuckled. "Nice try. You set foot outside this house without my permission, I'll come looking for you. And that's a promise."

Jason swallowed hard. For an old guy, Mr.

Stanton was in pretty good shape. And a good four inches taller. "Yes, sir."

But even buff old guys needed to sleep sometime.

And, as it turned out, Mr. Stanton went off to sleepy-land a little after eleven. That meant Jason, if he was very, very careful, could catch the last hour or so of the party. And make sure Cassie hadn't left with Kirk Trainer.

Transportation could be a problem though. He went into the bathroom and ran the water while he tried a few friends on his cell phone. They refused to leave the party to pick him up. They also said Kirk was putting the moves on Cassie big-time.

Desperate times required desperate measures. Jason used all his stealth skills to get past his brothers sleeping on the floor of the Stanton family room without waking Beau or Nancy.

Once out the front door, he was home free— literally. He hopped on his bike and pedaled home. Retrieving the extra key from inside the fake rock by the back door, he let himself in. The house was eerily dark and quiet. He tried not to let it freak him out.

Hurrying to the door by the garage, Jason plucked his mom's car keys from the hook. Once inside the garage, he stared at the minivan, his gut tightening at what he was about to do.

Mom would have a fit if she knew he took the van. But she would never know. He'd be gone an hour or two, tops. Besides, she'd let him drive a few times when they were outside town limits.

He unlocked the door and settled himself in the driver's seat. His heart knocked against his ribs.

Turning the key in the ignition, he was almost disappointed when the engine engaged. If it hadn't, he could have shrugged his shoulders and pedaled back to the Stantons' house.

The mental image of Kirk kissing Cassie was enough to curb the butterflies in his stomach. Jason loved Cassie and there wasn't anything he wouldn't do for her. When she looked up at him with those big, brown eyes, he just about died and he knew he would never, *ever* feel this way about another girl. Borrowing his mom's car was a small price to pay.

Once he reached the party, Cassie's welcoming smile and Kirk's scowl were enough to tell him he'd done the right thing.

Cassie twined her arms around his neck and kissed him. "I was afraid you wouldn't be able to come."

"It was a little harder to get away than I thought."

"You're here now and that's all that matters." Cassie gave him the smile that turned his knees to jelly.

"Hey, Jase." His buddy, Matt, came up and tried to hand him a beer.

"No, thanks, dude."

"Aw, come on. It's a party."

"I'm, um, driving."

Cassie squealed. "Driving. You can take me home. We could even, maybe, um, park somewhere."

It was so tempting. Him, Cassie, alone. But, no.

Shaking his head, he said, "Can't. I'll be grounded forever if my mom finds out I took her car while she was out of town."

Cassie pouted prettily. "You're sure?"

Jason's mouth went dry when he realized what he might be passing up. His voice cracked when he said, "Um, I'm sure. Maybe when I get my permit."

"Promise?"

"It's a promise." He kissed her deeply, glad he'd taken the risk to get there.

And the next half hour was great. Then the cops showed up. Kids scattered.

Jason, as luck would have it, was too far from the minivan to escape. His gut twisted as the cop asked for ID.

His mom would find out for sure. He could just hear her Jason-I'm-so-disappointed-in-you speech. And he could hear her crying in her room afterward, too. That was the part that really got to him. To know that he'd been responsible for making her cry.

"Um, I don't have any ID."

"How'd you get here?"

Quickly calculating his options, Jason realized he didn't have many. Bad enough that he was out after curfew at a party with alcohol involved. No way was he going to admit to driving without a license. "I came with my buddies. But they left when you got here."

"You got a cell phone?"

"Yes."

"Then you better call your folks and have them come pick you up."

"Um, my mom's out of town."

"Convenient."

"It's the truth," Jason protested. "I'm staying with my mom's friend and her husband."

"Better call them, then. We don't have the manpower to chauffeur you home."

Jason clicked open his cell phone and searched his phone book. Thank God he had the Stantons' number. Otherwise, the cop acted like he'd take him to jail for the night.

A sleepy male voice answered on the third ring.

"Beau, it's me. Jason."

"What the hell?"

"Um, can you come pick me up?"

"Where are you?" Beau's voice was low, alert.

"At the quarry." Jason winced at Beau's swearing.

But when he spoke again, Beau's voice was filled with worry. "Are you okay?"

His concern only made Jason feel worse. "Yeah, I'm okay. But, um, the police are here and they want to talk to you when you pick me up."

"The police. What's going on, Jason?"

"It was just a party. No big deal."

"The cops wouldn't be there if it wasn't a big deal. I'll be there in fifteen minutes."

Jason shut his phone and went to sit on a fallen log next to another kid who was trying not to appear scared shitless.

When Beau arrived, he looked like two hundred pounds of avenging Texan.

Jason swallowed hard. His eyes burned. No way was he gonna cry.

Beau spoke to the cop for a couple minutes, then stalked over to Jason. He towered over him, scowling. "You don't think your mother has enough to worry about without you pulling a stunt like this? What the hell were you thinking?"

How could he explain so an adult would understand? An adult who probably never loved a girl so much it hurt? "I dunno."

"That doesn't wash with me, kid. You were planning this from the get-go. Asking to sleep out in the tent. I still don't know how you managed to get out without me hearing you. But we'll discuss that later."

"Yes, sir."

"What I want to know is how you got here."

It took all Jason's will not to glance in the direction of the parked van. If Beau realized he'd taken his mom's car and driven without a license, he'd be toast. "One of my friends picked me up." The lie just about stuck to the roof of his mouth.

Beau turned to the cops. "Officers, I'm taking this one home. Thanks again."

The officers nodded and waved them on.

Beau grabbed Jason's arm and none-too-gently propelled him toward the truck. Thank God he was too pissed to really look around.

Jason sank into the passenger seat, just wanting the night to be over. He wanted to be in his own home, in his own bed, where it was safe. Beau looked mad enough to kill him.

As they headed for the road, Beau glanced at the handful of cars left, parked under the trees.

Holding his breath, Jason prayed he wouldn't see the van.

But his luck was holding true.

Beau did a double-take, then stomped on the brake. "Do you want to tell me what your mother's van is doing here?"

No. That was the last thing Jason wanted to do right now. Sighing, he gave in to the inevitable. "I brought Mom's van."

"You mean you stole your mom's van."

"No way. It's ours."

"You were driving it without her permission. That means she could report it stolen and you could be looking at grand theft auto."

"She wouldn't do that."

"No." Beau shook his head. He sighed heavily. "But maybe she should."

Jason thought it wise to keep quiet. Yet he couldn't help but ask, "Are you going to tell my mom?"

"You've put me in a really tough position. I don't want to ruin your mother's trip."

A part of Jason wanted just that—to have his mom come home and leave the PTO business to Mr. Stevens. *If* she'd been telling the truth. Then again, he was pretty sure his mom wouldn't lie to them. At least, not on purpose.

His sense of self-preservation kicked in. He didn't want to be grounded for the rest of his life. And that's what would happen if his mom found out about him borrowing the van. "I'm sorry, sir."

"You can cut the 'sir' crap. I don't buy it for a second."

"No, si— I mean, no."

They were silent the rest of the way back to the Stanton house.

When they pulled in the drive, Beau shut off the engine and turned to Jason. "I'm not going to call your mother. But when she returns, I'll have to tell her about the party. I haven't decided yet whether I'll tell her about the van. She probably deserves to know. Then again, the cop says you weren't drinking—one of your friends even offered you a beer and you declined." Beau shook his head. "Because you were driving." His voice sounded strangled, as if he were trying not to chuckle. "There are a lot of adults who don't show judgment that good. And I *was* your age once. I remember what it's like being almost fifteen. I pulled a few stupid stunts myself."

Jason was careful not to let his astonishment show. There was no way he would have thought Beau Stanton, old guy, husband, father and taxpayer, had done anything remotely wild in his youth.

Shaking his head, Jason thought he might, just possibly, come out of this okay.

But Beau's next words dashed his hopes. "The fact alone that you snuck out to a party against my express wishes will be enough to hit your mother with when she gets home. You kids just don't understand how much parents worry."

"Thank you." His voice was barely above a whisper. He had a pretty good idea how much his mom worried—he'd listened to her cry herself to sleep more nights than he cared to think about. But somehow, he just couldn't seem to quit screwing up. It was like his brain was hardwired to make the worst possible choice, the one most likely to get him into trouble.

"I'll have to tell Nancy about the van, because I'll need her to go with us to drive it home tomorrow. Whether she is quite as understanding as I am remains to be seen. There's still the chance she might decide your mother deserves to know. And I'll stand behind her."

Sweat beaded Jason's upper lip. There wasn't a snowball's chance in hell Nancy wouldn't tell his mom. They were best friends and he was pretty sure they talked about *everything*. He'd even overheard them discussing his dad and Larry-the-jerk from time to time, though they always changed the subject when they knew he was around. His mom tried really hard to act like his dad wasn't a total loser. But Jason knew better.

No birthday cards, no phone calls, no nothing in years. He figured his dad had forgotten he even existed.

But Jason could start proving he was a better man than his dad. He, at least, would accept responsibility for his actions. "I understand. Thanks for trying. And it had nothing to do with you. You and Mrs. Stanton have been really great to have us over this weekend. I'm sorry."

Beau nodded. "Enough said."

EMILY CLAPPED HER HANDS with excitement, managing to restrain herself and not jump up and down with joy. "I won."

Patrick was beside her at the roulette table. "I noticed. You're on a roll. Want to quit and get some dinner?"

"Now? While I'm on a hot streak? Forget it." Why, if she won a couple more rounds, she might be able to fly with the kids to Florida next time instead of driving. Or she could make an extra payment on the mortgage. She made a face at the thought. Being responsible was tiresome.

"You're sure? Remember, you want to quit while you're winning."

"I have the feeling my luck's going to hold a while longer." She grinned, enjoying every moment of excitement.

"Whatever. It's your money."

"Yes, it is. And I want to stay a while longer, okay?"

A smile twitched at Patrick's lips. "Okay." He seemed to be having a good time, too.

Emily held her breath as the ball zoomed around the wheel, making little clicking noises as it went. Finally, it dropped into a slot. "I won again."

This time she flung her arms around Patrick's neck and kissed him right on the mouth.

He grinned. "I sure hope you keep winning. I could get used to this."

"Watch."

She placed another bet and didn't even bother to hold her breath this time, so sure she'd win.

Only she lost.

And the trend continued. It took less than fifteen minutes to lose what it had taken hours to accumulate. Emily was shell-shocked when they stepped away from the table. "Can you believe that?"

"Yes, unfortunately, I can."

She eyed him sideways. "That's an 'I told you so' if I've ever heard one."

He chuckled. "Your words, not mine."

"Patrick, I'm such a fool. I should have quit when you suggested it. Now, all that money's gone."

"Fortunately, you're only down twenty bucks."

"Why doesn't that make me feel better?" She slipped her hand in his.

"Because you got caught up in gambling fever. It's not hard to do."

"Did you ever get gambling fever?"

He shook his head. "No, I know too much about probabilities. The house is going to win sooner or later."

"What about luck? You can't factor that."

Shrugging, he said, "I guess I'm not much of a risk-taker. You want to go eat? There are a zillion buffets we haven't tried yet."

Emily sighed. "Now that I'm coming down off the high of winning, I'm kind of tired. And as exciting as it was at first, I'd like to get away from all these people. How about room service and a rented movie?"

"Whew. You must've been reading my mind."

"Your room or mine?" She tried to keep any hint of suggestion out of her voice, but it was there all the same. The glint in Patrick's eye told her he'd heard it, too. Emily rushed to assure him, "Room service and a movie only. That's it."

"Darn. I guess I can live with that."

"My room, then. I want to call home real quick and make sure everything's okay." She glanced at her watch. "Oh my gosh, is it really nearly 1:00 a.m.?"

"Yes."

"No wonder I'm so tired. It's too late to call. You should have said something—you're probably starving."

He shrugged. "You were having too much fun. I enjoyed being there."

His simple admission touched her. She reached up and trailed her fingertips down his cheek. "I've enjoyed being with you, too." Way more than she'd enjoyed being with a man in a very long time.

CHAPTER FIFTEEN

WHILE PATRICK WANTED the sci-fi flick, Emily leaned toward a coming-of-age drama. They compromised with a romantic comedy, purchased from the hotel TV menu.

"Since you sprang for the movie, I'll handle room service. They can put it on my bill," Patrick said.

"We'll split it."

"That's not necessary."

"Yes, it is." It was very necessary for her not to feel like a charity case on this trip. Or a kept woman.

Patrick shrugged. "We'll bill it to my room and you can pay me later."

"That'll work. Just make the call. I'm starving." She realized it had been ages since they'd had a late lunch. Time seemed to lose all meaning in Atlantic City.

"What do you want?"

"Bacon cheeseburger, french fries, salad on the side and a diet cola."

"Sounds good. I'll make it two." Patrick phoned in their order.

When room service arrived, Emily checked her watch. "We timed that about right. The movie should be starting in five minutes."

Patrick signed the check and they arranged the plates and condiments on the table.

They chatted about minor stuff until the movie started. Then sat back and ate and watched the movie.

Although she'd enjoyed herself almost the entire trip, Emily thought the quiet, companionable evening with Patrick was the very best part.

In that way, her friendship with him was different than any relationship she'd had with a man. Maybe if she'd tried to be friends first with her ex-husbands instead of jumping into a hot and heavy fling, things might have been different.

Shaking her head, she decided the only difference would have been that, without hormones clouding her judgment, she might have noticed Walt and Larry's foibles before the wedding, not after.

She watched Patrick out of the corner of her eye. He had a wonderful laugh, full and masculine. When he relaxed, his unselfconscious charm was appealing.

When they'd finished eating, she cleared the dishes and put the tray outside her door. Instead of returning to the stiff side chair, she kicked off her shoes and sat on the bed.

Patrick glanced at her inquiringly.

"That chair was killing my back." She plumped a pillow, placed it against the headboard and leaned back, with a sigh. It had been such a lovely, lovely weekend, she never wanted it to end.

Regret washed over her. Why couldn't she have found a guy like Patrick when she was younger, when she didn't have four kids and a mortgage? That was an awful lot to ask any man to take on.

"Hey, whatcha thinking about?" The movie had ended sometime during her reverie and Patrick's eyes were warm with concern. "You're a million miles away."

"Do you ever think about the path you've chosen? How life might be different if you'd made better choices?"

"Sure. I bet everyone does. What choices do you regret?"

She thought about it for a moment. "If I had one thing to do over, I think I would have gone to college. Because then I would have had an education and confidence and wouldn't have fallen for the first guy who came along. But then again, I wouldn't have my kids and I wouldn't trade them for anything."

Patrick sat on the edge of the bed. He reached for her hand. "Is that why you picked someone who didn't treat you like you deserved? *You* didn't think you deserved better?"

"Something like that." Emily gazed at their clasped hands. His fingers were strong, but artistic, twined with hers. "What about you? If there was one thing in the world you could do over, what would it be?"

He released her hand and glanced at his watch. "Whoa, almost 3:00 a.m. I better head back to my room and let you get some sleep. We have to be at the airport by eleven."

But he didn't make a move to rise, so she took a shot in the dark that deep down he really wanted to talk. "I was honest with you about something I don't normally talk about. It's only fair you do the same."

He sighed. "There's only one thing I'd want to do over."

She waited for him to continue, watching the emotions play over his face. Fear, anger, guilt. Whatever his story was, it was a doozy. She resisted the urge to touch his face and smooth away the frown lines.

"The day my brother nearly drowned." He started to rise, but she grasped his arm.

"Please, tell me."

He held her gaze, searching her face, as if trying to determine if he could trust her. But hadn't he said everyone trusted her? Everyone found her easy to talk to?

Finally, he sank back down. "It was February. The pond by our house always iced over hard by February. But that year, we'd had a couple unseasonably warm days. Anyway, Roger and I were on our way to school. He teased me about a girl, so I grabbed his lunch box and flung it out on the ice."

Emily ached at the haunting regret she saw in his eyes. It was her turn to clasp his hand in sympathy.

"The ice was thin in only one spot—right by his lunch box. But not thin enough so we could tell. Roger told me to go get it. I was the big brother. I didn't take orders from him. So, I told him to quit acting like a baby and go get it himself."

"And he fell through."

Patrick nodded. "I panicked. I didn't know what to do. I ran to get help from a neighbor." His voice broke. "I ran as fast as I could."

Emily squeezed his hand. "I'm sure you did."

"The neighbor called my folks after he called the paramedics, but my dad and mom got there first. My dad tried to help Roger, but the ice kept cracking under his weight. I was small enough, I should have done it."

"You could have fallen in, too. Then you both might have drowned and your parents would have been without both sons."

He hesitated, his voice low and raw. "Sometimes, I think maybe that might have been best. By the time the paramedics got there, Roger'd been under water a long time. He'd sustained irreversible brain damage."

"Oh, Patrick, how horrible for you, for your family."

"I didn't care about me." The words were wrenched from him. "I just wanted Roger to be all right. To wake up and find out it was all just a bad dream. I wanted my mom to stop crying and my dad to quit looking like a zombie."

His eyes shimmered with moisture.

The instinct to comfort had Emily scooting closer, wrapping her arms around him. "It's okay."

He leaned back and held her gaze. "No, it's not okay. I could have let his teasing roll off. I was older, I could have been mature and ignored him. But, no. I had to retaliate. I had to pull one prank too many." His voice was choked. "And my brother paid the price."

His anguish broke her heart. What a terrible

burden he'd lived with all this time. Her voice was soft when she said, "Tell me about Roger."

He took a deep breath and released it. He didn't seem to realize they were hip to hip, arms wrapped around each other. "Roger has the mental capacity of a two-year-old. He can't speak, he can't control his bowels or bladder, can barely sit up."

"You said your parents care for him?"

"Yes. I send money. A couple times a year, I'll spend the weekend with him so they can get away. I intend to have him live with me once they're...gone."

"That's a heavy responsibility, but I can understand why you want to do it." How many men would step up to the plate like that?

"Yeah, but I wouldn't have it any other way."

The steady resolve in his voice warmed her. She was starting to understand that he might just be the kind of man to follow through on his promises. "I'd like to meet Roger someday."

"Freak show?"

Emily couldn't have been more surprised if he'd slapped her. "You ought to know me better than that."

"I'm sorry." He rested his forehead against her neck. "I do know you better than that. You're one of the few women I would consider introducing to my family. Because you have a huge, genuine heart."

She was warmed by his statement, but flustered, didn't know how to respond. She fell back on humor. "Yeah, to go with my big, genuine body."

"That's not really how you see yourself, is it? Because you are absolutely gorgeous. Inside and out. You have a body to die for. You're smart and funny and loving." He kissed her gently on the lips.

She searched his eyes and saw only admiration. Her pulse pounded. This wonderful, intelligent, good-looking guy thought she was gorgeous and smart.

He brushed a strand of hair from her face. "Oops. I forgot. Compliments are off limits."

She chuckled, her voice husky when she said, "Whose dumb idea was that?"

"Yours. And I understood your point at the time."

"Now, it doesn't seem quite as important."

"I wouldn't intentionally hurt you, you know."

She cupped his dear, serious face with her hands. "I know. I want to thank you for telling me about Roger. It took guts. And it means you trust me."

"It's a time I'd rather forget, but I think about

it nearly every day. Sometimes, I wonder what my life would have been like if the accident hadn't happened. Would I have continued to screw around and just have fun? Not thinking about anyone but myself?"

"You're too hard on yourself. You were just a kid. Kids are the most self-centered creatures on the planet."

"But most kids' selfishness doesn't result in someone almost dying. Why did I have to push it too far?"

She shook her head slowly. "I don't know the answer to that. All I know is that sometimes terrible things happen to good people."

"Roger was good. He didn't deserve it."

"No, he didn't. But it was an accident. If you'd known the ice was thin, you wouldn't have tossed his lunch box there."

"You're sure about that? Because I really don't know. All I remember was the impulse and acting on it. There wasn't a whole lot of thought involved."

"Again, normal for a boy of that age. Kids don't think."

He sighed. "All rational arguments. Things I tell myself over and over again. But in here—" he tapped his chest "—I feel responsible. And I'd do anything in the world to change what happened to Roger."

Emily leaned over and kissed him, softly, tenderly, wanting to erase his pain. He was such a wonderful man. And so very, very sad.

He responded with a low moan, pulling her close, deepening the kiss.

Emily felt as if she'd come home. As if she'd always been meant to be held by him. She twined her arms around his neck and tried to show him how much she cared. Show him how much his story touched her.

His arms tightened around her. He shifted, pressing closer. She could tell he wanted her as much as she wanted him. She murmured his name.

His eyes opened. The passion clouding them faded and she saw something close to panic.

He moved to sit upright.

She shook her head. "Don't go."

"If I don't leave now, things are going to get out of hand. And I don't want to take advantage of the situation. I don't need pity sex."

"It wouldn't be pity sex. I need you. Please, stay the night with me?" A part of her wanted to retract the invitation the second it escaped her lips. But another part of her cried out to be loved.

"Em, we agreed we'd keep it platonic."

"I know what I'm doing, Patrick."

"Do you? Or are you just caught up in the fantasy of being in Atlantic City, far from home?"

"Maybe a little of both. Everyone needs a little fantasy in their lives." A little hope. And Emily realized she'd been living too long without hope. She'd nearly forgotten what it was like to feel this close to a man. Patrick's confidences, his scent, the warmth of his body, all drew her to him.

He didn't move. Need flickered in his eyes. "What about your family?"

"Patrick, I'm not expecting a happily-ever-after here. It's been a while since I've been held through the night. And I'd like to pretend I'm not a single mom with responsibilities. I just want to be a woman." The note of pleading in her voice embarrassed her. How sad to have to beg a man to bed her.

He made a noise low in his throat and pulled her close. "Em, you drive me crazy. I've wanted you all weekend long. I've wanted you pretty much since the day you came at me with the scissors."

She placed kisses on his neck. "Really? Since that first day?"

He nodded.

She moved against him, capturing his mouth with hers.

He returned her kiss with possessive strokes of his tongue. Clasping her hands, he pinned them above her head, kissing away her protests.

Patrick pulled away a fraction and simply stared at her, his eyes deep, unfathomable. "Em, you are so beautiful," he murmured.

Arching to meet him, she wanted to get closer. Her arms still pinioned, she caressed his hip with her knee, trying to convey how much she needed him.

He released her hands and she greedily ran them along his shoulders and back, reveling in the feel of him.

Slowly, he unbuttoned her blouse. His pupils dilated, a small smile played about his lips. "Beautiful."

The admiration in his eyes almost made her forget those last fifteen pounds. Almost made her feel as beautiful as he professed. Thank goodness she'd thought to wear her sexiest black bra and panties.

He unclasped her bra, trailing kisses down her neck as he caressed her breasts with featherlight, teasing touches.

She murmured his name, reaching for his shirt. Unbuttoning it, she slid her hands inside, enjoying the warmth of his skin against her palms. Then she trailed her hands down his stomach, surprised to find he was all muscle. He hadn't been exaggerating when he said he played basketball.

When she reached to unsnap his jeans, he grasped her hand. "Wait."

She gazed up at him through half-closed lids. "Why?"

"Do you have a condom?"

"No. Do you?"

"I normally keep a couple in my carry-on, you know, just in case. But I didn't want it to look like I expected to seduce you."

Groaning, she sat up. "And I was trying to exercise self-control. I didn't want to tempt myself, so I didn't bring any."

"The hotel gift shop. Wait here, I'll be right back."

Patrick vaulted off the bed, buttoning his shirt and pulling on his shoes all at the same time. It was clumsy, awkward as hell, but somehow endearing. She only hoped he didn't trip and hurt himself.

As he stumbled out the door, he called over his shoulder, "Wait right there. Don't move."

She stifled a chuckle. "I won't, I promise."

Emily's throaty chuckle warmed Patrick's heart. Her promise prompted him to sprint to the elevator and press the down button repeatedly until the doors opened.

The elevator seemed to take forever as it lumbered down to the lobby. Then a horrible thought struck him. What if the gift shop was closed? But this was Atlantic City, where businesses stayed open twenty-four hours a day.

Patrick prayed the hotel gift shop was one of them.

And his prayers were answered. He swung the door open and searched for a discreet display. Past the postcards and kitsch, he spied what he was looking for. Normally, he would have waited for the guy standing there to move on, but he didn't have the luxury of waiting tonight.

He strode purposefully to the display and was relieved to see one remaining package of condoms. Whew! That was close.

But the man reached for the lone package.

Patrick snagged the condoms right before the other guy's hand closed on them. "Sorry, pal, I need these worse than you do."

The other man cursed loudly, but Patrick ignored him.

The cashier, a middle-aged woman, took her time ringing up his purchase.

"Here." He threw down a twenty, grabbed the three-pack of condoms and jogged out the door, whistling a tune. He ignored the one-fingered salute from the guy who would have to drive to a drugstore to buy his.

All was fair in love and war.

CHAPTER SIXTEEN

EMILY STRETCHED and yawned and came completely awake when her arm made contact with another human form. A naked, *male* form.

Then she remembered. Patrick.

Her body tingled as she recalled the night they'd spent together. She smiled slowly, more content than she could ever recall. Not only had she enjoyed making love with Patrick, she enjoyed waking up next to him in the morning.

Rolling on her side, she watched him sleep. His dark hair was tousled and his jaw was shadowed with new, scruffy growth. But he still had that dear, little-boy look that had first attracted her.

She couldn't stop herself from caressing his face. He was such a wonderful guy.

His eyes opened and he smiled.

If she weren't already half in love with him before, she would be now. Because his smile was so genuine and tender.

"'Morning," he said.

"'Morning." She brushed the hair from his forehead. Funny, she didn't feel that morning-after awkwardness with him. Making love with him had been as easy as breathing—as if they'd been together years and instinctively knew what the other liked.

"You're even beautiful when you first wake up." He trailed his fingers down her arm, then followed with kisses. "Your skin is so soft."

She snuggled close, twining her arms around his neck. "You're not bad yourself."

He grasped her hips, adjusting her position so she pressed against his erection. "I can't seem to get enough of you."

Desire flooded every molecule of her being. "Good. Because it's the same for me." She reached down and stroked him.

"Mm. Condom?"

Emily rolled on her side, searching blindly on the nightstand. Her fingers encountered only empty packets. She made the supreme effort to pull away from Patrick and sit up. Turning on the lamp, she blinked, willing her eyes to adjust to the light.

She counted. One, two, three.

Groaning, she picked up the packets and showered them on Patrick, like cellophane rose petals. "Guess what, stud. We're all out."

"Damn. Are you sure?"

"Count 'em. I'm sure. And now that I think about it, that should be right. There was the first time, when we barely made it to the bed. Then in the shower. And in the middle of the night…"

"Yes, that makes three."

"You should have gotten the twelve-pack."

He threw his head back and laughed. It was a beautiful sight. "I didn't tell you what I had to go through to get those. It was the last package and some other guy almost got them." He told her the rest of the story.

She laughed till the tears trickled from her eyes. "Oh, Patrick, and here I thought you weren't spontaneous. Did you really tell him you needed them worse than he did?"

"Scout's honor. And it's true. It's been a while for me and, well, I've been lusting after you for two solid days and I thought if we didn't finish, I'd—"

"Explode?"

"Exactly."

Emily leaned over and kissed him. "You managed to control that explosion quite nicely."

"It wasn't easy, believe me. If I haven't told you before, Em, you're one hell of a woman."

"Yes, you have. But you can keep on telling me. I've decided to allow you all the compliments you want."

"Even when we're back in Elmwood?"

His question brought her up short. How would they handle their blossoming relationship back in Elmwood? It sounded like he wanted it to continue, and she certainly wanted it to continue.

Taking a leap of faith, she said, "Especially when we're back in Elmwood."

Patrick rewarded her with a huge grin and a hot, wet kiss.

She enjoyed his passion for a few moments, then pulled away. "Down, boy. Remember, we're out of condoms."

"Remind me to buy a huge box when we get back to Elmwood."

"Buy them at the airport." She winked. "We don't want people to talk."

"Good point. Although I don't really care what people say. We're two consenting adults."

Emily glanced at the bedside clock. "Yikes. What time did you say we had to be at the airport?"

"Eleven. I set the alarm for nine."

"Then it didn't go off. It's nine-twenty now."

Patrick swore under his breath. "We better get moving."

Emily glanced around the room, trying to absorb the last fleeting moment of their weekend. "I wish we could stay longer."

"Me, too. But duty calls. I have class tomorrow and you have a meeting with Principal Ross."

It was Emily's turn to swear under her breath. No doubt about it, she'd have to hit the ground running the minute they got home.

JASON WATCHED Nancy replace the handset to the phone base. His neck knotted with tension.

"Good news guys, your mom's plane just landed."

Mark and Ryan shouted with joy. Jeremy even managed to whistle. Jason remained silent. His day of reckoning was here.

He'd thought it had been bad enough facing Beau this morning. And then Beau had told Nancy and she gave Jason his mother's patented I'm-so-disappointed-in-you look. What was it with mothers? Was that look part of an international motherhood training course?

Nancy'd been mostly quiet since then. Except when she argued in whispers with Beau in the front seat of the Stanton SUV during the trip to the quarry. She'd thought Jason couldn't hear, but he got it all loud and clear.

"I don't like keeping secrets from Emily," she murmured.

"I don't, either. But do you really want to hit her with all this when she gets home? What's the point of a relaxing weekend away if she's stressed out the minute she walks in the door? It'll be bad enough as it is."

"Poor Em. She really needed this weekend. And I was so hoping she and Patrick…" Nancy glanced at him in the backseat, apparently realizing his hearing was better than she originally thought. She leaned over and whispered the rest in Beau's ear.

Beau nodded. "I know."

It didn't take a brain surgeon to realize Nancy hoped his mom and Mr. Stevens had hooked up on their weekend away.

The very thought made Jason want to hurl.

They'd managed to get the van back to the house and in the garage. Jason replaced the keys, and they went back to the Stantons' place.

It galled him to watch Nancy pay a friend of Beau's daughter for babysitting the rugrats while they were gone. Jeremy was perfectly capable of watching them for a few minutes.

Or maybe it was just his conscience telling him the Stantons had done something really nice for his mom and he'd made a load of trouble for them. He really hadn't meant to.

"She's here." Ryan bounced up and down in front of the window. Mark quickly joined him.

All three of the younger boys crowded

around her when she came through the door. Only Jason hung back.

She dispensed hugs and kisses and the real babyish part of Jason wished he could be on the receiving end, too. He'd be lucky if she was speaking to him after Beau and Nancy told her about the party.

"How was your weekend?" Nancy asked.

"Fabulous." His mom smiled, her eyes sparkled, her skin glowed.

His stomach threatened to hurl.

"How'd everything go this weekend? I hope the boys were good for you."

"They were wonderful." Nancy's voice was overly enthusiastic. Even he could tell she was lying through her teeth.

"What happened?" His mom's eyes narrowed.

"They really were lovely, Emily." Nancy gazed helplessly at Beau.

Beau cleared his throat. "Yeah, they were great. Except for a little misunderstanding last night."

"What kind of misunderstanding?" Mom's voice was sharp. She glanced right at him. "Jason, do you know anything about this?"

Jason looked down at his shoes. He could feel everyone staring at him. He should be a man, take responsibility for his screw-ups. But his mom had looked so happy when she first came in, he didn't want to be the one to spoil it.

Beau jumped in to save him. "Um, well, Jason misunderstood me and thought it would be okay if he attended a party last night."

Jason was grateful. Beau made it sound almost like a harmless mistake.

"Did he ask you to go to the party?"

"Um, no, not exactly."

"Did you know he went to the party?"

"No. Not till later."

"So what you're saying is he snuck out."

Beau glanced at Jason and shrugged helplessly. Apparently Beau hadn't realized Jason's mom could do the interrogation thing really well. Nothing got past her.

"Yeah, I guess that's the gist of it."

That's when his mom brought out the big guns. "I'm so disappointed in you, Jason."

He raised his head and met her gaze. The tears shimmering in her eyes prompted a similar moisture in his own. "I'm sorry, Mom."

"You're always sorry. But nothing ever changes."

Mr. Stevens put his arm around Mom's shoulders. His gaze was hard.

Great. He'd thought things couldn't get worse,

but they had. It was obvious Mr. Stevens was looking to be the next Daddy Dearest.

Jason would be lucky if he didn't get shipped off to military school before the ink was dry on the marriage certificate.

PATRICK SIPPED HIS COFFEE in the teachers' lounge, hoping the caffeine would kick in soon. It almost seemed like Monday again, only his calendar told him it was Tuesday.

The physical education teacher entered the room and poured herself a cup of coffee. She came over and punched him on the arm. "Nice strategy, Stevens. Although, honestly, I didn't have you pegged as a player."

His sluggish brain cells couldn't wrap themselves around her cryptic statement. "What strategy?"

"Romancing the new PTO president. I hear you got two hundred fifty bucks for your trip fund. Chump change, but better than nothing. And it looks like nothing is what the rest of us are going to get." She sighed. "No new PE equipment this year."

All sorts of denials sprang to his lips. He couldn't, in all truthfulness, deny having a relationship with Emily. Didn't want to, as a matter of fact. But gossip was putting an ugly spin on their friendship. "Where'd you get the idea I'm romancing Emily Patterson?"

"Come on, Stevens, it's all over school—your little weekend getaway to Atlantic City."

"It's not like that. Who started that kind of rumor?"

She shrugged. "Who knows. News travels fast. Could be one of the Patterson kids let something slip."

Patrick stifled a groan. "I am *not* romancing Emily to get preferential treatment."

"Sure you're not. It's her stimulating conversation you're interested in."

"As a matter of fact, that's part of it." He tried to rein in his anger. "Emily is a terrific person once you get to know her."

"If you say so. You gonna be at the PTO meeting today? Cheer your girlfriend on?"

His spirits sank. He'd intended to go to the meeting to provide Emily with moral support. But now, that didn't look like such a good idea. "I'm not sure."

He made a mental note to call Emily and let her know what she might be walking in to.

EMILY RESISTED THE URGE to rub her temples. It had all looked so simple, listed on her agenda. A few minor items to discuss.

Wrong.

Every item had been debated backward, forward and sideways. And to top it off, Patrick hadn't attended. They'd played voice mail tag most of the afternoon. His last message had been cryptic. Something about people talking. And tests he needed to grade so he wouldn't be at the meeting unless she absolutely needed him to be there. She hadn't responded to the last message. What could she say without appearing needy and clingy?

"Next item," she said. "We recovered a two-hundred-and-fifty-dollar deposit owed to us from the casino gaming company. The funds have been pegged for the sixth-grade Sea World trip. Since it's a small amount, no vote is needed."

Whispers greeted her ears. The PE teacher grinned and winked. What in the world was going on?

She moved rapidly to the last item, a reading under the stars evening. Fortunately, there were plenty of volunteers and a committee was formed. "I'll have your budget to you by the end of the week."

Moving to the podium, she asked for a motion to end the meeting, received the motion and a second. Her first PTO meeting as acting president was over. She exhaled slowly.

All in all, it had gone well. Not easy, but well. She'd been able to answer the questions posed to her and retain an air of authority. Nobody stood up and pointed or shouted, "imposter."

Now that it was over, Emily was proud of herself. She'd stepped out of her comfort zone and it had worked out fine. Emily had proven she could do the job.

If only Patrick had been there to see it.

PATRICK DRUMMED HIS FINGERS on the tabletop, waiting for Emily to show.

When she entered the coffee bar, it was like she brought a breath of fresh air with her. His mood lightened, his pulse accelerated.

He watched her as she placed and received her order. She looked gorgeous. Tight jeans, a skimpy T-shirt and one of those crocheted vests that got his imagination going wild. The effect was only intensified because he knew for certain how gorgeous she was naked. It made him want to do just about anything to lose himself in the silky texture of her skin and fullness of her curves.

She frowned slightly as she approached his table. "Hi."

He rose. "Hi." Handing her a brownie and a bottled water, he said, "I got these for you."

"Thanks. But I'm not that hungry right now."

"Give it to one of the boys, then."

She sat down. "Yeah, that'll cause an all-out war. I'll save it for my lunch tomorrow."

"How'd the PTO meeting go?"

"It went okay. I was able to handle everything that came up. I kind of missed seeing you there."

Patrick felt like a real jerk. "I would have liked to have been there, too. But I was afraid it might complicate things."

Emily frowned. "What do you mean?"

"You got my message, didn't you?"

"Yes, but I have to admit I was distracted and didn't give it much thought. What does people talking have to do with the PTO meeting?"

Patrick cleared his throat. "They're, um, talking about us. Word's gotten around that we went to Atlantic City together. And right after that, I was awarded the refunded deposit money."

"So? What does one have to do with the other?" Her eyes widened as understanding dawned. "You're kidding? People are saying I awarded the money because you slept with me?"

He nodded glumly. "Yeah, I've taken a bit of ribbing at school."

"That's harassment." Her eyes blazed. "And totally untrue."

"You know that and I know that, but some people have tiny little minds and assume the worst. It's not right, but I'm not the kind of guy to go running to the administration complaining of harassment. This is something that will die down on its own."

"And what if it doesn't?"

"I figure if we kind of keep our relationship out of the public eye, people will find something else to talk about."

"What do you mean, 'out of the public eye'? Does that mean you're ashamed to be seen with me? That you want me to sneak around? Or is this the big kiss-off?"

Patrick's chest constricted. "None of those things. I wouldn't be meeting you here, if I felt that way." Emily was the best thing to happen to him in a long time.

"Well, what do you mean, then?"

"I mean, let's not flaunt our relationship. Atlantic City was a terrific thing, but maybe not the smartest thing we could have done. Hindsight is always 20-20."

"Jason has a basketball game tonight. I wanted to ask you to go with me. Is that 'flaunting' our relationship?"

"Um, well, it's a school event."

"A high school event."

"But, see, the educational community in Elmwood is pretty tight. Word travels fast."

"I take it you won't be going with me, then?"

He shook his head miserably. "No. My career is very important to me. So is the field trip to Florida. I'd like to think we can make it all work, but it's not a good idea right now."

"Patrick, I know I told you in Atlantic City that I didn't expect anything from you. But I guess I wasn't being truthful with you or myself. I'd like to think I'm important to you, too." Her voice was low.

"You *are* important to me."

Her beautiful brown eyes clouded with disappointment. "Yes, I can tell."

Patrick had rarely felt as helpless as he did now. Only waiting for the paramedics to arrive after his brother's accident had been worse. He wanted the chance to allow things to develop with Emily, but he couldn't honestly say he was prepared to sacrifice his career if it came down to it.

"Have you talked to Jason?"

She nodded. "I just don't know what to do with the child. He admits what he did was wrong and he seems genuinely sorry for causing trouble for Nancy and Beau. But he's got an attitude now that I've never seen in him. Hard, disillusioned almost. I get the feeling he figured out we're more than just friends."

"You can't allow him to control your choice of, um, friends."

"Easy for you to say. A little gossip starts and you're ready to call it quits."

"I didn't say that. I just said we might want to be more circumspect."

"That's just a fancy way of saying we need to sneak around. You know what, Patrick, I deserve better than that." She stood, slinging her purse over her shoulder. "When you decide what we've got is important enough to fight for, you let me know."

Then she marched out the door.

CHAPTER SEVENTEEN

EMILY WAS ABLE to hold her head high and keep her back straight all the way to her van. She even managed to keep it together exiting the parking lot.

But halfway down the street, tears started to fall. She'd been such a fool to think having sex with Patrick wouldn't change things for her. As much as she tried to pretend to be a woman of the world, she still didn't give her heart or her body freely. And she was afraid she'd given both to Patrick.

Hurt welled up and threatened to swallow her whole. She kept making the same stupid mistakes over and over again. All she wanted was to be loved enough, important enough, to come first in a man's life. Not all the time, just some of the time. And, with both of her ex-husbands, she'd known she wasn't even in the top half of the list. That knowledge had eventually eaten away at her confidence and eroded her pride.

Shaking her head, Emily promised herself she wouldn't go down that road again. But then doubt reared its ugly head, citing dismal statistics for a woman remarrying after the age of forty. Maybe having a man who didn't put her at the top of his list was better than no man at all? Maybe she'd just chased off her last chance to be a part of a couple.

"No." Emily smacked the steering wheel. "I refuse to believe that."

Oh, great, now she was talking to herself.

Her cell rang. A spark of hope ignited. Patrick might have realized what he was throwing away.

Disappointment soon followed. The readout said it was a call from home.

She pulled into a parking lot, uneasy about driving and talking on the phone at the same time.

"Hello."

"Mom, you haven't forgotten my basketball game, have you?" Jason asked.

"No, I remember. Have you and the kids done your homework?"

"Yeah. When are you gonna be home? I need to get there early to warm up."

Emily could have sworn she heard the *Mission: Impossible* theme song dogging her trail. It seemed she was incessantly running from one place to the next, barely keeping up with kids' schedules, work and PTO. The two days in Atlantic City seemed like a lovely dream.

"I'll run through the drive-through at Burger Barn. You can eat in the car. Jeremy can watch Mark and Ryan while I run you to school."

"Okay. Mom?"

"What, hon?"

"You're never here anymore."

She sighed. "I know, Jase. It's probably going to be like this until I finish out the year as PTO president."

"Why don't you just quit?"

Why indeed. She'd been asking herself the same question. It would make life so much easier and nobody would be able to say she was giving Patrick preferential treatment. And Patrick's precious career would be safe.

But it had felt good to lead the meeting yesterday. It felt good to challenge herself. And she knew she was contributing something worthwhile to the kids' school.

"Because I made a commitment and I intend to see it through."

Even if it kills me

The next hour and a half was a whirl of driving, feeding children, getting the younger kids presentable, driving some more. By the time her rear hit the bleacher seat, Emily didn't think she had the energy to cheer.

But when she saw Jason on the court, her

energy returned. He was so focused, so gifted when he was on the basketball court. Her heart swelled with pride.

When he made the first three-pointer of the game, she whistled and clapped and stomped her feet. He glanced up in the stands and nodded slightly.

Jason's team was playing their archrival. The game was close and exciting. Emily got caught up in the play. But not so caught up that she didn't glance toward the double doors every once in a while, hoping Patrick had changed his mind and joined them.

The game was nearly over when she decided he wasn't coming. She tried to regain her earlier excitement, but the disappointment was hard to ignore. She *did* deserve better than what Patrick had offered her today.

A few minutes later, someone squeezed in between Emily and Mark. Emily turned, ready to greet Patrick. But it wasn't him.

"Hi," Linda Price said.

"Hi, Linda."

"I heard you went to Atlantic City."

Emily's stomach tightened. Had *everyone* heard? "Yes, I did."

"And found a deposit owed to Elmwood?"

"Yes, a small deposit."

"Good. I'm glad. I wanted to tell you about it, but, well, things are complicated. Tiffany had a bit of a gambling problem and I didn't want to be responsible for people finding out."

Gambling problem? Interesting.

"I didn't know," she murmured.

"Brad's been through enough already." She nodded toward the bleacher section where he sat with her children and his own. He stood up and cheered when Linda's son made a free throw.

Emily felt a pang of pure envy. Even though there were rumors circulating about their relationship, Brad apparently didn't mind supporting Linda. Putting her first over the gossips.

"I imagine it's been difficult for him."

Linda stood. "I better get back."

"Linda, one question. Was Tiffany active with the Elmwood Heart Association?"

Nodding, she said, "Very. Ever since her father's heart attack a few years back. She wanted to leave a legacy."

"Thanks."

Emily tried to keep her attention focused on the game, but she kept returning to the information she'd received about Tiffany. Her instincts told her the gambling problem was related to the missing PTO money. But, even if she could prove that, it probably wouldn't do the school any good.

The game went into overtime and Emily forced the issue from her mind. This was Jason's time to shine. And he did, contributing to the win.

Emily glanced once more at the empty doorway. No Patrick. She came to the painful realization that he wasn't who she'd thought he was. Or didn't return her feelings.

She managed to smile and make a fuss over Jason when she met him outside the locker room. But her heart was heavy. Saying goodbye to a dream was never easy. Especially a dream she hadn't realized she'd had.

PATRICK RELEASED A MOUSE in Arnold's enclosure. He always felt a twinge of remorse when he fed Arnold, but rationalized that he hadn't created the food chain. This time, he felt like the lowest life form on earth.

Or maybe just in Elmwood.

Glancing at his watch, he figured the basketball game had been over for an hour. He itched to pick up the phone and call Emily to see who'd won, but knew he didn't have the right.

He'd been thinking about the situation all evening long. His suggestion to Emily was perfectly rational. But he knew she was right, too. It was like his dilemma in feeding Arnold. He could rationalize all he wanted, but his gut told him it was wrong. Or maybe it was his conscience. The question was, why did he keep Arnold around when he presented such a moral dilemma?

Because the boa was his friend. Sad, but true.

Before sex, Emily had been his friend. Now, he wasn't sure where they stood. But he had a pretty good idea he was losing her friendship and maybe something a whole lot more precious.

So, if he could bear some discomfort for Arnold, why not Emily?

Because Emily scared the hell out of him. She was so much more than he'd expected. And she had the power to disrupt his life more than a thousand boa constrictors.

And that was without considering the complication represented by the package deal of four children.

Shaking his head, he called himself every kind of coward. Other men could commit to a ready-made family, why couldn't he? Maybe if Emily's children were younger, it wouldn't be so hard. But the mere thought of parenting the demon teen made him break out in a cold sweat.

EMILY WAS SURPRISED to see Patrick sitting in Principal Ross's office. She quietly took the chair next to him, waiting for the principal to finish her phone conversation.

"Hi," he whispered.

"Hi." She wasn't in the mood to talk to him. Her emotions were still too raw.

"Do you know why she called this meeting?" Emily shook her head.

"How was Jason's game?"

"Good. They won." *You'd know that if you were there.*

"I'm glad."

Principal Ross hung up the phone. "This won't take long. I just wanted to let you know I'm implementing new measures when dealing with the PTO fund. Any expenditure or releasing of funds over fifty dollars will require a second signature."

"I understand completely." Emily's mind whirled. Was it because of Tiffany or because of the rumors about her weekend in Atlantic City?

"I should have done this sooner, I admit. Patrick, I would also like you to start looking into alternatives to the Florida trip for your sixth graders. It's becoming apparent the trip won't happen this year. Perhaps next year."

Patrick frowned. "What if I raise the funds?"

"I don't see how you can through regular fundraising channels."

"I can't just give up. Those kids are depending on me."

The principal sighed. "I understand you don't

want to disappoint the children. Feel free to continue with car washes and bake sales. But I'd also like to see a contingency plan in place."

"But—"

"No buts." She turned to Emily. "And Ms. Patterson, though I applaud your dedication in ferreting out that deposit, your efforts would be better spent on damage control here. Possibly one of the local companies would be willing to coordinate a last-minute fund-raiser."

"I'll call and see."

"Thank you." Her tone held a note of dismissal.

As they rose, she said. "And by the way, there are no rules stating a teacher can't date a parent, if the parent doesn't have a child in the teacher's class. But I'd ask you to be circumspect."

Circumspect. The same word Patrick had used. Why didn't educators just come out and say what they meant? Sneak around. Because it wouldn't do for a teacher with an impeccable reputation to date the most unsuitable Ms. Patterson.

Emily raised her chin, the tune to "Harper Valley PTA" ringing in her ears. All she needed was a pair of Nancy Sinatra–style white go-go boots.

She shook off Patrick's hand on her elbow.

When they reached the front doors, he said, "Emily, wait."

Turning slowly, her heart banged in her chest as she looked at his dear face. Why did love have to hurt so bad? "We don't have anything to talk about."

"Yes, we do. Can I walk you to your car?"

Emily shrugged. "Suit yourself."

She was acutely aware of his presence as he walked beside her. His silence unnerved her.

When they reached her van, he said, "I didn't like the principal's suggestion any more than I liked it when it came out of my mouth. No wonder you think I'm a lowlife. I probably sounded like a condescending asshole."

"Yes, you did."

"And you're right, you deserve better than that."

"Tell me something I don't know."

"I missed you last night."

Her chest ached at the sincerity in his eyes. But she refused to be putty in this man's hands.

"You knew where to find me."

"I thought about you all evening. Wondered how the game was going, how Jason was doing."

"So why didn't you come?"

"Because a part of me still believes I might jeopardize my career."

"Obviously, you were right."

He stepped closer. His voice was low. "What if I decide I'm willing to take the risk?"

"And I'm just supposed to fall into your open arms?"

He grinned sheepishly. "Would that be so bad?"

"Believe it or not, I have pride, Patrick. And a life that's way too complicated already, without you blowing hot and cold."

"I know. That's another reason I stayed away. I can't make any promises about where our relationship will lead. But I'd like to give it a chance."

"Prove it."

"How?"

"Jason has another game tomorrow night. An away game. We can all go together."

He hesitated for a fraction of a second. "Great. What time do I pick you up?"

"As soon as I get home from work at five-fifteen. We'll need to grab takeout on the way."

"Sure, no problem."

"See you then." She unlocked her car.

"Em?"

He leaned over and kissed her quickly on the lips. His voice was husky when he said, "I really did miss you."

I missed you, too. But she wouldn't allow herself to say the words. Instead, she nodded and got in the car.

THE NEXT DAY, Patrick hurried home from school. He could grade a few tests, then it would be time to pick Emily up for Jason's basketball game.

It seemed like only moments later that his watch alarm went off. Good thing he'd set it, or he might have been late.

Shaking his head, he wondered how Emily did it. She would have to rush home from work and head out again almost immediately. No time to unwind, no time to attend to any business she couldn't finish at the office. And this was the second game of the week.

He whistled a tune as he entered the garage. It seemed odd to add the optional third bench seat to his SUV. He'd never needed it, until now. Still, it was kind of nice.

As soon as he pulled into the driveway at the Pattersons, they filed out of the house, Emily in the lead with Mark and Ryan jostling each other close behind. Jeremy played a handheld game. Jason carried a gym bag, his mouth set in a grim line. Pre-game nerves or an active dislike of his mother's boyfriend?

"Hop in," he said as Emily opened the passenger door. The boys piled into the back, a jumble of voices. The aroma of sweaty boy wafted through the interior of the SUV.

Patrick opened the windows a crack.

Ah, blessed fresh air.

Emily grinned wickedly, as if she knew exactly why he did it.

"Where to for supper? Burgers, Chinese, chicken?" he asked.

"Burgers," Mark and Ryan exclaimed.

"Chicken," mumbled Jeremy.

"Chinese." Of course Jason would have to give a dissenting opinion.

Patrick shrugged helplessly. "Emily?"

"We had burgers Tuesday. Chicken or Chinese, boys?"

"Chicken."

"Chinese."

She laughed. "Looks like it's split down the middle. What would you like, Patrick?"

"Oh, no, I'm not falling into that trap. You can be the tie-breaker."

"Smart man."

"I have my moments."

"Chinese is hard to eat on the go. Chicken, it is."

Patrick tried hard not to wince, thinking of greasy fingers all over his leather interior. It was only a car.

The drive-through turned out to be just as frustrating. Nobody could agree on anything. Patrick could see the driver behind him through the rearview mirror. His gestures indicated he was rapidly losing patience.

As was Patrick. "Okay, corporate decision. We'll get a bucket. Eat what you want. Don't eat if you don't like it. The choice is yours."

All four boys groaned in unison.

Emily eyed him. "Very decisive. You might get the hang of this yet."

The question was, did he want to get the hang of this?

Patrick honestly wished he knew the answer. Because right now, all he wanted was several aspirin and a shot of whiskey. And not necessarily in that order.

As he'd feared, none of the boys seemed to know how to use a napkin. *Don't sweat the small stuff,* he told himself.

Shaking his head, he thought he must really have it bad for Emily, because even the specter of ruined interior didn't dim his enjoyment in being with her.

When they got inside, Patrick attempted to appear casual while surreptitiously scanning the bleachers for anyone from Elmwood. Linda Price and Brad Bigelow were there, but so far no one else he knew. He exhaled slowly.

Emily chose prominent seats in the front row, half court. She threw a challenging glance over her shoulder.

He smiled and nodded, reminding himself never to make her angry again. The woman could be downright vindictive.

But sitting next to her on the bleachers, he thought there was nowhere else he'd rather be. Mark and Ryan entertained themselves by running up and down the stairs.

"Do you want them doing that?" he asked.

"They'll wear themselves out before the game starts."

Patrick turned to Jeremy, who was still playing his handheld game. He didn't think the kid had come up for air. "Whatcha playing, Jeremy?"

The boy kept on playing.

Patrick covered the game screen with his hand. "I said, what are you playing?"

The boy glanced up long enough to glare. Then he jerked the console away. "Mario Brothers." He was quickly immersed in the game again, and Patrick gave up on trying to connect with him.

When the teams came on the court and the game started, he was pleased to find it was fast-paced and Jason played well. The kid was a gifted player. But Patrick had as much fun watching Emily as the game. She radiated excitement. When Jason made a good play, she stomped, she clapped, she yelled his name. Being circumspect wasn't a part of her nature.

And he fell a little more in love with her.

Love? No way.

Maybe?

He shelved the internal debate for another time, when he could properly dissect each aspect and come to a solid conclusion.

Then Patrick did something he hadn't done in decades. He took a risk.

Wrapping his arm around Emily's shoulders, he pulled her close and kissed her temple. Right there in the middle of a crowded gym.

It was his attempt at showing Emily and Elmwood exactly how he felt about her.

CHAPTER EIGHTEEN

EMILY LEANED BACK in her chair and sighed with contentment. After veal parmesan, tortellini, a Mediterranean salad and cannoli for dessert, she couldn't eat another bite. "That was a fabulous meal, Patrick. I still can't believe you cooked that."

"I took an Italian cooking class." He shrugged. "I like to feed people."

It was Saturday night and Nancy had magnanimously offered to sit with the boys for the evening. She said it was because Beau was out of town, but Emily suspected her friend was trying to help the budding romance along.

She nodded toward the kitchen counter, where a large box of muffins resided. "I've noticed. For a smart guy, you sure are pretty dumb about buying muffins in large quantities. They go bad so quickly. Have Kat and Ari ever caught on?"

"No. Or if they have, they don't say."

"That's really sweet." Thinking back, she was

surprised to discover this facet to his personality. "You really *do* like to feed people. You brought pizza to my house that first night. And every time I've met you at the coffee bar, you've already bought me a cookie or a brownie."

He shrugged. "A quirk."

"Yes, I guess it is." But something nagged at Emily's memory. Something somehow significant with his feeding people. But try as she might, she couldn't pull up the elusive thought.

"You're sure you don't mind doing some brainstorming tonight?" he asked.

"Hey, I'll do just about anything to get out of cooking supper."

"Anything?" His tone was suggestive.

Emily's face grew warm. Had he been reading her mind? "I thought we were going to take this slow."

"Yes, I guess that's best. Not easy, but best." He stood and started to clear dishes.

She helped, wondering at her good luck in finding a man who not only cooked, but cleaned up afterward, as well. How in the world had he evaded marriage so far? She wouldn't voice the opinion, though. Didn't want him to think she was tossing around marriage hints. Though she did daydream about it from time to time. Interesting that in those daydreams, the kids were never present.

Maybe because Patrick was a different person around them. He was very good with Mark and Ryan, but he became stiff and uncomfortable with Jason.

"Glass of wine?" he asked.

"That would be nice."

He poured a glass of burgundy for each of them and led her into the den. She sat on the couch, while he removed a large folder from his desk. His Sea World file.

After handing her a legal pad and pen, he selected a pad for himself. "So far I've got down another bake sale and car wash. Any other ideas?"

"I called the local candy company and a school cancelled on a project, so I was able to grab it. We should have the kits within the next week or so."

"Excellent." He grinned.

"Um, Patrick?"

"Yes?"

"Even with these projects, I don't see how you can raise enough to do the Sea World trip. It's an ambitious idea during the best of circumstances."

"I'll *make* it work."

"Don't get me wrong. I admire your dedication. I'm just wondering if there might be something closer the kids might enjoy as much."

"Nothing is like that first trip to Sea World."

"How about the aquarium at Atlantic City? It's closer and I bet we might be able to get together some sort of package for a lot less money."

"They don't have whales or dolphins."

"But there are other things the kids would find interesting."

"Not as interesting as Sea World."

Emily chuckled. "You remind me of Jason when he's got an idea he's just positive he can make work by sheer force of will. That don't-confuse-me-with-facts attitude."

"Hey, I'm a scientist. I deal in facts every day. But this is different. This might change kids' lives."

"Are you sure you're not just a frustrated marine biologist?"

Pain flashed in his eyes. "No, Roger was going to be the marine biologist."

Emily scooted closer. "I'm sorry, I didn't realize. And here I stuck my size ten foot in my mouth."

He wrapped his arm around her shoulders. "You didn't know."

"How do you want to schedule the bake sale and car wash? I'd say let's have them at the same time, but we might be short on manpower."

"Do you think we could organize the bake sale for next Saturday if we started first thing Monday morning?"

"Normally, I'd say give the parents more notice. But we don't have a whole lot of time. Besides, I've always got a kid telling me at the last minute he needs cupcakes or cookies for school the next day. That's what they make bakeries for."

"I always send out the notices in plenty of time for my class." His tone was aggrieved.

"I don't doubt that. It's the way kids are. They always wait till the last minute to tell me."

"Okay, next Saturday it is. Then the car wash the Saturday after that?"

"If the weather stays warm like it has been, that should be fine. But what if we get a late snowstorm? The children will catch their death of cold."

"In April, the chances of snow are pretty slim. We'll just have to schedule the car wash anyway and hope for the best. I'll tell the kids not to get wet."

"So that's exactly what they'll do. Haven't you figured that out yet?"

"I guess I'm just now realizing what complex creatures children are."

Emily forgave him a little for not being there for Jason when he was a student in Patrick's class. She was now convinced he'd been cold out of ignorance, not anything personal.

"Do you want to go to Jason's game on Thursday?"

"Sure."

"I think he really enjoyed having you there, even though he wouldn't show it."

"Yeah, he did a pretty good job of covering. All those frowns and evil glares. He's more protective than most fathers."

Emily sighed. "You've got to understand that he's been the man of our house for a long time. It wasn't right for me to allow him to take on so much responsibility. But it was too big a relief to have someone to share the burden."

"He's still just a teen. Do you think he'll accept me eventually?"

She couldn't bring herself to lie to Patrick. Jason seemed more resistant to Patrick now than when they first started dating. "He's a hardheaded boy."

"I'm sure he'll come around."

Emily wished she could be half as sure. "Did I tell you what Linda Price told me? Tiffany Bigelow was very active in the Elmwood Heart Association. And they, coincidentally, had a hefty deposit with the casino gaming company for a fund-raiser. Do you think we could find anything online?"

"We don't know unless we try." He went over to his computer.

She followed, resting her hand on his shoulder.

It felt natural to share such a mundane moment. "What're you doing?"

"I'm looking to see if the heart association has any chat rooms."

"You think she might have said something there?"

"Anything's possible."

As it turned out, Tiffany had been active in the chat room. But her posts were a carbon copy of all she'd espoused for Elmwood. How she'd planned a fabulous fund-raising event sure to bring in big bucks in donations.

"I don't recall any publicity about a casino night for the heart association." He searched for the heart association Web site and went to their events page. "Nope. No mention of a casino night. I'd love to know what went wrong with the casino gaming company."

"I'd like to know why the heart association didn't ask for a refund—they had a credit balance. I wonder why our deposit was so much smaller than the heart association's?"

"Bigger event? We'll probably never know for sure."

It was on the tip of Emily's tongue to tell Patrick about Tiffany reportedly having a gambling problem. But she didn't want to be responsible for starting unfounded rumors about the dead woman. Her family had enough to deal with as it was.

"Want to go watch a movie? I've got the movie channel."

Emily was relieved at his suggestion. She wasn't intentionally keeping something from him. She just wasn't volunteering all the information she'd received. "Sounds like a good idea. I've still got a couple more hours until I turn into a pumpkin."

"Too bad the kids aren't spending the night at Nancy's house."

She wrapped her arms around his shoulders and kissed the top of his head. "Jason pretty much ruined that. Besides, I wanted to talk to you about what happened in Atlantic City."

"That we slept together?"

"Yes. I want you to know I don't sleep around. When I'm with a man, it's because I care about him very much."

"I care about you, too."

"Did you see Jason's expression when we returned to Nancy's house? It was as if he knew we'd made love. And that I'd somehow disappointed him."

"Jason's just at that age. He'd probably like to think he was conceived by immaculate conception."

"That's part of it. But there's more. I've put that child through so much. Although he was only nine at the time, he had a front row seat to the train wreck that was my marriage to Larry. It breaks my heart to think of how it's affected him. I think that's why he's so protective."

"You're too hard on yourself. Other kids have step-parents move in and out of their lives and they adjust."

"You don't understand. I was barely functional the first few months after Larry left. Ryan was just a baby and it was all I could do to care for him. Jason pretty much took over with Jeremy and Mark."

"That was an awful lot of responsibility for such a little guy. I'm glad you told me. It helps me understand Jason better. And it means you trusted me enough to tell me."

"Mostly, I told you so you'd understand why I want to slow things down between us. I want the boys to have time to adjust to the idea of you being in my life before we get hot and heavy. And I think it's important for me to have time to adjust, too. Instead of jumping in with both feet like I did with Larry."

Patrick stood and pulled her into his arms. "Em, I'm not saying it will be easy to take it slow, particularly when I remember how good we were together in Atlantic City. But if it's important to you, then it's important to me."

She wrapped her arms around his waist and rested her head against his shoulder. Could it be that she'd finally found a man who put her feelings first?

"It won't be easy for me, either, Patrick. Self-control isn't one of my strong points. And what we shared in Atlantic City was…special."

Her pulse pounded as she remembered their lovemaking. Fanning herself, she knew she was in dangerous territory. Even thinking of making love with Patrick seemed to be out of bounds.

He tipped her chin up with his finger. "Em, I meant what I said earlier. I really care about you."

"I know you do." *But can't you care about my sons, too? Even just a little?*

He kissed her, his tenderness bringing tears to her eyes.

When the kiss intensified, Emily pulled back, smiling sadly. "Now's not the time to test my self-control."

"I'm willing to prove myself to you."

Nodding, Emily didn't trust herself to speak. She didn't think he had any idea how desperately she wanted him to do just that, but couldn't allow herself to hope. Only time would tell whether he cared enough to try to reach her children.

Patrick led her to the family room, sitting right next to her on the couch, his arm around her, his thigh warm next to hers.

Sighing, she decided she could very happily stay exactly where she was for the rest of her life. When he kissed her, she felt as if she'd always loved this man.

That's when Emily knew she was in way over her head. Whether they were having sex or not, she loved Patrick.

EMILY WAS RESTLESS, her adrenaline rush from the close basketball game nowhere near abating. Even after Jason's team won. As promised, Patrick had attended and cheered nearly as loudly as she did. He'd joked around with Mark and Ryan and even managed to get Jeremy to smile.

After Patrick had dropped them off, she sent the younger boys to bed and realized she had some time for herself.

Emily sat down in front of her computer. Chat rooms. She wondered if maybe there was a chat room for people with gambling problems. The search engine turned up a long list of sites. How to narrow it down? She'd try the ones geared toward women first.

Two hours later, she'd scanned the chat logs for the women's sites starting a couple months before

Tiffany's death. She didn't see anything that remotely looked like Tiffany might have posted.

Stretching, Emily shut down her computer. This was like searching for a needle in a haystack.

Why she bothered, she didn't know. Probably all the unanswered questions. She needed answers, needed to understand the dead woman. Maybe Patrick was right. Emily had a more scientific brain than she'd ever known.

PATRICK SET UP the last rectangular table outside the local discount store. "Kat, would you spread this out?" He handed her a festive paper cloth.

"Yes, Mr. Stevens."

"Ari, you can help me set out the baked goods."

"Cool."

It took Ari a lot longer than most kids, but he was very conscientious. The fierce determination on his face underscored his physical struggle to maneuver his hands without dropping anything.

Patrick suppressed his natural instinct to simply do it himself, instead allowing Ari to take as long as necessary. He knew it was good for the boy to exercise his motor skills and feel he was contributing.

"Here's the sign you asked me to make." Kat held a poster board aloft for his inspection.

"Absolutely perfect. You did an excellent job, Kat."

She flushed with pride.

He handed her a roll of masking tape. "Why don't you tape it to the front of the table, so everyone will know that this is a fund-raiser."

Patrick set out the cash box and counted the money for a second time, noting the amount on a pad of paper. When he glanced up, his world took on the cheerful glow of Emily's smile as she walked across the parking lot. She carried a cardboard box and each of the boys carried a bag, even Jason.

"Hello, Kat, Ari."

"Hello, Ms. Patterson."

"I'm glad to see you, but your shift isn't until noon." Patrick kissed Emily quickly on the cheek. "And you already brought by chocolate chip cookies yesterday."

"The boys were in the mood to bake last night. They did brownies and more cookies. I baked a few loaves of bread."

"You bake bread?" He tried not to allow his shock to show, but he must have failed.

She laughed. "It's one of my few talents in the kitchen. And then Nancy sent one of her red velvet cakes and a couple of pies."

He took the box from her. "I'm impressed. Thanks."

"We're also volunteering our services for the day. Nancy's going to stop by later to pick up Mark and Ryan. Jeremy, Jason and I will help."

"I hope we get enough traffic to keep you busy. There are a couple more students scheduled for the 11:00 a.m. shift."

"Oh, you leave that to me. If there's one thing I know, it's how to drum up business. Now, Jason has a real knack with numbers, so if you'd like, he can be your cashier. Jeremy and I will start sending people in this direction. That'll free you, Kat and Ari to serve customers."

Patrick marveled at her military precision. "You never cease to surprise me."

"I know. Isn't it fun?" She winked at him.

He threw back his head and laughed. "Yes, it certainly is." For the first time in years, he felt like he was actually a participant in life, not just observing. And it felt awfully good.

He admired everything about Emily as he watched her work the crowd of Saturday shoppers. She was so open and friendly, very few people refused her plea to patronize the bake sale. They also accepted flyers she'd printed to publicize the car wash.

And, surprisingly, Jeremy was just as good a salesman as his mother. His earnest expression seemed to soften the hardest heart. And when the other children from Patrick's class arrived to help, he took them under his wing.

Soon, Patrick was too busy to watch Emily. He and Kat and Ari served a steady stream of customers while Jason made change with amazing agility.

When they ran out of baked goods by two o'clock that afternoon, Patrick felt as if he'd been run over by a steamroller. "Sorry, folks, it looks like we're all out," he said to the customers lined up.

One woman stepped up to the table and placed a couple of dollar bills in the donation jar, which was already brimming with folding money and change. Several other people followed suit. One gentleman put a twenty-dollar bill in the jar and didn't take any change.

Patrick's heart swelled at the goodness he'd observed today. People really cared.

Emily approached, her smile still as bright as it had been this morning. "Jeremy says we sold out."

"We sure did. I owe it all to you." He hugged her quickly.

"We were glad to help."

"That's it, Jason. We're done." Patrick could hardly believe the stack of cash in the box. None of their fund-raising efforts had been nearly this successful. He hesitated, unsure whether he wanted the unpredictable teen in charge of that much cash. But then he realized Jason had been handling the money for hours and hadn't done anything the least bit suspicious.

Jason held his gaze, his chin slightly raised, as if he sensed Patrick's indecision. "Do you want me to count it?"

Patrick took a deep breath and decided to trust Emily's son. "Yes, Jason. If you want to count the till, we'll clean up."

CHAPTER NINETEEN

JASON FINISHED COUNTING the bills, carefully separating the new, crunchy bills that sometimes stuck together. He wanted to make sure he got it right. Then came the change.

"Three hundred sixty-seven dollars and thirty-five cents."

Patrick clapped him on the shoulder. "All right. That's awesome."

"Yeah, that's way more than I figured when I got here this morning."

"You did a good job handling the money. I'm impressed."

Jason shrugged, trying not to let Patrick's praise mean much. "I'm good at math."

"I appreciated your help." Patrick glanced at Jason's mom, and the expression in his eyes made Jason swallow hard. The guy had fallen hard for Mom.

And Jason wasn't as sure as before whether it was a bad thing. Today had been kind of, well, okay. Almost like a real family pitching in together.

Maybe he'd been wrong about the guy. Maybe Patrick really did love Mom and would be good to her.

Shaking his head, he wondered if that was how Larry-the-jerk had started out. The early times were kind of fuzzy to Jason. The end was crystal-clear, though. Lots of yelling and Mom crying. Then, it was just the five of them.

Still, he couldn't help but long for a real family with a mom *and* a dad.

PATRICK TOOK the Pattersons out to supper that night to celebrate their bake sale victory. Emily was amazed that a man with no children had managed to pick the most popular hangout for kids age two to seventeen. Not only was there pizza, there were games galore and prizes. Even pinball and video games to entertain the teens too cool to hang out with their families.

Emily propped her chin on her hand. "Okay, how did you know this was our favorite place to eat?"

"It's that science geek thing again." He grinned. "I overhear lots of kids at school talking about Chuckee's like it's the Holy Grail. I asked a couple of teachers this week, too."

"Ah, so this was premeditated?"

"I kind of hoped I could persuade you to join me. And maybe get to know your boys a little better. I'd like to see things between us work out."

"That's really sweet." She sipped her soft drink. "There's no better way to a woman's heart than through her children."

"My own sterling qualities aren't enough, huh?"

"Oh, they weigh heavily in your favor. But I couldn't get serious with someone who wasn't good to my children. You and Jason got off to a rough start, but you're really trying to understand him. And I think it's working. He seems to be thawing a little."

"Yeah, he did a good job today. All the kids did a good job."

"Ari and Kat seemed to be enjoying themselves, too. They've both come a long way since that first day I met them. You know, I wonder if maybe it's a matter of having your attention. You really listen to those kids."

"I try. Their parents are great. But they both work two jobs to make ends meet. That doesn't leave a whole lot of time and energy for doing stuff with Kat and Ari."

Emily reached across the table and touched his cheek. "You're an incredible man."

Patrick's face darkened with embarrassment, but he cupped her hand in his. "And you are an extraordinary woman, Emily." For a moment, she thought he was going to say something else, like maybe verbalize the affection shining in his eyes.

Instead, he kissed her palm and placed it on the table.

"Too much PDA? What, is there someone here we know?" Emily glanced around the room, waving at Linda Price when their eyes met.

"Just about the whole place." He nodded to another couple dining with a boy and a girl. "I've decided I don't care what other people think. We're not doing anything wrong. And now that Principal Ross has implemented her checks and balances for funding, no one can say I coerced you into giving me funding."

The door opened and Nancy, Beau and Ana entered. They smiled and waved, making their way through the crowd of milling children.

"Hey, you two," Beau said.

"Hi." Nancy leaned down and hugged Emily. "How'd the bake sale go?"

"Terrific." Emily managed to smile in welcome, even though she wanted a few moments alone with Patrick. "We raised almost four hundred dollars. Your pies were a big hit. And the red velvet cake went almost immediately."

"Good, an old Southern specialty of mine."

Emily touched Ana's shoulder. "The boys are over playing games, if you want to go find them."

Ana beamed. She was almost like a little sister to them, though she'd sworn at one time or another to marry each boy when she grew up.

"Please, join us?" Patrick asked.

Emily wanted to kick him in the shin, but she also couldn't help being grateful he was nice to her friends. Larry had never wanted her to have friends, and, as a consequence, he was rude until he drove most of them away.

Nancy moved toward the booth, but Beau gently grasped her arm. "Thanks for the invite, but we're gonna find our own table." He glanced meaningfully at Nancy and nodded in their direction. He might have as well as come out and said in pig Latin, *eave-lay em-thay alone-ay*. His sensitivity to their budding romance warmed her heart, though. He was quite a guy. Nearly as terrific as Patrick.

Understanding sparked in Nancy's eyes. "Oh, yes." She laughed. "I see a table way over on the other side of the room. We'll see you guys later. Let's tell Ana where we'll be."

After Nancy and Beau disappeared into the throng of children and parents, Patrick said, "Tactful. I like them."

Emily chuckled. "I get the feeling they like you, too."

They had a whole thirty seconds to themselves before Ryan ran up to the table. "Mom, the skeet ball game ate my money," he complained.

Raising an eyebrow, she commented, "Did it eat your money, or did you spend it all and not get enough tickets for a prize?"

He shifted from foot to foot. "It's not fair, Mom. Jeremy and Jason won't help me and Mark has like a thousand tickets."

"You need some help with skeet ball, buddy?" Patrick asked.

Ryan nodded. "Will you help?"

"Sure thing. I'll have you know I was the skeet ball champion of my neighborhood growing up."

"Cool. Come on."

Emily's eyes misted as she watched her son lead Patrick by the hand. When they reached the skeet ball machine, Patrick held Ryan's arm as he demonstrated throwing the ball and following through. Like a real dad. Then he encouraged Ryan to try on his own. Just like a real dad.

Ryan frowned in concentration, pitched the ball and actually scored. He jumped up and down as the machine spewed out tickets.

Ryan beamed up at Patrick. The moment was so precious, she wanted to treasure it always. And cry for the simple memories like these the boys would never have with their own fathers.

But she managed a warm smile for Patrick when he returned to the table.

"Ryan went to get his prize," he said.

"That was very kind of you."

He shrugged and grinned. "No problem. I still like to play games as much as the next kid."

She reached across the table and grasped his hand. "I appreciate it anyway."

He met her gaze. "I'd do just about anything for you, Em. Besides, he's a great kid."

In that moment, Emily wondered if maybe dreams did come true. Wondered if maybe she'd finally met the right man.

Patrick cleared his throat. "I'm going to my folks' house the weekend after the car wash. It's just a regular visit, not the kind where I give my parents a breather from care taking. I was, um, wondering if you'd come with me. I'd like you to meet Roger."

Knowing his history with Roger and how protective Patrick was of his younger brother, Emily felt honored by his request. She squeezed his hand. Her voice was husky when she said, "I'd love to."

EMILY KNOCKED on Jason's bedroom door.

"Come in." His reply was muffled, just barely discernible.

Opening the door, she stepped into his room. It looked like a war zone, as usual. She didn't have the heart to get on his case about it. Not only had he been super helpful at the bake sale, he seemed to be making a real effort to get along with Patrick.

He looked up from reading a book. Yet another surprise. Although it was *Manga* and she had a hard time understanding the appeal, it was still a book, with a beginning, middle and end.

"Jase, I wanted to discuss something with you."

He eyed her warily. His body language screamed, "I didn't do it."

"It's nothing wrong. It's actually something right."

His shoulders relaxed. "What?"

"I've noticed you've been making an effort to get along with Patrick and I appreciate it." She smoothed a wrinkle in his bedspread. "He's… special to me."

"Um, okay."

"And I wanted to tell you before I told the other boys. He's asked me to go to his hometown with him the weekend after the car wash. I'd be meeting his parents and his brother, who is severely handicapped."

"Oh."

"Usually when an adult meets a person's

family, that means the relationship is getting pretty serious. How do you feel about that?"

Jason hesitated. "I'm still not his number one fan, but he seems to treat you good. I guess I can live with it."

"That's all I ask, Jase. For you to give him a chance."

"But if he hurts you, the guy is history."

"I really believe he's one of the good guys. I didn't think there were any more of them out there—I always figured Nancy got the last one when she found Beau."

"Yeah, Beau's okay."

"That's the second part. Nancy and Beau have agreed to have you boys stay at their house again that weekend. I can't consider it unless you promise, I mean *promise*, you will be on your very best behavior. No parties, no sneaking out. Totally on the straight and narrow."

Jason grinned. "No problem, Mom. I doubt I could get past Mr. Stanton a second time. He's one scary dude when he's mad."

"Then don't make him mad. Promise me?"

"I promise."

"Good." She leaned over and kissed him on the top of the head, just as she'd done when he was a little boy. "I love you."

"Yeah, um, me, too." He picked up his book

and resumed reading. Or at least gave the impression of reading.

Emily smiled and rose from the bed. "Don't stay up too late, okay?"

He grunted in response.

Glancing at her watch, she found herself with a few spare minutes on her hands. She went downstairs, turned on the computer and sat down on the office chair.

She knew it was probably a wasted effort, but she'd started scanning gambling addiction chat rooms, hoping she'd find some clue or explanation to what Tiffany Bigelow had done with the PTO money.

An hour later, her eyes started to burn and she knew it was a lost cause. Tiffany could have logged on under any name. Or even gone to other Web sites.

"Mom?"

Emily swiveled in the chair. "What, Jeremy?"

"You need to sign off on my agenda."

"Bring it here."

She glanced through the spiral-bound notebook the junior high used to keep kids on track. With Jeremy, that was rarely a problem. Except this time. "It looks like you're missing a social studies assignment. Why?"

Jeremy frowned. "It's a stupid assignment.

We're supposed to break these dumb old codes, like they did in World War II."

"Sounds kind of fun to me. Like being a spy."

"Well, yeah, if they used something halfway challenging. But the stuff they use is so lame a two-year-old could figure it out."

Emily hid a smile behind her hand. Sometimes understanding her gifted son was almost as hard as understanding Jason. Boredom was the only common denominator in their rebelliousness. But she didn't want Jeremy to think he could get away with blowing off his homework just because he was too smart for it. "Show me the assignment."

He flipped through his binder and handed her the photocopied page. She glanced at the instructions and understood his frustration. It looked more geared to a fourth-grade class than seventh-graders. "You're right. It is pretty lame. But the idea is cool. Tell you what, why don't you rip right through this silly stuff, then for fun you can develop your own code. One so tough, the Germans would have never figured it out."

He seemed to weigh her suggestion. She held her breath, hoping he wouldn't think her idea was as totally lame as the school assignment.

Slowly, he smiled. His eyes lit with challenge. "Awesome. I could figure out one *nobody* could ever crack."

"I'm sure you can. Now, give me a hug and finish up your homework. You need to get to bed pretty soon."

Flinging his arms around her neck, he squeezed tight, then was gone, her baby/soon-to-be teen.

ON SATURDAY, Patrick arrived early at the gas station to set up. The air was chilly, but the weatherman had predicted a bright spring day. Soon, the sun would chase away the chill.

He hummed as he unloaded boxes of towels, car washing detergent and window cleaner. Try as he might, he found it difficult to concentrate. Instead, images of Emily flashed through his brain. Emily sharing a joke with one of her boys. Emily naked, wearing only a slow, seductive smile. Emily arguing a point with him until he had to see things her way.

They'd had supper together almost every night this week. Either she'd invited him over and cooked for him or he'd brought takeout to her house. Last night, he'd invited the Pattersons over for a spaghetti supper at his apartment. On the whole, it had gone very well. The two younger boys were captivated by Hairy S. Truman, Newt and Arnold—his Republican convention as Emily referred to them. Jeremy had fiddled with the telescope Patrick kept on the balcony. Even

Jason seemed to have mellowed, giving the thumbs-up on Patrick's cable selection.

To top off the evening, Emily had told him she had Beau and Nancy lined up to babysit the weekend after next and Jason had agreed to behave himself. The trip to meet the Stevens family was a done deal.

Patrick smiled when he thought of his mom and dad meeting Emily. They would love her as much as he did. And Roger would respond to her warm, open nature. Somehow he knew Emily wouldn't be the type to freak out or freeze when she met Roger. Maybe it was because she was so levelheaded about her own children's foibles.

Hearing another vehicle pull up, he turned to see Emily's van. Contentment stole over him as he waited for her to herd the kids out of the car. She carried a large box of doughnuts and a thermos he presumed contained coffee.

"Good morning." Nodding toward the card table he'd erected, he said, "You can set the food over there. Great minds think alike."

She chuckled. "I should have known you'd bring food. Sometimes you've got to allow someone else to feed the world."

"What? And miss out on all the fun?"

She placed the doughnuts and thermos on the table.

He stepped up behind her and slid his arms around her waist, nuzzling her neck. "I missed you."

"You just saw me last night."

"Way too long to go without you."

Ryan tapped his elbow. "Can I have a doughnut, Mr. Stevens?"

"Sure thing. You'll need some energy to wash all the dirty cars that'll be coming through here."

The rest of the boys converged on the snack table.

Eyes bleary, Jason raised his hand in acknowledgment. "Too early," he croaked.

Emily leaned closer and murmured, "He doesn't wake up before noon on a Saturday if he can help it."

"I did the same thing when I was a teen."

"What can I help you with?"

"I'll hook up the garden hoses to the faucets." He studied the layout of the parking lot in relation to available water. "Then if you want to fill the buckets with detergent and water?"

"You got it."

They worked companionably in silence. Mark and Ryan played chase around the back of the station. With no entrance near there, it was the ideal way for them to blow off steam.

After a doughnut and a cup of coffee, Jason

seemed to revive a bit. He joined Patrick setting up the drying station. "Some of the kids from school are going to come help out. I hope that's okay?"

Patrick paused. Was this an olive branch? "I think that's great. We can use all the help we can get. Maybe you and your friends can organize the small kids from Elmwood."

"Sure."

"That'd be a big help." He clapped Jason on the shoulder. The boy tensed for a moment, then relaxed. He even managed a small smile. "No problem." Jason turned to walk away, but stopped. "Mr. Stevens?"

"Yes?"

Jason glanced around, as if he didn't want to be overheard. His mom and the other boys were over by the table. His voice was low. "You really like my mom, don't you? You're not just messing with her?"

Patrick had to respect him for still trying to protect his mother. "I care a great deal for your mother. I'd never mess with her or intentionally hurt her."

Jason nodded, apparently satisfied. He turned and walked away, whistling a tune.

Student and parent volunteers from Elmwood started arriving, and of course all the vehicles they arrived in had to be washed—the resulting donations were way above the cost of a car wash.

Patrick waved to Ari and Kat's father as he dropped them off in his old station wagon. He was probably on his way to his second or third job.

Everyone was assigned a station, Ari and Kat drying, along with Mark, Ryan and Jeremy.

"Hey, Jason, you want to take over at the hose?" he called.

Jason nodded.

Patrick and one of the fathers manned the sponges and buckets. Emily joined them.

It was intricately timed chaos, but it seemed to work. Cars, SUVs and trucks lined the parking lot and snaked into the street. Everyone was patient. No mean feat on an early Saturday morning.

At lunchtime, Patrick ordered pizza and they ate in shifts. Jason's friends from high school appeared as if by magic, surely drawn by the aroma of food.

"Mr. Stevens, do you think we might want to separate into two drying stations now that we have more volunteers?" Jason asked.

"Excellent suggestion. That seems to be where the bottle neck is. Maybe if you can have a few high school kids and a few Elmwood kids on each team?"

Jason nodded. "Yeah. That's kind of what I figured."

He turned to go, but Patrick grasped his arm. "Hey, Jason, thanks for helping out. It, um, really means a lot."

"Sure. No big deal." But the hunger in Jason's eyes told him it *was* a big deal. The kid was starving for approval. Why hadn't he noticed that before?

"Well, thanks." He released Jason's arm.

Patrick washed vehicles by rote for the next few minutes while he pondered the mystery that was Emily's oldest son. Was he seeing Jason differently because the kid was finally letting down his guard? Or because Patrick was finally willing to set aside his biases and accept the child, difficulties and all?

While he wanted to think he was pretty adept at judging character, he had to admit he might have had a blind spot where Jason was concerned. The thought troubled him.

"Hey, why the frown?" Emily playfully flicked sudsy water on the front of his T-shirt.

"Just thinking." He flicked water at her.

She laughed. "Good thing it turned out to be warm today. Almost swimsuit weather."

His imagination went wild at the thought of Emily in a string bikini, one of those crocheted numbers that left very little to the imagination.

She leaned close and whispered in his ear, "Hold that thought. I like it when you look as if you want to take me to bed for a week."

Tucking a strand of hair behind her ear, he said, "Sometimes that's all I seem to think about."

She sighed. "Me, too. I have the feeling I'm not going to be able to keep my hands off you much longer."

Shouts and laughter invaded his lust-inflamed brain. He glanced up to see what all the commotion was about.

It looked as if the drying teams were having a friendly competition. To see who could get the other team the wettest. A fifth-grade girl had commandeered a bucket, took a soapy sponge and threw it at one of the teens, nailing the guy between the shoulder blades. Which resulted in the teen grabbing a sponge from the wash team and brandishing it like a weapon. The girl giggled and tried to dash out of range, but the teen's aim was true.

Patrick smiled at the horseplay. It was a joy to watch.

He glanced at Emily and she grinned.

A cry of outrage made them turn. The teen who had thrown the sponge was drenched from the chest down. A boy who appeared to be in about third grade held an empty bucket aloft.

The teen shouted, "Hey, Patterson, a little help here?"

"You got it, dude." Laughing, Jason turned on the hose and advanced on the boy. "You're really going to pay for that."

The boy stuck out his tongue and beat a hasty retreat.

But not hasty enough.

Jason twisted the nozzle and nailed the kid in the rear end.

Cheers erupted from the high school kids.

The boy laughed. "You barely got me."

"Oh, yeah?" Jason ran toward the boy, the hose uncoiling as he went.

The boy screamed in mock terror, turned and ran.

Jason pursued. It was all in good fun.

Until the boy swerved unexpectedly into the street, where a car pulled out to pass the line of vehicles snaking into the car wash.

Patrick shouted a warning. Time slowed to a crawl. He heard the screeching of tires and saw the child's glee turn to fear.

CHAPTER TWENTY

OUT OF THE CORNER of his eye, Patrick saw Jason drop the hose. It took on a life of its own, whipping and undulating, spraying randomly across the parking lot.

He heard Emily's cry of terror.

Patrick grabbed his cell phone and dialed 911. Sweat beaded his upper lip as he told the operator they needed an ambulance at the corner of Cedar and Main Street.

"Is the boy conscious?"

"I don't know." His chest grew tight. "Other adults are administering aid." He jogged to the curb, where Emily spoke soothingly to the boy.

A man asked the boy questions Patrick assumed were meant to assess his medical condition.

"Paramedics are on the way," Patrick said, his voice sounding thick and unnatural. "I've got the 911 operator on the line, wanting to know about his condition."

"I'm a nurse," the man said. "I'll talk to her."

Patrick handed him the cell phone. Although he was trained in CPR, he was relieved to have a professional take charge.

Patrick rested his hand on Emily's shoulder as she knelt by the child.

She glanced up. "Do you have a blanket or dry towels? Anything to keep him warm? He's shivering."

"I keep a blanket in the back of the SUV for emergencies." He sprinted to his Lexus and removed an old afghan. Returning, he handed the blanket to Emily. "Here you go."

Emily shook out the folds and gently spread it over the boy, who was struggling to get up.

A few soothing words from Emily convinced him to lie still. She had that effect on people. Especially children. And lonely science geeks.

Glancing at the pale boy, Patrick felt helpless. "Is there anything else I can do to help?"

"Check the driver," the nurse replied. "He looks like he's in shock."

Patrick walked around the car. The door was open, the engine still idling. An older gentleman sat on the sidewalk, mumbling, "I never saw him."

After switching off the ignition, Patrick went to the man. He squatted next to him. The remorse in the driver's eyes was almost Patrick's undoing. He patted the man's thin shoulder. "It was an accident. You didn't mean to."

Patrick swallowed hard. His eyes burned. Oh, how he would have loved it if someone had said those words to him twenty-five years ago. But they hadn't. He'd stood off to the side, trying to make himself inconspicuous, so no one would see the guilt written all over his face.

And today, the old man had to deal with similar guilt. Tears trickled down his face. His shoulders started to shake.

Patrick patted his arm. "What's your name?"

"Leonard."

"Leonard, the little boy is going to be okay. There's a nurse and some nice people helping him. And the paramedics are on the way."

The paramedics are on the way. The phrase echoed through his mind. They'd said the same thing when Roger had almost drowned. But it had seemed like forever until they got there.

Patrick's mouth went dry. He had to get himself together. "You're shivering. I'll go find a blanket."

The man grasped Patrick's arm. "Don't go."

Panic tightened his chest. He had to get out of there or something bad would happen. "I'll be back." He glanced wildly around. He gestured toward one of the onlookers, a kindly looking middle-aged woman. "Ma'am, would you sit with him until I come back with a blanket?"

"Of course." She sat down next to the gentleman on the curb.

"His name is Leonard."

She grasped the man's hand. "Leonard, everything is going to be okay."

Patrick rose on stiff legs. His knees felt as if they might give under his weight. He glanced at the boy, lying so still on the street.

But instead of that injured child, he saw Roger, wet and nearly lifeless. Pale and still, lips blue. Patrick gazed at the boy, then the car. He'd had something important to do. What was it?

Then his gaze stopped on Leonard.

Blanket.

He walked toward his car, but it wavered, seemed to grow more distant with each step he took.

Someone grabbed his arm. He forced himself to focus on the face. Jason.

Jason's mouth moved and words came out, but Patrick couldn't seem to string them together in a coherent sentence. So, he concentrated on Jason's eyes. The raw grief and guilt made him recoil. It ignited a response in Patrick so deep and primal it scared him.

He tried to shake off Jason's hand, but the boy only hung on harder.

Staggering, he wrenched his arm free. "What the hell did you think you were doing?"

Jason's eyes widened. "I didn't mean to. It was an accident." The unspoken question mark at the end of his words begged for Patrick to utter the same platitudes he'd given Leonard. But there would be no forgiveness for this child who thought pranks were harmless and didn't have consequences.

Images flashed through Patrick's brain. The mousetrap, the overflowing toilet, the ruined dance, an injured boy who would never be the same again. All because of a prank that proved to be far from harmless.

Poison boiled in Patrick's blood, demanding release. Demanding penance. "If that boy dies, it will be your fault."

The rational part of Patrick's mind told him the boy wouldn't die. The rational part urged him to wrap Jason in a bear hug and comfort him. But the sight of the quiet, injured child wouldn't allow him to listen to reason. Guilt and vengeance merged into one. He enunciated clearly. "Don't speak to me. Don't touch me. If there was a just God, you would be lying there instead of that child."

Jason reeled. A few feet away, he vomited in the bushes.

Bile rose in Patrick's throat. If only it were that easy to get rid of the guilt. He knew from experience Jason could never purge himself of his responsibility.

Patrick turned. His gaze locked with Emily's. Her mouth made an O of surprise. Her eyes widened with shock. He jogged to his car, fumbling in his pocket for his keys. He was vaguely aware of Emily rising. He ignored her as he guided his SUV out of the parking lot, tires screeching. Escape was the only thing that mattered. It was all he'd wanted to do for the past twenty-five years. Escape from the self-hatred.

JASON STARED UP at the ceiling, ignoring the tap on his door.

"Jason, may I come in?"

"Go away."

"Honey, you've got to eat something."

A hysterical laugh built in his chest. No, he didn't have to eat. He'd proven that over the past eight hours. "Later, Mom. I'm not hungry."

He held his breath, hoping she wouldn't come in and try to give him a pep talk. Nothing she said could make a difference. He kept replaying the whole thing in his mind, wishing he could concentrate hard enough to change the outcome. But no matter how hard he focused, no matter how much he prayed, it didn't change. Tyler Jones was still in ICU with a head injury and a broken leg. They didn't know yet whether he'd have brain damage.

If there was a just God, you would be lying there instead of that child.

Oh, how Jason wished he could trade places with Tyler. The physical pain couldn't be as bad as what Jason was experiencing. He knew he was to blame. He knew he was the biggest screw-up ever to walk the planet. And was pretty sure no one could love someone who had done something as horrible as he'd done.

Mr. Stevens's tirade had pretty much clinched the deal in Jason's mind.

His gut ached as he remembered the hatred gleaming in the man's eyes. After Mr. Stevens had left, his mom had told him it was just an accident. She'd acted all concerned about Jason. But it was only a matter of time before she realized what a monster her son was and gave up on him like everyone else.

He closed his eyes, but all he saw was the boy lying in the street, his scalp covered in blood. Opening his eyes, Jason sat up as if spring-loaded. If he didn't do something, it felt like he would explode.

Climbing out his window, he lowered himself

to the ground. A jog would help. Jason started running, not caring where he headed. Because it really didn't matter anymore.

PATRICK REPLACED the receiver without saying goodbye. When the hospital cited privacy laws and wouldn't release any information on the Jones boy, he'd called the mother of one of his students. The woman knew everyone in town and made it a point to ferret out gossip the minute it hit the grapevine. And she hadn't let him down.

Tyler Jones was in a coma.

Patrick went to his bedroom and removed his duffel bag from the closet, his motions jerky. He had to get out of there. Had to escape before regret swallowed him whole, then spit out his brittle, decaying bones. He shoved a couple of shirts and two pair of jeans in the bag.

He turned off the light and went to the den, making sure his Republican convention of pets had enough food to last them several days.

Against his will, a smile twitched at his lips. He would miss Emily and her irreverent sense of humor. Patrick picked up the handset. He should call her before he left, make everything right with Jason. But how could he when he knew one screw-up would haunt the boy for the rest of his life?

Shaking his head, he knew there was really nothing he could say. He didn't have the wisdom to save Jason from the hell he knew the boy would endure. And it would destroy him to watch history repeat itself.

EMILY DISCOVERED Jason was missing around midnight. She panicked, imagining worst-case scenarios. Although he hadn't confided in her beyond saying he was sorry the Jones boy was injured, Emily could tell Jason was hurting inside. She'd seen the horror, then the sad acceptance on his face when Patrick said those awful things to him.

She'd tried to wrap him in a hug, protect him as only a mother could, but he hadn't allowed her that luxury.

What should she do? Call 911? There was no note, so maybe he hadn't run away. Maybe she and the Stantons could find him.

She picked up the phone and called Nancy. They would be right over. Already she felt a little calmer, knowing help was on the way.

Her hand hovered over the phone. Every instinct cried out for Patrick. How could she long so desperately for the reassurance of a man who had hurt her son? Surely he hadn't meant the cruel things he'd said to Jason. Maybe Patrick would want to know Jason was missing? Maybe he was regretting his harsh words this very minute. And maybe, once Jason was home safe and sound, Patrick would apologize to the boy and they could all work through this together.

Emily picked up the phone and dialed Patrick's number, but all she got was voice mail. She hung up without leaving a message.

When Nancy and Beau arrived carrying a sleeping Ana, Emily was pacing, wondering where her firstborn was and if he was okay.

Nancy hugged her. "I'll stay with the kids while you show Beau some of Jason's hangouts. If Jason returns home, I'll call immediately."

"Thanks, Nance."

"Any word from Patrick?"

"No."

"I'm sorry."

"So am I."

Beau placed Ana on the couch. "I'm sure Jason's fine. Just probably needed to blow off some steam. Have you called his friends?"

Emily nodded. "No one's heard from him. Not even Cassie."

He patted her shoulder. "We'll find him. Come on, let's go."

They found Jason an hour later, trudging down the old quarry road. He wouldn't speak, just stared right through her. But he did obey her command to get into Beau's truck.

Jason stared off into the night as they drove home in silence.

Finally, Emily couldn't stand it anymore. "What were you doing?"

"Jogging."

"It's almost two o'clock in the morning."

He shrugged, his hollow-eyed glare telling her it didn't matter what time it was. He'd apparently felt the need to run from the horror of the day. And he'd done just that, until exhaustion had slowed him to a walk.

When they returned home, Nancy and Beau retrieved their daughter and slipped quietly from the house.

Emily followed Jason upstairs. He went to his room without turning on a light, falling into bed fully clothed. Slight snores reassured her that he hadn't died from his ordeal.

She pulled his beanbag chair toward the bed and grabbed an extra blanket. Scrunching down in the chair, she spread the blanket out and tucked it around her. She had the feeling dawn would be a long, long time in coming.

A few moments later—or what felt like it—something woke her. She bolted upright. Sunlight peeked around the window blinds.

"It's okay, Mom. It's just me." Jason looked like hell. Bags under his eyes, hair standing straight up. But there was a new resolve in his stance. "Will you take me to the hospital?"

Lack of sleep fuddled her mind. "Are you sick?"

"I want to tell Tyler Jones's family I'm sorry. That it was an accident and I didn't mean to hurt him."

Emily had never been as proud of her son as she was in that moment. Or as concerned about him. "Are you sure? Now might not be the best time—"

"If I don't do it now, I'll chicken out. You've always told me to accept responsibility for my actions. That's what I intend to do."

"What I'm saying is that his family is stressed and they might not be...receptive right now."

His mouth twisted. "Yeah, like Mr. Stevens wasn't 'receptive'? I've already thought of that. They can't say anything worse than I've already thought myself."

She brushed a strand of hair from his forehead. "I'm very proud of you."

His eyes clouded. "Don't be. I don't deserve it."

"Jason, it *was* an accident. You had no way of knowing Tyler would run out into the street." She shrugged off her own conflicting emotions and concentrated on how best to explain something she didn't understand herself. "Patrick didn't mean what he said to you, Jase. I—I've never seen him like that before. Some people react to stress in weird ways."

"He told the truth, Mom. *I* wish I could have traded places with Tyler." His voice broke. He swiped his sleeve across his eyes.

She longed to take her baby in her arms and soothe him. But he wasn't a baby anymore. And he was doing a courageous thing many adults would never attempt.

Cupping his face with her hand, she held his gaze. "You are a smart, courageous boy with a good heart. We'll get through this together. But please don't talk about taking Tyler's place. I need you too much."

Slowly, he nodded.

Emily exhaled, for the first time admitting to herself she'd feared he might harm himself. Being needed seemed to give him a reason to keep going. Just like it had given her a reason in the dark times after Larry had left.

"Now, get showered. I'll call Cassie's friend Sarah and see if she'll sit with the other boys while you and I go to the hospital. Unless you change your mind."

"I won't change my mind." His voice was husky, but firm.

CHAPTER TWENTY-ONE

PATRICK SKIPPED A ROCK across the pond. He'd been down here every afternoon for the past three days. Usually after lunch, the walls started closing in on him and made him feel as if he might smother. Spending time with Roger didn't even help like it normally did. Instead, it reminded him of all they'd lost through one thoughtless act. And showed the grim reality of what the Jones family might face.

He'd kept in touch with the Elmwood Elementary grapevine, grateful for once that a student's mother was a gossip. He knew Tyler Jones was still in a coma. He knew Emily and Jason spent a lot of time at the hospital. And that Jason had faced the Jones family like a man and apologized.

Shame burned Patrick's gut. Jason was a better man than he.

And then there was Emily. She reputedly had been a tower of strength to the Joneses. She'd set up a team of volunteers to make sure the Jones family had a hot meal delivered to their home nightly and she herself took a full meal to whichever parent stayed by Tyler's side. She'd also organized volunteers to entertain the two other Jones children, giving them a break from the crisis, if for just a short time. And, finally, she'd utilized her PTO president skills and gotten the ball rolling for a white elephant sale in the school parking lot.

With each tidbit of information, he fell more in love with her. But along with that, his resolve to stay away from her grew. Two wrong relationships had nearly destroyed her and he had no intention of adding a third. Besides, she was like a mama bear, her children her cubs. She would never forgive him for treating Jason so abominably.

Hell, he would never forgive himself for treating Jason that way. His actions at the car wash had scared and confused him. He had no idea why he'd suddenly lost control. And now, the mere thought of returning to Elmwood made his hands shake.

"Thought I might find you here." Patrick's father sat down next to him, gathering a few flat stones.

Patrick rolled a stone over and over between his fingers. "It's quiet here."

"It is that." His dad drew his arm to the side and skipped a stone across the pond.

They sat in silence for a few moments. The only sound was the wind rustling through the trees.

"Something happen in Elmwood?"

"Why do you ask?"

"Because you've never called in sick before unless you were unable to move."

Patrick shrugged. "I'm overdue for some R & R then."

"I get the feeling it's more like you're running from something. Or someone."

"I'm not running from anything. I just needed a break." *Liar.*

Patrick tried hard to focus his mind long enough to make polite conversation. It would be the only way he could convince his dad everything was okay and leave him in peace. "Roger's looking good."

"Yes. He's managed to avoid all the flu and upper respiratory stuff that went around this winter."

"Mom's looking tired though."

"She is tired. But she loves every minute she spends with Roger."

"Do you ever regret, um, keeping him at home?"

His dad sighed. "Usually your mom and I burn out at different times. So when one of us is tired, the other props him or her up. Once we both burned out at the same time and it was pretty rough."

Patrick's chest ached. He almost wished he hadn't asked. "I'm sorry."

His dad shrugged. "There's nothing for you to feel sorry about. You give us those weekends away. Looking forward to that is what keeps us going when things get hairy. And during the good times, Roger's smile is reward in itself."

"Yeah. And he's got that chuckle thing, too."

"Exactly. You know we're the only ones who can get him to laugh—you, me and your mother?"

He nodded. "That's why I know he's happy." He skipped another stone. "But I still can't help thinking how life might have been for him. If he hadn't fallen in the pond."

"I won't lie to you, Patrick. I used to think that myself sometimes. But that train of thought was only driving me crazy. I wouldn't be much good for Roger or you and your mother if I wallowed in all the would-haves and could-haves."

Patrick hesitated. "I've been doing some wallowing lately."

"I figured it was something like that."

"I'm the one who caused Roger's accident."

"Son, you've got to forgive yourself. I blamed myself for not getting him out of the water sooner. And I was an adult. It's not either of our faults we had an unseasonably warm spell that year."

"But if I hadn't been such a jackass and tossed his lunch box on the ice—"

"Roger might have ended up out there anyway. The only way I can live with myself is by believing there's a greater plan."

"What kind of greater plan could there be for Roger to end up the way he did?" His voice was louder than he intended. Anger burned in his gut.

"I didn't say I understood completely, but Roger touches a lot of lives. He's a favorite of the nurses and everyone always makes a big fuss over him in the grocery store. People are just drawn to him. His simple spirit, his joy in life."

"Oh, come on, Dad. How about the children who stare? The ones who point and giggle? Or the adults who look away?"

"Yes, there are a few. But the people who take the time to know Roger adore him."

As suddenly as his anger came, it disappeared. "Yeah, he makes me feel like I'm the most important person in the world when he smiles at me."

His father's voice was gentle. "That's a pretty big gift, isn't it?"

"Yes, I guess it is." He hesitated. "Dad, I still intend to take care of Roger when you and Mom can't do it anymore."

His dad nodded. "I know you do."

"But I'm wondering if I could ever ask a woman to share my life with me. Sure, there are probably women who would agree to taking on Roger. But they wouldn't have any idea what it's really like."

"I'm not sure anyone knows what it's really like. Even you, son. And it worries me sometimes. All I ask is that if it's more than you can handle, you find a good place to take care of Roger."

"I *won't* let him go to one of those places."

"I'm just saying keep an open mind. I don't intend to sacrifice another son because of one tragic accident."

"I'll remember. But I've taken care of Roger for the weekend before and I think I can do it."

"I think you can, too, or I wouldn't leave him in your care. And it eases my mind to know you'll always be there for him, whether he lives in your home or in a care facility."

Patrick's throat got all scratchy. "You can count on me."

His dad pitched another rock.

Patrick followed suit. He and his father'd had conversations like this for a long time.

"Patrick?"

"Yes?"

"Have you met someone special?"

"Yes, I have."

"I thought so. When do we get to meet her?"

"You might not meet her…. It's complicated."

"Because of Roger?"

"Lord, no. She's a remarkable woman with a huge heart. I know Emily would love Roger."

"Then what's the complication?"

Patrick's chest constricted. Even as a child, he'd thought his dad was the smartest, funniest, most together guy on the planet. The years had only intensified that impression. "I don't want to disappoint you, Dad."

"Is she an axe murderer? Escaped ex-con? A Republican?"

Patrick chuckled. "I'm not sure about her party affiliation. But she's the most astounding woman. It's well, her kids."

"Ah, a woman with a past."

"I can accept that she's been married before. And I like being around the younger boys, Mark and Ryan. I've even gotten where I can hold a conversation with her seventh-grader, Jeremy."

"That's a challenging age. So this Emily has three sons?"

Patrick's chest tightened. "Four."

"Ah. Is it the fourth son who's the problem?"

"I'm that transparent?"

"Yes. And I have excellent deductive reasoning skills."

"He's a difficult kid. But what really worries me is my reaction to him."

"You don't have warm, fuzzy, stepfatherly feelings for him?"

"Pretty much the opposite. There's something about Jason that seems to bring out the worst in me. I don't like the way I am around him."

His dad laughed aloud. "Boy, that sounds like hard-core parental guilt if I've ever heard it."

Patrick was shocked. "You've felt that way about me?"

"When you were a teenager, I wondered on a daily basis if I was going to be able to make it as a father. There were a couple times when I could have easily throttled you."

"Wow. I remember you getting mad once or twice, but nothing like that."

"Because I managed to keep it on the inside most of the time."

"I can't seem to do that." He picked up another

stone, rubbing his thumb over the smooth surface. "I, um, said some horrible things to Jason."

"Did you apologize for losing your cool?"

"It was way more than losing my cool, Dad."

"Why don't you explain?"

Patrick took a deep breath and told him about his power struggle with Jason.

His father grinned. "Sounds like a strong-willed young man. And you're a strong-willed adult. Vying for the same woman's attention."

"Dad, don't make it so Freudian."

"Sounds like he's been the man of the house for a long time. It may be the only thing he knows and you're threatening his position."

"I understand that. And I've been making a special effort to hold my temper around him. And he seemed to be trying to get along, too. But last Saturday, the whole thing blew up in my face."

"That explains the timing of your surprise visit. We weren't expecting you for a week. What happened?"

Patrick described the accident, recalling each vivid detail because he'd relived it over and over in his nightmares.

Then he slowly told his dad all the horrible things he'd said to Jason.

His father was silent so long, Patrick was afraid to look at his face. Afraid of the hatred and condemnation he would see there. Or almost as bad, sad disappointment.

But when he looked up, it was worse than he could have imagined. Deep pity was etched in every line on his dad's face.

Finally, his father said, "Who were you really blaming?"

The question took him by surprise. Who else was there to blame? Then sick realization hit him between the eyes.

"I was in charge. I should have stopped the horseplay. It was as much my fault as it was Jason's. Even though it was only a matter of time until someone got hurt as a result of Jason's pranks."

"Sounds like an accident to me. Not anyone's fault. I think I understand now."

"Understand what?" Patrick was mystified. Frustration coursed through him. "Explain it to me, then."

His father held his gaze. "You'll figure it out when you're ready."

"What if I don't? My life is falling apart. I can't work at the best job I've ever had—I've let my students and principal down. I can't pursue a future with a woman I love, because her son makes me crazy. I can't eat, I can't sleep. Please, Dad?"

His father stood. Hesitating, he said, "You'll

find your answer there." He nodded toward the center of the pond. "And in your heart." Then he turned and walked away.

Anger started a slow burn in Patrick's gut. How could his father turn his back on him, now, when he needed him most?

JEREMY FROWNED. "How come Jason gets to handle the money? I'm better at math."

Emily took a deep breath and counted to five. It seemed as if the kids had been bickering constantly since they'd arrived at the white elephant sale an hour earlier.

Several answers to Jeremy's question popped into her head, none of which she would verbalize. Like she figured Jason needed to be involved helping the Jones family in some concrete way. Or schoolwork came so easily to Jeremy, he ought to allow his brother this one task to make his own. Or worse yet, Jason had been so damn brave throughout this whole crisis, she thought he deserved a little attention.

So, Emily fell back on a mom's last line of defense. She ignored the question. "Here." She handed Jeremy a pad of paper from her canvas bag. "You can write a story, draw a picture or develop more top secret code if you're bored. But you need to quit picking on Jason."

Jeremy rolled his eyes, but accepted the pad and pencil.

Karen Hendrix sidled up, her close-set eyes gleaming with interest. "And how is poor Jason doing? I imagine you kept him out of school this week?"

"No, I felt it was important to continue with his normal routine." Emily busied herself sorting through baby clothing she'd already sorted twice. She had a pretty high tolerance level for most people, but gossips made her blood boil. And Karen was a gossip of the first degree.

"Have you heard from Patrick Stevens?"

Tilting her head to the side, Emily managed a light tone. "Why do you ask?"

Karen flushed and tittered. "Well, you know, um, it's common knowledge you two are dating."

Emily wasn't about to be reeled in. "No, I didn't know."

"Patrick's called me several times."

Now that was news. "Oh?"

"Checking on Tyler's medical condition and how your family's holding up."

"That's very kind of him."

"He's at his parents' house you know."

Emily made a noncommittal noise, keeping her expression slightly bored.

"I asked him when he intended to return."

Emily was dying to know the answer, but refused to ask. Instead, she sorted another stack of clothing.

"He didn't give me an answer. Don't you think that's odd? He up and took personal time for an urgent family matter and he's not sure how long he'll be gone. But he doesn't sound like anyone in the middle of a family crisis."

Turning, Emily planted her hands on her hips. "What makes you the expert on what someone in the middle of a family crisis sounds like? Maybe some people want to keep their personal life personal."

"You needn't get snippy."

Oh, great, now Karen would broadcast that Emily had a nervous breakdown at the white elephant sale. If she couldn't locate gossip through snooping, Karen manufactured it on the barest of information.

"I'm sorry for being rude, Karen. Now, if you'll excuse me, I have clothes to sort."

"Of course." Karen scuttled off, probably looking for easier prey.

Jeremy muttered something under his breath. Emily couldn't hear the exact term, and she was pretty sure she didn't want to. Because if it was unflattering to an adult, even as unworthy an adult as Karen Hendrix, she'd feel honor bound to give him the respect-your-elders lecture.

Flipping a page in the notebook, Jeremy's face brightened. He started scratching out letters and making arrows and notations in the margins. Emily sighed with relief. He'd finally found something to hold his interest for more than a nanosecond.

When did Patrick plan on returning?

She had considered driving up to Syracuse to talk some sense into him. Force him to explain himself. Make him see he'd hurt Jason badly and needed to make it right. Reassure herself that he was okay. Do her damnedest to fix something she didn't understand.

A sense of déjà vu nagged at her. There was something familiar about this almost overwhelming need to fix a situation, fix a person. Frowning, Emily thought about the last time she'd felt the same compulsion. It dated back to the day she'd caught Larry-the-jerk with a cocktail waitress at the Lazy Eight Motel.

Yes, Emily had reacted with understandable anger. She'd screamed and thrown breakables. She'd dumped all his clothes on the front lawn. She'd had the locks changed on the doors and refused to let him in.

But, later, she'd actually tried to salvage their marriage. Practically begged him to go with her for counseling. Suggested he quit drinking. And he'd laughed at her. Because the problem wasn't with him, it was with her. In his convoluted reasoning, her two pregnancies had driven him to stray.

And for a long time, Emily had believed a portion of what he'd said. She'd believed it even though neither of her brothers-in-law had strayed when her sisters had retained a few post-pregnancy pounds. Fortunately her mother and sisters had convinced her the only responsibility she had in his infidelity was how she reacted to it. Trying to fix someone who didn't want to be fixed wasn't the answer. So, she'd divorced Larry-the-jerk and vowed to devote her energies to raising four kind, ethical boys rather than seeking out any more men who needed fixing.

Somehow, Patrick had gotten past her guard. Emily had thought she'd finally found a man who loved her for who she was and wouldn't let her down. Boy, had she been wrong.

"Hey, Mom, I cracked the code."

Emily realized she'd been staring off into space. "What, Jeremy?"

"I cracked the code in your notebook. It was pretty easy."

"Code? Notebook?" She had a hard time following his train of thought. Then she noticed she'd given him Tiffany's PTO notes. "Let me see."

He handed the notebook to her, his eyes sparkling behind his glasses. "Yeah, at first I couldn't figure out what all the red and black notations meant, but I remembered the toy roulette wheel you got us when you were in Atlantic City. Then the numbers threw me for a couple minutes—the negatives and positives."

Emily stared down at Tiffany's grocery list. Between Jeremy's scratchings and arrows, a pattern emerged. It appeared to be a detailed accounting of Tiffany's gambling wins and losses. Roulette, blackjack, poker, slots, it seemed Tiffany had been an equal opportunity gambler. The losses outweighed the wins, leaving a negative balance of nearly five thousand dollars.

"Jeremy, you're a genius."

He grinned. "Tell me something I don't know."

PATRICK STARED out over the water. It had been two days since his dad had made the cryptic remark about looking into the pond to find the answers. And no matter how hard he'd tried to draw him out, his father had refused to discuss the topic further, saying Patrick would understand when the time was right.

What if he didn't? Or what if he was so darn dense, he didn't understand until it was too late?

Until his career and his relationship with Emily were both only memories.

It scared him to think things had gotten so far out of control. He'd had a plan, a job he enjoyed, enough money to get by. And now, he sat, useless, by the pond most of the day, waiting for illumination. Kind of like Linus waiting for the Great Pumpkin to appear.

Okay, it was obvious his dad meant Roger's accident. And Patrick felt more than partially responsible for Tyler Jones's injuries.

And okay, if he were being brutally honest, he blamed Jason for the accident. But his problems with Jason had started long before the car wash.

The kid rubbed him the wrong way. There was no deep-seated, psychological reason. The boy was a troublemaker and Patrick didn't like troublemakers.

Frowning, he realized that wasn't quite true, either. Most of the time, he could see past the misbehavior to find some common ground with the child.

But with Jason, there was absolutely no common ground. Was there?

Thinking back, he tried to recall Jason's time in his class. The mousetrap incident certainly hadn't helped. Neither had some of the rest of his pranks.

Pranks. Jason loved pranks more than any

other boy Patrick had seen. Except maybe Patrick himself when he was that age.

Of course, when Patrick was that age, he'd grown out of playing pranks. Or more likely, he'd been scared straight. Roger's accident had made Patrick change.

Patrick was concentrating so hard, he barely noticed the crunch of approaching footsteps on gravel. He didn't glance up. He wasn't in the mood for any more of his dad's cryptic messages.

"Hi. Your mom said you'd be here."

"Emily." His mouth went dry.

She perched on a rock next to him.

"What are you doing here?" he asked.

"I wanted to make sure you'd heard that Tyler came out of his coma and will make a full recovery. No brain damage."

Patrick felt as if a great weight had been lifted from his shoulders. "I'm glad."

"But I guess I could have told you that by phone— your parents are listed in the white pages."

"It's good to see you, Em." He reached out to touch her hand, but let his arm drop. He had nothing to offer her.

Shrugging, she said, "I'm still not sure why I used up my last personal day to drive all this way to see you. Except for one thing. I'm not here to fix you."

"That's a relief." He chuckled, but it sounded hollow. Truth was, he'd give his right arm for someone, anyone to fix him, so he could get back to living his life.

"I promised myself I'd wait for you to come back to Elmwood. That you'd have to come find me."

"Oh."

"But I couldn't do it. I needed to see you, make sure you were okay."

"I'm okay."

"You look like you've been through hell."

He scrubbed his palm over his stubbled chin. "Vacation beard."

"This isn't a vacation, Patrick. You're running away, pure and simple."

"So what if I am?"

"You pursued me. I allowed you into my family. Let my kids get attached to you. I didn't figure you for the running kind."

He shrugged, steeling himself against the hurt and confusion in her eyes. Because if he allowed himself to feel her hurt, he wasn't sure there would be room for his own.

Whoa. Where'd that come from?

"I believe you owe me an explanation for why you talked to Jason the way you did. Why you left everything you love to run away."

"I don't know, Em." The tortured words were wrenched from him. "If I knew why, I'd know how to correct it. There's deficiency in me. No matter how hard I try, I can't relate to Jason. How can you and I contemplate a life together, if I have such an intense, negative reaction to your son?"

"We haven't discussed a life together. I haven't asked for that kind of commitment."

"You don't have to. It's the next logical step in our relationship."

She laughed. "Logic has nothing to do with love."

He grasped her hand, caressing her palm with his thumb. "I wanted a future with you. But it doesn't look like that's going to happen."

"We can take things slow."

"No, we can't. I love you, Em. Taking things slow isn't an option. I want the whole shebang. Marriage, family. But we'd be doomed to failure before we ever began."

"Because of Jason."

"Yes, because of Jason."

She was silent. "Have you thought about how he feels? The child was racked with guilt as it was. Then a man he was learning to accept as a father figure told him he wished he'd been the one injured. You might as well have told him you wished he were dead."

Patrick swallowed hard. "I've thought of little else."

"Are you going to make it right?"

"Em, I'm so sorry about all the stuff I said to Jason. But, there's no way I can ever make it right. I won't lie and pretend to feel something I don't."

"I was afraid you'd say that." She released his hand and stood. "I love you, Patrick. But I won't put my life on hold while you find yourself. And I won't tell Jason to expect an apology from you. Somehow, we'll need to get past it without your help."

"I'm sorry." If only she knew how truly sorry he was. How he ached bone deep to make things right. But couldn't find his way through the maze of conflicting emotions to do so.

"So am I," she murmured. Folding her arms over her chest, she asked, "What about Kat and Ari and the rest of the kids in your class? Are you just going to desert them, too?"

"I'll explain to them somehow when I get back."

"And what about Sea World?"

It seemed like years since he'd planned the field trip with such enthusiasm. "There was no way we could have swung that financially anyway. Unless you've found a ton of PTO money?"

"No, I haven't. As a matter of fact, I'm pretty sure Tiffany gambled our money away or funneled a portion into deposits for other charities' events. But that doesn't mean we can't figure out a less expensive alternative for the field trip."

"It's too late." Too late for so many things.

Emily tilted her head to the side. "Maybe it's too late for us, but I won't let the students down. I'll see that the sixth-graders have a trip to remember." She turned and walked away.

As her steps receded, Patrick busied himself collecting flat stones. He'd just gotten his skipping rhythm reestablished when he heard footsteps again.

He glanced up eagerly. The welcoming smile froze on his face. "Dad, it's you."

"Yes, Emily left. She said goodbye on her way out. She seems like a nice woman."

Patrick cleared his throat. "The best."

"She asked to meet Roger before she came down here."

"She did? She didn't mention anything."

"I don't think Emily did it for you. She did it for herself. Roger liked her, in case you wondered."

"I'm sure he did. She's wonderful."

"So why are you letting her get away?"

"She chose to leave." Patrick's face grew warm

as he realized he was trying to blame her. "Because I couldn't tell her what she needed to hear."

"I thought it was probably something like that. Son, I've been waiting for you to figure things out on your own. But for the first time in your life, your powers of observation seem to be nonexistent." He set something next to Patrick. "Maybe this will help jog your memory. Remember, your mom and I love you very much." He turned and walked away.

Patrick stared at the metal box.

Roger's Scooby-Doo lunch box.

Patrick stared at the box as if it contained plastic explosives. Slowly, carefully, he unclasped the hinge and raised the lid.

Empty. Harmless.

But not harmless in his memory. He recalled the way the handle had rattled when he'd grabbed it away from Roger. His brother's holler of outrage when Patrick had tossed it out on the ice. The crackle of ice giving way under Roger's weight. The way he'd slipped beneath the water with barely a sound. And how lifeless he'd looked after he'd been dragged from the water.

Chills raced up Patrick's skin. He started to shiver, as if it was he who'd been submerged in the freezing water.

Of all the children he'd encountered, Patrick knew Jason would be the one most likely to pull a stunt like throwing his brother's lunch box in the middle of an iced-over pond. How could he ever forgive Jason for sharing the same flaw that drove him crazy with remorse?

CHAPTER TWENTY-TWO

EMILY STOPPED BY the school on her way home from work, meeting with Principal Ross.

"Thank you for seeing me." Emily handed the notebook to the administrator. "This appears to be a record of Tiffany's gambling wins and losses. As you'll see, her losses are roughly five thousand dollars."

The woman frowned. "That would still leave an additional ten thousand dollars missing."

"I have the feeling she might have been juggling event deposits for at least two nonprofit groups to float her gambling. When we went to Atlantic City, the casino games company records indicated she made a deposit for ten thousand dollars—on behalf of the Elmwood Heart Association."

"I still don't know why she thought the school or district would condone an event tied to gambling, even if there were just prizes involved."

"Judging by how much she gambled those last months, I figure she wasn't thinking too straight about a lot of things."

The principal nodded. "So it would seem. So we're pretty much out of luck recovering the ten thousand if she funneled it to another charity, unless she left a paper trail."

"I got the impression she dealt in cash. And I don't know all the legalities. That's why I brought this to you."

"I'll run it by the school's attorney. But I imagine he's going to say we'd have to try to collect from Tiffany's estate. The district might choose not to risk the bad PR."

Emily nodded. "I figured as much. And it looks like the Sea World trip definitely isn't going to happen, even if Mr. Stevens were here to finish planning it."

"You're right. I was afraid it was a rather ambitious project. But Patrick was so enthusiastic." The principal sighed. "And Tiffany seemed to be a whiz at raising funding."

Out of her gambling wins. Or the Elmwood Heart Association's coffers.

Emily shifted in her chair, chastising herself for being unable to think of a single good thing about the dead woman. "What about the money Patrick raised? Is that part of the PTO general fund?"

"Yes. Technically, it is."

"Then I would like to make a proposal for its use." She slid a copy of her request across the desk. "I've researched an alternative—the Atlantic City Aquarium. I've attached their educational brochure."

Principal Ross flipped through the pages. "We could afford this?"

Emily leaned forward. "The tour bus company is willing to give us a steep discount. If we do a turnaround trip, there would be no hotel costs and the kids can bring snacks and sandwiches in ice chests. The entrance fee at the Aquarium is quite reasonable. They have some interesting eco-tours—with one of the tours, the kids would take fifty-foot pontoon boats to the Inter-Coastal waterway. There are some great hands-on activities and the kids would get the opportunity to see marsh islands and nesting shore birds. I think the children would enjoy this field trip every bit as much as they would enjoy Sea World. And they still have a few openings in May."

Ms. Ross glanced up from the proposal, smiling slowly. "Emily, you're a genius."

Emily allowed herself a small moment of pride. It was a pretty good solution, if she did say so herself.

Clearing her throat, she said. "There would be

very little out-of-pocket cost to the students, if any. And if I've figured correctly, we might have a couple hundred dollars left over. I'd like to propose that the PTO make a gift toward Tyler Jones's medical fund."

"Thank goodness Tyler came out of the coma. His mother says the doctors are calling him a miracle child, because tests indicate he didn't sustain permanent brain damage."

"Yes, Tyler's mother called me with the news, too. He had a lot of people praying for him."

"Unfortunately, I doubt we'll be able to contribute to his medical fund. It would open up a whole can of worms. But we can certainly see that the children here at Elmwood make sure he knows how much he's been missed. I know several classes are working on cards and posters."

Emily nodded. "It's been great to see everyone pull together."

"The community has you to thank for that. You got the whole ball rolling. Just as you've kept the PTO moving in a positive direction." She leaned back in her chair. "You know, Emily, I initially had doubts about whether you could handle the PTO position, but you've done an outstanding job."

Emily's face warmed at the principal's praise, but she knew she would treasure her words all the same. "Thank you. I had my doubts, too. But it looks like everything will work out in the end." Everything except her mess of a personal life.

After leaving the principal's office, Emily slowly drove home. She didn't want to spend another evening without Patrick. The boys had done everything in their power to cheer her, but she still missed him.

When Emily pulled into the driveway, she frowned. A figure sat on the porch, but was partially concealed by the early evening shadows.

She clutched her keys as a weapon and climbed the steps. The back of her neck prickled. The aroma of Italian spices and pepperoni made her stomach growl.

"Hi." Patrick's voice was low. "I come bearing pizza."

"You just about scared me to death."

"Sorry, I wanted to talk to you alone for a minute. Then if you see fit, I'd like to talk to Jason."

Warning bells went off in her head. Hadn't he done enough harm already? But she had to be fair, didn't she? Let him explain, if he could?

She sat next to him on the steps. "Okay, talk."

"I'm sorry I ran out on you during a really difficult time. It was inexcusable."

"I needed you, Patrick. We *all* needed you."

Her voice was husky. She hadn't realized how much she'd trusted Patrick until he'd broken that trust.

"I wish I could have been there for you like you deserved." He brushed a strand of hair from her forehead. "I love you, Em."

She jumped to her feet. "Wait a minute, Patrick. When you love someone, you stick by them, no matter how hard it gets."

He stood, too. "I'm sorry. I think I can explain and maybe persuade you to take another chance on me. I want us to be a real family. You, me, the kids, and later, Roger, if he comes to live with us."

"Roger isn't the issue here. I can understand wanting to take care of him later—as a matter of fact, I wouldn't have it any other way. But you need to explain the problem between you and Jason. He was trying to get along with you and you dumped on him."

Patrick frowned, his eyes were dark with regret. "I know. And Em, I'm truly sorry. I've been dealing with some stuff for a long time and Tyler's accident brought it all back. That's why I dumped on Jason."

"What kind of stuff?"

"Roger's accident."

"What does it have to do with Jason?"

He cleared his throat. "I've wondered from

the start why I had such a strong reaction to Jason, when other oppositional children don't get under my skin."

"Oppositional?"

"Troublemakers." He smiled to soften the term.

Smile or no smile, it made Emily mad. This was her son he was talking about. She propped her hands on her hips, ready to give him a piece of her mind.

Patrick held up his had. "Wait. Hear me out. My dad pointed out in a roundabout way that maybe Jason reminds me of another troublemaker."

Emily managed to control her temper at his second use of the term. "Who?"

"Me."

"You said you quit playing pranks early on."

"Only after Roger nearly drowned."

Emily started to understand, but she wanted to make sure. "What does that have to do with Jason?"

"Nothing. And everything. I've always blamed myself for Roger's accident. I tried so hard to make up for it. Studied hard, got good grades, quit playing pranks. But it was never enough. *Nothing* I could do could ever make up for what I took from Roger."

Emily's anger dissolved. Her heart ached at the

pain in his voice. Grasping his hand, she said, "It was an accident."

"Yes, just like what happened to Tyler was an accident. But somehow when I see Jason, I'm thinking of me at that age."

"And blaming yourself."

"Yes." He ran his hand through his hair. "I think that's why I lost it with Jason at the car wash. It was like the pond all over again. And I couldn't seem to control what came out of my mouth."

"I'm trying to understand, but it's hard…. Are you punishing my son for your mistakes?"

Patrick opened his mouth, then clamped it shut. He paced a few feet away, turning his back.

She waited. Not patiently, but she waited. Emily had the feeling her future hinged on the outcome of this conversation.

"I guess maybe I was." His voice was low and anguished.

Emily exhaled slowly. "In a twisted way, I think I understand. Doesn't mean I excuse it or would allow it to continue, but I can almost understand. It's better than thinking you have a random prejudice against my son. Or worse yet, a mean streak."

Patrick stepped close. "Believe me, Em, you're not thinking anything I haven't been thinking about myself. And it made me sick. I'm still not sure if I buy all this stuff, but if it's true, it means it's something I can work on. I'm willing to do whatever it takes. I don't want to give up on what we've got. I love you and I want us to be a family."

She wasn't about to muddy the waters by telling him she loved him. "Patrick, I wish that were enough. But I can't risk putting my kids through another unstable relationship."

"I don't want you to. All I want is a chance to prove I can be the kind of man you deserve. The kind of man your children deserve."

Emily made a noise low in her throat. The old Emily would have welcomed him with open arms, convincing herself that everything would be okay. She wasn't that woman anymore. "How are you going to do that?"

"I want to talk to Jason tonight. I want to explain in terms he can understand."

"That's a start, Patrick. But there's more at stake here than a simple misunderstanding."

"I know." He released her hand. "I've made an appointment with someone who helps people deal with grief. My dad saw him after Roger's accident and he helped a lot—because in a way, the Roger we knew died that day at the pond."

Emily hesitated. "I never thought of it like

that, since he's still here physically. You never grieved, did you?"

"No, it doesn't seem like I did. I thought, maybe, um, if this guy helps me get a handle on what's wrong, maybe the five of us could try family counseling?"

She cupped her hands around his face. "Oh, Patrick, I wish I was twenty-one again and believed in miracles. I've promised myself I wouldn't fall for another man who needs fixing."

"But don't you see, Em? Everyone needs fixing of some sort. But I'm not expecting you to do it for me. I'm willing to work my rear off to make it happen."

Emily saw a glimmer of hope. He wasn't like Walt, running away from the problem. He intended to face it head-on. And he wasn't like Larry-the-jerk, blaming everyone else for his mistakes. Patrick was accepting responsibility and looking for a solution.

A smile started somewhere in her heart, reflected in Patrick's eyes. "You're right. You don't need me to fix you. You're more together than you give yourself credit for."

"I can't promise it'll be easy. But I promise I'll do everything in my power to work things out."

His courage gave her hope. She kissed him,

her mouth featherlight on his. "I love you, Patrick. I'll try to be there with you every step of the way."

A MONTH LATER, Patrick closed his eyes, enjoying the feel of the salty spray on his face, the wind ruffling his hair. Best of all was the excited chatter of his students. He was disappointed when the pontoon boat docked.

When they were back on shore, Emily clasped his arm. "So what did you think?"

He wrapped an arm around her. "It was a wonderful experience." He nodded toward the children clustered around the guides. "One they'll never forget. Especially Ari and Kat."

Kat chatted animatedly with Ari, who'd been able to participate in the tour with minor accommodations to his condition. He'd even helped reel in the otter trawl net.

"You're not disappointed?"

"Not at all. I wanted the Sea World trip because it was the last trip my family took together before Roger's accident. But it was a mistake to think I could rewrite history. The aquarium tour is the start of new memories."

"I'm relieved. I was afraid you'd be disappointed."

"I could never be disappointed in anything you planned, Em."

"Better wait till after the wedding to say that."

He groaned. "Just tell me I don't have to wear a lavender tux."

She grinned wickedly. Leaning close, she whispered, "Only on our wedding night."

Patrick laughed. "You are a very twisted woman."

"I know. That's why you love me." Her smile faded and she grew serious. "About the wedding. It was really sweet of you to ask Jason to be your best man."

"I'm honored he said yes. It takes a special guy to forgive his future stepdad for being an idiot."

"After he met Roger, Jason thought of how he would have felt if Mark or Ryan had been injured on his watch. There were a lot of times when he wouldn't have intentionally hurt them, but something tragic could have happened. Like the first night I brought you home and he was making out with Cassie instead of watching his brothers."

"Yeah, we talked about that. And the fact that when he's mad at himself he'll sometimes say cruel things to his brothers, even though he doesn't mean them. He's a pretty insightful kid. Maybe because he's got such a terrific mom."

"And to think you once told me Jason needed a reality check." Mischief sparkled in Emily's eyes.

"No, it was me who needed the reality check." He drew her close.

"That's okay, I love you anyway." She kissed him on the cheek. Her breath was warm on his ear as she whispered, "And tonight I'll show you how much."

The muffled giggles coming from behind his back told him they were being watched.

"Come on, Mr. Stevens, Ms. Patterson." Kat walked over and took Emily's hand. "You don't want to miss a thing."

"No, we don't." Emily caught Patrick's gaze and winked.

EPILOGUE

JASON POSED for more pictures than he cared to, but figured his mom and Patrick deserved the photo op.

Patrick handed the camera to Jeremy. "Okay, now a picture of your mom and me with the graduate."

Jason wrapped an arm around his mom's shoulders and rested his hand on Patrick's. He still wasn't sure about this public display of affection with another guy, even if he was his stepfather. But he humored Patrick anyway.

"Okay, now the grandparents get some time with the grad." Grandpa Phil was followed closely by Grandpa Stevens, the two grandmas right on their heels. Grandpa Stevens wheeled Uncle Roger at a pretty good clip.

Jason figured he had about five minutes until his aunts and assorted cousins descended on them, too. "Hey, Uncle Rog. How about a high five?" Jason gently grasped Roger's wrist and raised his hand for him, playfully slapping some skin.

Roger grinned that crooked grin of his, complete with a trickle of saliva at the corner of his mouth. Then he made a noise halfway between a cackle and a cough.

Jason loved making his uncle laugh. "See, works every time."

Patrick punched him on the shoulder. "You telling him dirty jokes again?"

"Nah. All very clean, huh, Uncle Rog?"

Roger nodded, a very loose approximation of a gesture others took for granted.

"I'm so proud of you." His mom hugged him, her eyes moist.

"Don't cry, Mom. It's a happy time."

"It's a *very* happy time." She smoothed a wrinkle in his graduation gown and adjusted his cap. "I won't know what to do without you around the house."

"I'm not leaving for college until September."

"I know. But I'm preparing myself."

"I'll be home for holidays."

"You'd better."

He kissed her on the cheek.

Patrick waited patiently a few feet behind Jason's mom.

Jason extended his hand. "Thanks, Patrick. For all your help."

"You did it all on your own, son. You wrote one

hell of an application essay. NYU had no choice but to accept you. And in four years, I'll be proud to have another educator in the family."

Jason swallowed the lump in his throat, hoping Patrick realized how much he'd inspired Jason's choice of majors. He glanced at Uncle Roger. "I think I'll like Special Ed."

"I'm sure you will. You'll be damn good at it, too. You have a way with Roger like nobody I've seen. And your students will respond to you every bit as much. Because you care."

"Just like you care for your students. Even the troublemakers."

The regret in Patrick's eyes made Jason want to kick himself for being an inconsiderate jerk.

"Hey, you've been in my corner every day since you told me about you and Uncle Rog at the pond." In four short years, Patrick had been more of a father than Jason's own dad, who hadn't even bothered to respond to the graduation announcement. "It's, um, meant a lot."

"You *are* my son, Jason." He tapped his chest with his fist. "In here."

"Yeah, I know, Dad."

Patrick tilted his head to the side, his eyes bright with emotion.

Jason held his breath, hoping Patrick wouldn't say something completely lame and sensitive about Jason finally calling him Dad. Another part of him hoped he would. Progress, Jason supposed, due to learning a new way of doing things.

He could still feel the giddy sense of freedom he'd experienced when the family shrink had taken him aside and pointed out it wasn't Jason's job to protect his mom anymore. Once they'd married, it had become Patrick's job. The shrink had also said Patrick and his mother were totally responsible for raising the younger boys. Jason's only job as a teen was to be kind and respectful to his family, earn good grades and help out with chores.

What a revelation that had been. It was as if the weight of the world had been lifted from his shoulders. And, soon, he'd been too busy studying and socializing to play any pranks. Better yet, he didn't even *want* to play pranks.

As his aunts and grandmothers descended on Jason in a chattering group, he held Patrick's gaze over Aunt Lisa's head.

Patrick nodded slowly and mouthed, "Thank you, son."

Jason mouthed back, "You're welcome, Dad."

 **Harlequin Historicals®**
Historical Romantic Adventure!

*From rugged lawmen and
valiant knights to defiant heiresses
and spirited frontierswomen,
Harlequin Historicals will
capture your imagination with
their dramatic scope, passion
and adventure.*

*Harlequin Historicals . . .
they're too good to miss!*

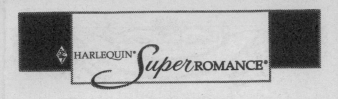
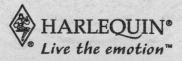

HARLEQUIN®
Presents~

**The world's bestselling romance series...
The series that brings you your favorite authors,
month after month:**

Helen Bianchin...Emma Darcy
Lynne Graham...Penny Jordan
Miranda Lee...Sandra Marton
Anne Mather...Carole Mortimer
Susan Napier...Michelle Reid

and many more uniquely talented authors!

Wealthy, powerful, gorgeous men...
Women who have feelings just like your own...
The stories you love, set in exotic, glamorous locations...

HARLEQUIN®
Presents~

Seduction and Passion Guaranteed!

HPDIR104

HARLEQUIN®
INTRIGUE®

WE'LL LEAVE YOU BREATHLESS!

If you've been looking for thrilling tales of
contemporary passion and sensuous love stories
with taut, edge-of-the-seat suspense—then
you'll love Harlequin Intrigue!

Every month, you'll meet six new heroes
who are guaranteed to make your spine tingle
and your pulse pound. With them you'll enter
into the exciting world of Harlequin Intrigue—
where your life is on the line
and so is your heart!

THAT'S INTRIGUE—
ROMANTIC SUSPENSE
AT ITS BEST!

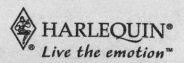

HARLEQUIN®
Live the emotion™

eHARLEQUIN.com

The Ultimate Destination for Women's Fiction

The eHarlequin.com online community is *the* place to share opinions, thoughts and feelings!

- Joining the community is easy, fun and **FREE!**

- Connect with **other romance fans** on our message boards.

- Meet your **favorite authors** without leaving home!

- **Share opinions** on books, movies, celebrities…and *more!*

Here's what our members say:

"I love the friendly and helpful atmosphere filled with support and humor."
—Texanna (eHarlequin.com member)

"Is this the place for me, or what? There is nothing I love more than 'talking' books, especially with fellow readers who are reading the same ones I am."
—Jo Ann (eHarlequin.com member)

Join today by visiting
www.eHarlequin.com!

eHARLEQUIN.com

The Ultimate Destination for Women's Fiction

Visit eHarlequin.com's Bookstore today for today's most popular books at great prices.

- An extensive selection of romance books by top authors!

- Choose our convenient "bill me" option. No credit card required.

- New releases, Themed Collections and hard-to-find backlist.

- A sneak peek at upcoming books.

- Check out book excerpts, book summaries and Reader Recommendations from other members and post your own too.

- Find out what everybody's reading in Bestsellers.

- Save BIG with everyday discounts and exclusive online offers!

- Our Category Legend will help you select reading that's exactly right for you!

- Visit our Bargain Outlet often for huge savings and special offers!

- Sweepstakes offers. Enter for your chance to win special prizes, autographed books and more.

Your purchases are 100% guaranteed—so shop online at www.eHarlequin.com today!